MIND GAME

"Am I going to learn to read *your* mind?" she asked. "Things are awfully one-sided now."

He raised himself up on one elbow and looked over at her lazily. "You will learn."

Then he slowly ran his dark eyes over the length of her before lying back down again. It was the first blatantly sexual thing he'd done, and the effect on Emily was such that for a moment she simply stopped breathing. Then she let out her breath with an involuntary sound and he chuckled.

"Perhaps you'll have some incentive to learn."

The Enchanted Land

SARANNE DAWSON

LEISURE BOOKS   NEW YORK CITY

A LEISURE BOOK®
November, 1991

Published by

Dorchester Publishing Co., Inc.
276 Fifth Avenue
New York, NY 10001

Printed in the United States of America.

The Enchanted Land

Chapter One

Emily could not believe her eyes. She actually shivered with delight as she clutched the slim, tattered volume to her chest, squeezing her eyes shut and then opening them again to stare at it. The title was nearly illegible in the age-darkened leather; it was nothing short of a miracle that she'd spotted it in the first place. With great care, she opened it to the title page:

"Azonyee and Mevoshee: The Magic Races"
By Alonzo P. Neville

In much smaller print that she had to squint to read, she saw the words: "Privately printed, 1874."

She turned a page, then another, her eyes devouring the difficult print. Words leapt out at her. Phrases echoed through her mind. She might well have stood there in the bookstore until she'd read it all if another customer hadn't brushed past her in the narrow aisle.

With great reluctance, Emily tore her gaze from the book and closed it. There was no price on it, but that wasn't unusual for this particular shop. She watched the owner for a moment as he engaged in some lively bargaining with the woman who had roused her from her reading.

Did he know what he had here? Could he possibly know that this was almost certainly the only copy remaining in existence?

Emily knew that the owner's personal tastes ran to Victorian literature and journals; she'd shopped here before. But he'd never shown any interest in folklore.

Her conscience inconveniently reared its nagging head. If he didn't know, was she morally obligated to tell him? Was the opposite of that old caveat "Let the buyer beware" also true? Should the seller be made aware?

What she preferred to think of as logic began to beat back the untimely intrusion of her conscience. The little book wasn't really all that valuable—except to folklorists like herself. And even among that small group, this particular volume would have little more than curiosity value, thanks to its author having subsequently disavowed it.

In fact, she thought, it was entirely possible that no one else in the world would have any real interest in this book.

Besides, she'd already overspent her book budget for the year—and it was only April.

Striving for a casual demeanor and still struggling to ignore the grumbling of her conscience, Emily started toward the checkout counter.

Only someone with his hair-trigger reflexes (and there were *very* few of them) could have reacted to the blow as quickly as Alec did. His shields went into place in less than a second—even before his mind told him that the psychic force was benign in nature, nothing more than a sudden, powerful release of surprise and pleasure not directed at himself.

The little bookstore was crowded with rows of floor-to-ceiling shelves, all of them filled, making it impossible for him to see other customers only a few feet away. He slid past a pair of latter-day hippie types and a well-upholstered middle-aged woman and moved around the corner to the next row. He was certain the burst of psychic energy had come from somewhere in that direction.

Despite the fact that his shields were now firmly in place, and despite the certainty that the blow hadn't been directed at him, Alec moved cautiously. Or perhaps it would be more accurate to say that he *increased* his caution, since he was always careful out here among the Tiyazh.

He rounded the corner into the next row and paused with a slight frown. The only person in that row was a young woman who appeared to be deeply engrossed in a small, shabby book. When she gave no indication of being aware of his presence, he edged closer.

He stared at her curiously. On a few occasions in the past, he'd come across Tiyazh who were psychically gifted and could brush against his mind when it was relatively unshielded—but this somehow felt *different*.

Emboldened by her lack of awareness of him, Alec gave up pretending to search the shelves and simply stared at her. She was, he decided, definitely worth staring at.

He couldn't guess her age precisely but supposed she must be in her twenties. Seen in profile, her features had an appealing delicacy, and he liked her pale blonde hair braided into a single, thick plait that hung down her back. She was small, but a quick scan of her tight, faded denims revealed a pleasingly curved body.

He abruptly cut off his thoughts. Was it possible that she could be one of *them*?

No, he decided quickly. She remained totally unaware of his presence, and she couldn't be *that* good, simply because he himself wasn't that good—and he was the best.

She turned another page, still totally absorbed in the book, and he reached out carefully to probe her mind, prepared for the remote possibility of discovery.

But just then, a woman brushed past them both, interrupting the younger woman's reading. Alec withdrew quickly, but a frown knitted his dark brows. An uneasiness that came astonishingly close to outright fear swept through him. Alec trusted his instincts; his life had frequently depended upon that unquestioning trust. In that brief moment when he'd made mental contact, he'd sensed something wholly unique.

Then, still without glancing in his direction, she closed the book and started toward the checkout counter. He followed, his curiosity growing beyond his uneasiness.

Emily dropped the book onto the counter with an attempt at casualness. When the proprietor picked it up, she asked how much, her tone trying to suggest that the answer would be barely worth his ringing up the sale.

He opened it, glanced through it quickly, then shrugged. "Ten dollars?"

Emily lowered her head quickly, pretending to search through her bag for her wallet. Ten dollars! Now she was beginning to feel *really* guilty! She would have paid five or even ten times that much for it. But she didn't feel guilty enough to quibble. Besides, there was someone waiting behind her. She paid for the book, then turned to glance briefly at the man in line behind her before leaving the shop.

A true New York miracle happened as she stepped out into the rain: a taxi had just disgorged its passengers right in front of her! She jumped in and gave the driver her friend Susan's address, then settled back just as the full impact of the man hit her. She leaned forward again and peered through the dirty, rain-streaked window, catching one last glimpse of him as he came out of the store. He was staring straight at her.

The cab pulled away, but the image of the man remained with her. What was it about him? She cast about in her mind for an answer to that powerful awareness of him.

Okay, so he *was* darned attractive: rather long, thick black hair—really black, the shade that brought to mind descriptions like "raven" in silly romance novels—and a thoroughly masculine face, slightly harsh with an aquiline nose above a wide mouth and a squared chin that even had the requisite cleft. His eyes had been dark, too—as dark as his hair.

Slowly she began to understand what she'd felt. It wasn't his looks, however attractive he was. No, it was something else entirely: an arrogance?

The cab rumbled, swerved, and blared its way uptown, and still Emily could not put the man from her mind. Manhattan was full of fascinating characters; it was one of the things she loved best about the city. But even here, he had stood out somehow.

As she thought about him, her mind began to drift back to ancient times, to a time of kings and other assorted tyrants who had wielded absolute control over their worlds—power utterly without limits that no modern leader could gain.

Then she uttered a self-deprecating laugh. How on earth had she come up with that? A few seconds' glance at a total stranger and she was imagining him to be a reincarnation of Attila the Hun. In all likelihood, he was a very ordinary man. At most, he must have been some actor, getting into a role.

The taxi screeched to a halt in front of Susan's building, and Emily was shocked to realize that she'd spent the entire trip thinking about the stranger. She paid the driver and got out, dismissing him from her mind as she hurried into the building, clutching her precious find. As soon as Susan opened the door, Emily burst out eagerly:

"Susan, you'll never guess what I found!" Then

she stopped and laughed. "No, of course you won't. But I have to tell you about it."

Susan obligingly dropped into a chair. "So tell me. I just hope it isn't a man, since I went to a great deal of trouble to find you an interesting one for tonight."

The dark stranger's face flickered briefly through her mind, but Emily shook her head. "No, not a man—a book!" She pulled the little volume from the bag and held it up triumphantly.

"This isn't supposed to exist! I'm sure it must be the only copy left—and it only cost me ten dollars!" Emily had long since beaten back her conscience in the face of such a bargain.

Susan read the title and frowned. Emily required no further encouragement.

"Alonzo Neville was a nineteenth-century folklorist. He came from a wealthy family and could afford to spend his life studying something that was only a hobby for others. In later years, he became a very much respected figure in the field, but he wrote this when he was quite young.

"He'd had it privately published and distributed copies to his friends. Then, years later— after he'd become a leading figure in the field— another folklorist happened to get hold of a copy. It was thoroughly trashed by everyone in the field and he was ridiculed for having written it. So he disavowed the story, claiming he'd written it after smoking hashish: a mere youthful indiscretion. And then he went around and collected all the copies and destroyed them. But he obviously didn't get them all."

Emily smiled and ran a hand caressingly over

13

the dirty cover.

"What was so terrible about it?" Susan asked.

"Well, he claimed to have interviewed an old woman who was a member of a magic race called the Azonyee."

"A magic race? You mean a whole tribe of them—like gypsies?"

"No, not like gypsies. *Serious* magic. And she told him there were two tribes of them—the Azonyees and the Mevoshees—and they lived separately and waged some sort of battles with each other."

"And where was he supposed to have run into this old lady?"

"Somewhere in the Adirondacks, as I recall. Some colleagues of Neville's actually went up there to check out his story. They claimed no one in the area had ever heard such stories. Some of their letters on the subject have survived; it was quite a scandal among them. But they never mentioned the name of the village or the exact location."

"Em, I hate to put a pin in your balloon, but if the people up there didn't know anything about it and then Neville himself admitted that he'd dreamed it all up under the influence—why is the book so important?"

It was a good question, and one Emily was hard put to answer without sounding as if she were off in Never-Never Land again.

"I first heard about it when I was in graduate school, and the story intrigued me. You see, there have been other veiled references to two magic tribes in old tales all over the world. Always two tribes and always the battles between them—and always the fact that they live among us—but not *with* us."

"You've lost me."

"They're supposed to exist in some sort of enchanted place—a place they can come and go from, but where the rest of us can't enter."

"Well, all that means is that Neville's hash dream wasn't even original."

"But, Susan, doesn't the notion intrigue you: real, honest-to-God sorcerers walking among us, living in a place that isn't there?"

Susan regarded her old friend with a smile. Emily both amused and fascinated her. In most ways, Emily was a very sensible person, but it seemed to Susan that a part of her had never quite grown up. It never failed to bring to Susan's mind the story of Peter Pan. With her white-gold hair and her petite figure, Emily even resembled Tinkerbell. In fact, she'd once dressed up as that very character for a Halloween party.

Privately, Susan had always wondered if that side of Emily had resulted from her extraordinary origins. She'd literally been left in a basket on the doorstep of Children's Hospital when she was only a day old. And no trace of her parents had ever been found. A history like that, Susan thought, could send one off into thoughts of fairies and magic and heaven knows what else.

She saw Emily opening the little book with that air of concentration that told Susan she would soon be lost in it. So she leapt from her chair.

"No reading! The sorcerers can wait. You promised to go shopping with me."

Emily closed the book reluctantly. Susan was right. She was here for the pleasure of a weekend in New York, not to hole up with a book. The magic people could wait a while longer.

"I had only a moment to probe her mind," Alec said, "but when I followed her to the cashier and saw the title of the book . . ." He shrugged eloquently. "It is very troubling, though of course it could have been only a coincidence."

"Why didn't you follow her—to learn more?" one of the Elders asked.

"That was impossible. She got into a cab outside the shop." He smiled ironically. "Another coincidence. To find a cab in the rain in New York is almost a miracle, and 'porting after her in such circumstances was impossible."

In the silence that followed, heads began turning slowly in the direction of a handsome, white-haired member of the Council whose expression hovered somewhere between hope and ecstasy. Alec, too, turned toward her, and like the others, his face showed the mark of a dawning possibility. That old story! He hadn't forgotten it, of course, but neither had he made the connection. He felt a wave of sympathy for Tapha and her hopes—but he also felt an even stronger sense of danger.

"So Morra's spirit returns to haunt us," the Leader stated, her tone annoyed. "But we had believed that Neville had destroyed all the copies of his book."

"Apparently we were wrong," said another. "But the book itself can do us no harm."

Alec agreed. "The book isn't important. What *is* important is her interest in it. Finding it triggered a very powerful psychic energy in her."

"Tell me about her," ordered Tapha, speaking

16

for the first time.

Alec stared at her, admiring the delicate bone structure that not even advanced years could alter. He described Emily Carr.

More silence followed. The unease in the ornate chamber increased, vibrating through them all.

"It is possible," Tapha said finally. "Yes, it is possible."

"You will find out more about her, Alyeka?" the Leader asked, disguising an order as a question. For all her authority, she was careful with Alec, as were the others, who were nominally his superiors.

"Yes, it shouldn't be difficult. I saw her name and address on her driver's license when she paid for the book. She lives in Connecticut."

Alec got up and took his leave of the Council. But when he met the hope-filled gaze of Tapha, he saw superimposed upon her face the face of a much younger woman, staring at him through the rain-dappled window of a taxi.

Emily was poring over the map when Ben arrived. She let him in, then returned to the dining-room table where the map was spread out. Ben followed her and slid his arms about her, but she deftly sidestepped beyond his reach as she continued to peer at the map.

"It isn't on here. But that doesn't mean it doesn't exist. Surely there must be villages too small to appear on a map."

Ben sighed inwardly. His first thought was that her obsession with this book would be yet another barrier she was erecting between them. But that thought was quickly canceled. This was pure Emily. When she was onto something new, she simply lost interest in everything else.

"Why don't you check an older map?" he suggested. "There must be old maps of the area somewhere."

She looked up at him with a smile that sent his hopes soaring, if only for a moment. "Yes, of course there must be. If the library doesn't have them, I'll call the New York State Historical Society."

"And if you find it, you'll go up there?"

"Of course. I know you think I'm obsessing over this—and you're right. But I have to follow it through to its end."

He nodded, then took her hand and led her back to the living room. "Emily," he said carefully, "I've seen you get lost in your work before, but this is different. You really *are* obsessed with this fairy tale. I sometimes wonder if you actually know the difference between myth and reality."

"The difference often isn't all that great," she stated with a faint trace of irritation caused by her knowledge that he was right. This *was* different. "Besides, what you refer to as 'make-believe' is my profession."

Ben nodded and chuckled, taking her hand in both of his. "You know, now that I think about it, I can't imagine you in any other profession. But how did you come to choose it?"

She shrugged. "I didn't; it chose *me*. I was a liberal arts major, casting about for some career that would satisfy a neurosurgeon father and a writer mother. In my sophomore year, I took a folklore course just to lighten up my schedule, the same way most of my students do now. And I knew after the very first class that I'd found what I wanted to do. All the other lit classes were just to make myself a respectable career."

"And were your parents satisfied?"

She laughed, a low, melodic sound he loved. "Surprisingly, they were. Mother said they'd called me their 'fairy child' when I was a baby, so it seemed to fit."

"Do you ever think about your real parents?" he asked curiously. He knew the story of her origins, but had never felt comfortable asking questions about it.

"Oh, I thought about them endlessly when I learned the truth, but over the years I've come to accept that I'll never know anything. Mother and Dad saved all the old records: the newspaper articles, even copies of the police reports. They knew I'd be curious. But there were simply no leads.

"For a time, they hoped someone would come forth and admit that they'd seen someone set a big wicker basket on the hospital steps, or maybe a cab driver would recall taking someone there at that time. But nothing happened. It's no wonder they thought I'd been left by fairies." She smiled.

Ben thought they just might have other reasons for believing such a thing, too. Ever since he'd first met Emily Carr nearly a year ago, he'd thought there was something almost unearthly about her. At the least, there was something very *different*—quite apart from her beauty.

But that difference defied description. It was, he thought, something one *felt*, rather than anything specific in her behavior.

That difference had made him very cautious in his pursuit of her, and he thought unhappily that he was still not really getting anywhere. She would let him into her life, but only on her own terms. And he had the unpleasant certainty that if he were to walk away, she would scarcely notice.

And yet, he couldn't in all honesty say that she was cold. The faculty colleague who had introduced them had called her just that: "as cold as she is beautiful" had been his description.

But Ben was sure he was wrong. Emily could be very warm and funny, but then she would just seem to drift off again—not withdraw icily, but simply move to someplace he couldn't go. He didn't think she was even aware of it.

She had started to talk about the book again, but her enthusiastic monologue was interrupted by a loud rumble from his stomach. She stopped and gave him a startled look.

"Oh, I forgot that I was going to cook dinner for us."

So they went out to their favorite Japanese restaurant, where he struggled to hold her interest and she wondered why she couldn't seem to fall in love with him.

It certainly wasn't the first time Emily Carr had asked herself that question. At twenty-nine, she'd had several other very nice men fall in love with her. And some not-so-nice ones as well. While other single women plotted and schemed and read articles about how to attract men, Emily often found herself in the uncomfortable position of having to fend them off.

She knew perfectly well that she was most men's dream-come-true: blonde, blue-eyed, delicate in appearance. There were times when she had wished for different genes from her unknown parents.

She had also occasionally wondered if the real reason she just couldn't find anyone she wanted to share her life with had to do with that mystery of her birth. How could she give herself to another person when she didn't even know who she truly was?

Ben took her home and tried to invite himself in, but she gently put him off, claiming that she had students' papers to review. It wasn't true, but it was easier than telling him she just wanted to be alone—to reread the book.

Emily lived in a pretty little bungalow she'd purchased a few years ago when she'd come to teach at the small, exclusive college in town. She'd wanted to put down some roots after spending nearly two years traveling to study folklore in various parts of the world.

Wellsford was one of those small colleges that would certainly survive the coming dearth of students that so threatened other schools. It had a huge endowment, thanks to many wealthy alumni, and an excellent reputation for turning out well-rounded graduates.

Emily's folklore classes were among the most popular on campus, because of her marvelous ability to spin out fabulous tales. Of course, it was also true that many of the male students came because of her beauty, rather than an interest in folk mythology. In general, they came too to escape the rigors of science and math and Greek philosophy—but every once in a while she found among them a few who, like herself, became intrigued by the worlds people had constructed over the centuries to help them understand the one they lived in.

She curled up in her favorite chair and opened the old book carefully. Immediately after her initial reading, she'd taken the precaution of having it copied, but she preferred to read the original.

An hour later, she put it down again with a sigh of disappointment. She'd been hoping to discover something she'd missed in her initial reading, but she'd apparently overlooked nothing. Still, it remained an intriguing tale that set her aquiver with wonder.

The tale Neville had set forth had supposedly been told to him by an old woman he'd encountered while hiking in the Adirondacks. He'd gone to that particular spot as a result of a veiled reference to it in some unspecified old manuscript.

The area, then and now, was sparsely populated. He'd gone to the hamlet mentioned in the manuscript: Traverton's Mill. There he spent several days questioning the inhabitants, but to no avail. No one had ever heard of "magic people" living in that area.

Then, since he was an avid hiker and birdwatcher, Neville had decided to spend a few days trekking through the forests. And it was there he'd encountered the old woman who provided him with his story.

He described her as being an "ancient crone, somewhat gypsylike in demeanor" and far too frail to have been wandering about alone in the forest. He was genuinely concerned about her, and when he inquired about her circumstances, she told him her story.

She claimed to be an Azonyee, a member of a magic tribe that she said lived there in the forest, in an "enchanted place" beyond his reach. He said that she spoke English quite well, although with an unidentifiable accent.

The woman told him that there were actually two such tribes: the Azonyee and the Mevoshee, and that they'd existed since the beginning of time, always living separately from each other and apart from the rest of the world, although they apparently visited the "outer world" quite often.

Then, according to Neville, she began to talk about something that sounded like "matrees," which after a while he began to understand meant powerful forces within the earth. Neville, who was already well-versed in folk mythology, likened them to the "ley lines" that had figured in many tales of mysterious "earth forces."

Such tales were nearly as old as mankind itself. Stonehenge and many other monuments were believed to have been erected along such lines of force, or at the junctures of those forces. Over the centuries, researchers had spent lifetimes studying these strange megaliths, which were quite common in Western Europe and North Africa, but existed elsewhere as well.

Neville had expected the woman to claim that her people had built these monuments, but when he asked her, she dismissed them as being the work of "foolish Tiyazh," which he later came to realize was her word for all the rest of the world's people.

Instead, she said that her people and the Mevoshee engaged in battles designed to "balance" the "matrees," or earth forces. There were, she told him, those among them who were highly gifted and specially trained to undertake these battles. They were called "Shekaz."

These battles, or "Shekaz-ma" as she called them, took place in predetermined spots where the earth forces were in danger of becoming "unbalanced." Although the woman was unable or unwilling to describe the actual battles, Neville wrote that it was his impression that they were fought with magic, rather than with conventional weaponry.

And the old woman claimed truly fabulous powers for her people: telepathy, psychokinesis, teleportation, mind control, etc. Nothing was beyond their abilities, and magic even played a strong role in their daily lives.

He plied her with questions concerning their society, and she claimed they had a true democracy where Elders such as herself were revered and (scandalous to Neville's nineteenth-century mind), men and women were truly equal.

She said that they moved back and forth from their world to the "outer" one at will, bringing back things they liked and even educating themselves in "Tiyazh" schools. The Shekaz in particular were educated "outside," since their work required them to be in the outer world regularly without calling undue attention to themselves.

"How would I recognize one?" Neville had asked.

The old woman had merely smiled and said, "If you encountered one, you would know."

Neville said he had given her a dubious look, and the woman had gone on to explain that she was quite old and her powers were greatly diminished—and besides, she'd never been a Shekaz.

And then she was gone. Neville wrote that he must have inexplicably fallen asleep, though he'd been anything but tired. It had seemed to him that he'd merely blinked and then discovered that he was once again alone in the woods.

Because of his concern for the old woman's safety—and his continued curiosity as well—Neville had searched the woods for her the remainder of that day and for some time thereafter. But when he'd questioned area residents about her, no one had any idea who she might have been. And he never saw her again.

It was a compelling story, and Neville's recounting of it, plus his many comments, made it very believable.

Emily sat there thinking about the paper she'd reread earlier on Neville and his work. The man had been intensely devoted to the study of folklore, and his research methodology had been flawless, commanding even the respect of modern-day researchers. He'd also apparently been a somewhat austere man, not given to self-indulgence despite his considerable wealth.

Why, Emily wondered, would such a man smoke hashish in the first place, let alone write a book based on a drug-induced dream? It seemed totally out of character for him. In fact, his colleagues had teased him unmercifully about it.

And perhaps some of them might even have half-believed it, since they took the trouble to seek out the place he'd visited, despite the difficulties of transportation in those days.

She got up and replaced the book on her well-filled bookshelves, then went to bed, her mind still filled with his marvelous tale. Even as she thought about it, she was aware of her undue fascination with the story. It wasn't all that different from other folktales, after all.

She was drifting down into sleep when the old woman's statement about the warriors called "Shekaz" came back to her: "If you encountered one, you would know." Something about those words nagged at her, but she was asleep before she could grasp it.

Alec drove the silver Honda onto the quiet, tree-lined street, staying under the speed limit, but not so far under as to attract attention. He enjoyed driving expensive, powerful sports cars like Ferraris and Lamborghinis, but such a car would be too obvious in this small, college community. Hondas, by contrast, were ubiquitous.

The homes were set back behind huge old trees and lawns that were just beginning to return to life. Most were smallish older houses, and all were well maintained. Number 247 was built of weathered cedar shakes, trimmed with cream-colored shutters. Crocuses and early tulips were blooming in abundance along the foundation and in beds that surrounded the big trees.

He cruised slowly past, taking in all the details. Then he saw several joggers coming down the sidewalk. He smiled. The popularity of jogging and walking was a great help to people like him, who sometimes had to fit in in places where their presence might otherwise be questioned. Tomorrow there might be a new jogger on the quiet street.

He returned to the campus he'd passed earlier, parked the Honda, and strolled about until he came to the main administration building. He was wearing an old but good tweed jacket and casual slacks with an open-necked shirt, and he drew no more attention than he usually did.

Upon discovering that Emily Carr's hometown was a college town, Alec had guessed that she must either be a student or a member of the faculty. If their suspicions regarding her were correct—and he still had trouble believing that —then she would most likely be a faculty member, since twenty-nine was a bit old to be a student.

A smiling gray-haired woman at the reception desk obligingly handed him a faculty directory, and he quickly discovered that she was indeed on the faculty: "Associate Professor of English Literature."

Then he asked for a class schedule and searched it. She was at this very moment teaching a class—on folklore!

He thought about that. It simply hadn't occurred to him that she might be a folklorist, but it could provide a totally harmless reason for her excitement over the book.

He spent some more time poring over the class schedule and saw that although she had only the one class this day, she had a full schedule tomorrow. That suited him just fine.

The woman gave him directions to the classroom building where she was teaching, and he started off in that direction. But when he reached it, he paused.

Was it really wise to let her see him again?

On the other hand, what was the harm? Besides, he *wanted* to see her again—and to see her reaction to him. He walked into the building, knowing that her class would be over soon.

There was a small lounge area at the end of the hallway where her classroom was located, and he moved in an unhurried way in that direction. A few students glanced up at him, then reburied their noses in their books.

He began to examine a photographic exhibit along one wall as he thought about her. The Council had made no decision yet about how to proceed with her—or even if any action at all should be taken. But they'd agreed with him that she should be separated from the book as soon as possible. That sudden burst of energy that had first attracted him to her argued that the book could indeed be some sort of psychic link.

On the other hand, his discovery that she was a folklorist could indicate that her reaction had been nothing more than jubilation at its discovery. This, he knew, was the explanation he wanted to accept.

He was about halfway through the photographic exhibit when the noise level rose suddenly, and he turned to see students pouring out of the classrooms. Alec hurried toward her classroom. He was only a few yards away when she appeared, surrounded by a small group of students. She turned in the opposite direction without glancing his way, and he followed along. The students surrounding her broke away to go into other

28

classrooms or down an intersecting corridor, and she was alone as she pushed open the door into the stairwell. He caught it before it could close.

He was just starting down the stairs behind her when she reached the turn and glanced back. Her eyes widened in shocked recognition and she stumbled, dropping her briefcase as she grabbed for the railing. He ran down the steps to retrieve it for her.

She was still standing there, gripping the railing and staring at him silently. He handed her the briefcase. Their fingers grazed lightly before she pulled away as though she'd been burned.

"I'm sorry if I startled you," he said pleasantly. "Are you all right?"

His words and the clattering feet of students coming down the stairs apparently shook her out of her near-paralysis. She managed a nod and a murmured "Thank you."

He started down the stairs behind the students, then paused to look back at her. She still hadn't moved. Their eyes met for a long moment. He had to restrain himself from reaching out to her, probing those thoughts that were so obviously about him.

Then he turned away and nearly ran down the remaining steps. Normally in control of *all* his senses, Alec now felt himself dangerously close to the edge. It had been a mistake to come here today—and he was a man who never made mistakes.

Emily clutched her briefcase tightly and continued down the stairs, oblivious to the greetings of passing students. What was he doing here? Or more to the point, who was he? She pushed through the exit door and scanned the green. By now, he was far ahead of her, striding quickly through the throngs of students.

For one mad moment, she envisioned herself running after him to demand that he answer her questions. Then, as reason reasserted itself, she turned instead toward her office.

But somewhere deep inside her, an uneasiness began to stir. Something had happened back there in the stairwell. Some sort of link had been formed. She was certain she would see him again.

Alec jogged down the sunny street. He appeared to be a man intent on nothing more than maintaining his fitness, but he was in fact scanning the nearby homes for any sign of life within. Then, satisfied that no one was watching him, he turned into her driveway.

On the driveway side, the house was fully exposed to view from the neighboring home. Even though he knew no one was there, he chose to cross the yard to the far side where a row of tall, thick evergreen shrubs hid her house from the other neighbor. He moved quickly into this shelter, then entered her home.

He liked it immediately: cozy, full of charm, but not pretentious, despite some very good antiques. And there were plants everywhere, all of them lush and healthy.

Then he saw a sudden movement on the stairs and a Siamese cat with eyes the color of its mistress's appeared, its sleek, creamy back arched as it growled at him. He stared at it, and a moment later it came to him and rolled over so he could rub its stomach. The growl was transformed into a low, rumbling purr. The cat followed along after him as he walked through the first floor, and rubbed against his legs when he stopped in the kitchen.

Everything was neat and orderly, though obviously well used. He scanned the spices on a large spice rack and examined the contents of the refrigerator. A large plastic container held homemade soup that smelled good.

With the cat still trailing after him, Alec went upstairs. He saw that there were three rooms and a bath. The room at the top of the stairs was obviously a TV room that doubled as a guest room. He checked the small collection of videos, noting that her tastes apparently veered from fantasies to serious drama.

The other room on that side was her bedroom. He paused in the doorway, catching a faint, floral scent—the same scent she was wearing the day before. He liked it and thought it suited her well.

The room was unabashedly feminine: delicate antique dressers, a floral-printed bedroom chaise, and a brass bed covered with a matching spread. Several more plants hung in the window in brass pots. On one of the dressers was a brass-trimmed mirrored tray with perfume bottles, and he began sniffing them until he found the one she'd been wearing: "Ombre Rose."

Then he opened dresser drawers and smiled at his discoveries. For a woman who had chosen highly feminine furnishings, she had surprisingly utilitarian tastes in underwear. He didn't find one frilly or lacy item.

He looked into the two closets as well. Not one clingy-looking dress. Obviously she wasn't a woman to advertise her beauty. But then she didn't have to. The attire of Tiyazh women—and lately the men as well—never failed to amuse him. To his people, clothes were simply a covering, and the only requirement was that they be comfortable.

Then he paused to examine some photographs in brass frames that stood on the other dresser. There she was in a formal portrait at about three or four years of age, a beautiful child with huge blue eyes and a nimbus of nearly white hair.

Beside it was what he guessed to be a fairly recent photo. It showed Emily Carr with two people who must be her parents. He picked it up and stared hard at it, trying to see a resemblance. Both of them were tall, and they looked more like each other than either of them looked like her. He wondered if her birth certificate might be around somewhere.

Just to be sure, he checked the contents of this dresser, too, but he'd already seen that there was no evidence of a man in residence. And she hadn't worn a wedding ring.

Finally he tore himself away from her bedroom and went to look for the book. The other room, as he'd suspected, had been turned into an office—and he saw it immediately, its drab, dirty cover standing out amidst hundreds of other books that lined two walls and part of a third.

He ignored it for the moment, and instead set about checking desk drawers and the contents of a large filing cabinet. Everything was neat and orderly, which made his search a lot easier. He found her passport—but no birth certificate.

Then his attention was drawn to her computer. He sat down and called up its contents, then scanned the words on the monitor. She must be working on a book. She wrote well, he thought.

Finally he picked up the book and went back downstairs, then reluctantly left her house.

Chapter Two

The moment she walked into her house, Emily was sure someone had been there. The feeling grew ever stronger as she walked through from the garage entrance into the foyer, where her mail had fallen through the door slot.

Then Chaucer came hurrying down the stairs to greet her, his behavior perfectly normal. She bent to pick him up and the certainty began to fade. He fancied himself the guardian of the house and had always protested loudly when anyone had been there in her absence—even when it had been someone he knew, like her neighbor or Ben.

Still, she couldn't quite shake that feeling of having been invaded, of a stranger walking through her house, touching her things.

Her gaze swept quickly over the living room.

Everything in order. Nothing missing. Burglaries weren't very common here, but she was a woman living alone, and she was always aware of that possibility.

Absently stroking Chaucer as he curved himself over her shoulder, she went to the small dining room, where the gleam of antique silver candlesticks and a handsome tea service further improved her state of mind. Even if a burglar had been able to resist her stereo, how could he have passed up all that silver?

Then she set Chaucer onto the kitchen floor and got out his food while he made his usual attempt to trip her by weaving himself around her legs. After feeding him, she peered into the refrigerator and decided to make herself an omelet to go with the soup she'd made the day before. But when she took the plastic container of soup from the refrigerator, that strange certainty returned.

It's that man, she told herself. I can't get him out of my mind. Who is he—and why did he follow me here?

Following the episode on campus yesterday, Emily had gone to the administration building, reasoning that a visitor to the campus would have gone there first.

The receptionist remembered him. He'd shown up not long before Emily had seen him, and had asked first for a faculty directory, and then for a class schedule. Any doubts Emily had had about the reason for his visit to Wellsford vanished when the receptionist belatedly recalled giving him directions to the building where Emily had been teaching.

All day long, she had expected him to be waiting outside her classrooms, or lurking in some stairwell. She'd even avoided her usual shortcut between buildings, because the path led through a stretch of woods.

Part of her actually *wanted* to see him again, though. She envisioned herself marching up to him and demanding to know just what the hell was going on and who did he think he was, following her around?

But the rest of her definitely did not want to see him again.

Just as she was about to go upstairs to change, the phone rang. She jumped nervously, half-believing that it would be him. But it was Ben, inviting her to dinner at his place. She thanked him but declined, pleading tiredness. It was true; she'd slept poorly last night, tossing and turning with unremembered dreams she was nevertheless certain were connected to the dark stranger.

Guilt washed over her after she hung up. What on earth was she going to do about Ben? She'd really been hoping that somehow time would resolve the situation. School would be over in a few weeks and he would be off to Europe for the summer. He was a professor of American literature and would be guest-lecturing at several European universities.

She, on the other hand, would be working on her book and spending a few days in Louisiana, doing field research with a colleague from Bowdoin for a paper they hoped to present next spring on the Cajuns.

But Ben had begun to push her to join him at the end of his lecture series in Rumania. The opportunity to explore that previously closed country was very appealing to her—and she knew that Ben knew it, too.

Could she go there and still hold him at arm's length? Emily thought about it as she went upstairs to change. Then, as she stepped into her bedroom, those thoughts were swept away by an even more powerful certainty that someone had been here.

She hurried from dresser to dresser and closet to closet. Everything was in its place. But this time the feeling would not go away. It clung to her, prickling her skin, worming its way into her every thought as she changed into sweats and went back downstairs.

She was sorting through her mail when it struck her. Bills and catalogues went flying as she ran back up the stairs, then stopped in the doorway to her office.

Still, when she saw that the book was gone, she searched frantically for it, trying to convince herself she might have put it somewhere else. Finally she returned to her office and sat down, staring at the space where it had been.

Chaucer came up and began to rub against her legs. She gave him a baleful glare. "Why didn't you tell me he'd been here? You *always* let me know when someone's been in the house—and this time it was a stranger."

But he merely backed off and began to clean his face.

Emily reached for the phone, then hesitated. How could she explain to the police that nothing was missing from her house except an old book, valuable to almost no one but herself? They would want to know what it was worth, and she could just imagine herself telling them of her bargain while they stared at her very much *not*-missing stereo and expensive antiques, not to mention the computer, the VCR, and a new, big-screen TV.

Chaucer still sat on the floor, washing his ears now, the picture of contentment. Why hadn't he told her about this intruder?

And there was certainly no doubt in her mind about who the intruder was. He'd obviously checked more than just her schedule for yesterday and had known she'd be gone all day.

But how had he found her in the first place? She relived their first brief meeting at the checkout in the bookstore. Yes, it was possible that he'd seen her license when she opened her wallet to pay for the book—but dammit, he would have had to be looking very carefully. How long had he been following her before that? And why did he want that book?

Besides, if he'd been planning to break into her house, why had he called attention to himself by being outside her classroom yesterday? That didn't make sense at all—unless, of course, he actually *wanted* her to know he was the burglar.

Thank God she'd had the presence of mind to make a copy of the book. But she still felt the loss of the original keenly.

Still undecided about calling the police, and with the unanswerable questions bouncing around in her head, Emily went back downstairs. She checked the locks on the doors and windows. They were good locks—or so she'd been told—

and none of them appeared to have been tampered with.

Her shock began to give way to anger and she became caught up in her amateur sleuthing. She went outside and began to walk around the house, searching for any signs that he might have forced a window, then relocked it from the inside. The entire exterior of the house was lined with flower beds, and the ground was still soft from several days of on-and-off rains. But there was no sign of forced entry, and no footprints in the flower beds.

Just as she was returning to the front of the house, her neighbor came out. She was an older woman who lived alone and was home most of the time.

"Is something wrong, Emily?" the woman asked, coming to the low fence that separated their properties.

"Something is missing from my house, Mrs. White, and I was trying to figure out how someone could have broken in. Did you happen to see anyone here today?"

The woman's expression became so horrified that Emily immediately felt guilty for having frightened her.

"Oh dear—and I've always felt so safe here."

"It *is* a safe neighborhood," Emily assured her. "All that was taken was an old book I bought recently."

"A book?" the woman echoed in surprise. "Was it valuable?"

"Only to me—or so I thought. Did you see anyone?"

But she hadn't. As luck would have it, she'd been out almost the entire day, visiting friends and shopping.

Emily went next to her other neighbor, a young couple with a new baby. He owned a photographic studio and she worked part-time as a psychiatric social worker at a hospital. Emily's home was less visible from their home because of a high, thick hedge along the property line, so even if Peggy had been home, Emily doubted that she would have seen anyone.

After expressing the same shock Mrs. White had (and making Emily feel like the neighborhood prophet of doom and gloom), Peggy said that she'd worked for a few hours in the morning, then had been home the rest of the day. She'd taken the baby with her to work, as she often did.

Emily was about to leave when Peggy suddenly frowned thoughtfully. "You know, it probably isn't connected, but I *did* see a stranger coming down the street as I was leaving for work. He was jogging. I didn't recognize him, and I know most of the neighborhood joggers. He sort of caught my eye—but he certainly didn't look like a burglar."

"What *did* he look like?" Emily asked, nearly certain about what she would hear.

"Very attractive." Peggy smiled. "That's why I noticed him. Quite tall, with really black hair that was kind of longish and a darned good tan for this time of year—unless that's his natural skin tone. Well-built, too. Athletic, but not too muscular."

Emily nodded. She'd described him perfectly —except for those darker-than-black eyes that Peggy couldn't have seen from a car.

She went home and called the police. They came quickly, and their reaction to her story was just what she'd expected: polite skepticism. They checked the locks and confirmed that they hadn't been tampered with. She asked if it was possible to pick them without leaving any traces, and the officer shrugged.

"Just about any lock can be picked by a professional, but you can usually tell it's been done. Besides, most of the burglaries around here have been amateur jobs."

She gave them the stranger's description and told them how he appeared to have followed her here after that meeting in the bookstore. They then lost interest in the theft and expressed concern about her safety.

"There are a lot of crazies out there, Ms. Carr—and you're a beautiful woman. You got to consider the possibility that he stole the book just as a way of getting your attention."

After they left, Emily thought about the possibility the officer had raised. But she quickly dismissed it. A man like that didn't need to do anything to get a woman's attention. He could get it just by existing. Hadn't Peggy noticed him? And the receptionist had recalled him quite clearly as well.

Not to mention the fact that she herself had behaved like a blathering idiot yesterday when she'd seen him.

"What do you want?" she asked into the silence of her house. And she was still asking when she fell asleep to another night of disturbing, unremembered dreams.

* * *

Emily cast a worried glance heavenward as she got out of her car and started toward the Barr Student Center. The blue sky was being overrun by smudges of black, and thunder growled in the distance. No doubt the approaching storm would add the perfect touch to her lecture, but it wasn't going to do much. for the lecturer's peace of mind.

She had always feared thunderstorms—a totally irrational fear, but too deeply imbedded to be driven out by logic. Even now, she could feel the onset of that peculiar sense of vulnerability that always took hold of her at such times.

A surprisingly large crowd awaited her in the main lounge. The Sunday Afternoon Series (SAS in the college's lexicon) had been a success from the very beginning, since students chose the topics. Emily was easily the most popular lecturer, and this was her third talk this year—but this was also the weekend before finals began and she'd been certain the crowd would be much smaller. Apparently they all wanted to escape from their studies for a while.

After greeting a number of students, Emily made her way to the refreshment table. The cake was nearly gone and the food service people were carrying in a fresh urn of coffee. She guessed that the staff hadn't expected this size crowd, either.

"Dr. Carr, I have some good news."

Emily turned, coffee cup in hand, to face a slim, intense youth. Toby Shaw was a freshman who was taking his second course with her. Nominally a philosophy major, he was planning to switch to English lit next year, and was one of those rare students who was fascinated by the study of folklore.

She knew what his news must be and smiled, even though she had mixed feelings about it.

"I've gotten permission to go to Louisiana," Toby exclaimed, flashing her that bright, quick smile that never seemed to her quite genuine.

Emily congratulated him and told him what a wonderful opportunity it would be for him to see what the study of folklore was all about. But she was thinking about his turn of phrase—so very typical of him. He said he'd "gotten permission," as though some committee had agreed to let him go. Most students would simply have said that Mom and Dad said okay.

As she made her way to the lectern, Emily tried to set aside her misgivings about Toby. He was a bright kid, with that deep but patient curiosity that made for a good researcher. But the truth was that he disturbed her for reasons she couldn't quite define. She felt drawn to him in some strange way—and yet she felt repelled by him just as strongly.

She'd noticed that the other students seemed slightly uneasy around him, although he was always pleasant and helpful and not given to overly demonstrating his considerable intellect. But if Toby was aware of this, it didn't show. He seemed quite happy at Wellsford, despite the lack of any close friends.

The room gradually began to quiet down as she arranged her notes. She looked up in time to see Ben slip into the room, taking a seat in the back where a few other faculty and staff had gathered. He hadn't told her he planned to attend, but she supposed it had something to do with her avoidance of him this past week while she'd been trying to decide what to do about him.

Emily's topic was "Practitioners of Magic Through the Ages"—a broad topic, but she'd managed to tailor it to the one-hour limit of the lecture. She'd given the same talk last year, but this year she planned to include material from Neville's book.

Neither the book nor the thief had turned up, although the police had done their best. As word had gotten around about the theft, the local newspaper had contacted her and had even done an article about the book. Several people had come forth with recollections of having seen the dark stranger on campus, but no one had seen him since.

Emily was soon into her talk, speaking with her usual vibrancy about the history of magic. The mostly blue-jeaned crowd gave her their rapt attention. One of her students had set up a slide projector and was showing Emily's collection of slides depicting ancient sorcerers and magicians. The final slide was made from a drawing in Neville's book of the old woman who'd told him the story of the Azonyee and the Mevoshee.

She concluded her talk with Neville's story. His statement that he'd been under the influence of hashish at the time brought smiles and laughter. There weren't many drug abusers here, but the distinctive aroma of pot had been known to drift about certain secluded areas of the campus from time to time, and the local police's semiannual drug busts were a campus joke for all but those who were caught.

The big room had one wall entirely of glass,

and in the final moments of her lecture the storm arrived, sending huge drops of rain thudding softly against the panes. The room was growing rather dark, since the big overhead lights had been left off for the slide show.

And for that reason, Emily had failed to see the stranger enter.

It was Toby who drew her attention to him. During the question period that followed, Emily's gaze was drawn to Toby, who sat near one of the questioners. He looked positively pale and his eyes seemed to be darting around the room wildly—almost, she thought, as though he expected to be attacked.

Then he abruptly swiveled around at an awkward angle and stared toward the dimly lit rear of the room. Emily's eyes followed his.

She caught her breath with an audible gasp, causing the long-winded questioner to pause uncertainly. But Emily had ceased listening to him. It was *him!* Even though he was little more than a shadow, she knew it was the dark stranger.

Toby suddenly turned her way again, his thin face taut with fear. Then he scrambled to his feet and fled the room through a side door. His movement galvanized Emily into action and she ran from the lectern toward the stranger, determined not to let him get away this time.

It took her precious moments to get through the confused crowd, but she saw him slip through the doorway, and she followed. She heard Ben calling her name, but she kept running.

She burst through the door into the lobby just in time to see the outer door begin to swing shut. Picking up her speed still more, she caught it before it closed and ran out into the storm.

Beyond her lay the broad expanse of the green that formed the heart of the campus. Visibility was limited, but Emily could see no sign of anyone out there. To the left lay a parking lot, and without a moment's hesitation she headed in that direction.

The lot was empty. A dozen or so cars were parked there, but none was leaving. Ignoring the pounding rain—and her own safety—Emily ran through the lot, convinced he must be hiding behind or in one of the cars. But he wasn't there.

She stopped in confusion. It simply wasn't possible that he could have driven off in such a short time. The lot fed into a road that led off-campus, but it was clearly visible for a considerable distance and she'd seen no cars on it.

"Emily! Em, what's going on?"

She turned reluctantly to see Ben running toward her. "Did you see him?"

"See who?"

For one brief, crazy moment, Emily wondered if she might have imagined him. But then she remembered Toby's expression—and that, of course, brought up an entirely new set of questions.

"The man who stole my book," she told Ben. "He was there in the back, near where you were sitting—and now he's gone. How could he have gotten away? I was sure he must have come in this direction."

Ben took her arm. "Do you think we could talk about this inside? We're both getting soaked."

Emily cast one last disbelieving look around the lot, then let Ben lead her back to the student center. She was so angry and frustrated that she hadn't even noticed how thoroughly soaked she was.

Someone had apparently called campus security, since an officer in a hooded rain poncho reached the building from the opposite side just as they were about to enter. Emily stood dripping onto the terrazzo floor of the lobby and explained the situation as curious students milled about.

Ben hadn't seen the stranger, but fortunately for Emily's peace of mind, several others remembered him. He'd come in late in the lecture.

She also discovered that the officer had come from the gymnasium, which lay on the other side of the student center, and he'd seen no one either.

"But that's impossible!" Emily protested, thinking about the open space between the two buildings. "He ran out this door; I saw it closing when I got into the lobby. And he wasn't on the green or in the parking lot."

The officer agreed that it seemed impossible he could have gotten away, then shrugged and pointed to the large poster advertising her lecture.

"You sure he didn't just vanish into thin air?"

Everyone but Emily laughed at that. She was still seething with frustration, but she was also beginning to shiver. Ben suggested that she go home to change, but she had just remembered Toby and insisted that she had to check on him first.

"He was terrified, Ben. You should have seen the look on his face. He must know who he is."

But there was no answer at Toby's apartment,

so Emily let Ben drive her home. She ignored his expressions of concern about the danger this man posed to her. Her mind was focused on Toby Shaw. When she found him, at least she'd know who the stranger was.

As soon as she got home, Emily tried Toby's apartment again, but there was still no answer. Confused and now worried about Toby, she went upstairs to change.

She was soaked through to the skin, so she toweled herself dry, changed into jeans and a sweater, then turned on the blow-dryer. While she dried her soggy hair, she thought about the stranger, about the three times now that she'd seen him, and about why he had stolen her book.

Strangely enough, until she thought about Toby's obvious fear of him, Emily hadn't really been afraid of the man. Ben seemed to think he might be a psychopath who had fixated on her, but Emily didn't believe that, even though it was just what the police had suggested.

Was she wrong to be more curious about than fearful of this man?

She turned off the blow-dryer and started to go back downstairs, then stopped. Round and round in her mind went all that she knew about him—beginning with that strange aura of invincibility she'd felt when she'd first encountered him.

She thought about his inexplicable entry into her house. One police officer had joked that he "must walk through walls." And just a short time ago, he'd managed to vanish into thin air. It was then that Emily caught that thought that had been lost to sleep the night she'd reread Neville's book:

"If you meet one, you will know."

"Shekaz," she murmured in a tone of wonder. A tremor that was part fear and part excitement ran through her, and she sank onto the bed. Shekaz. The highly trained warriors of the magic tribes, the ones in whom all their powers were greatest—including, according to the old woman, the power of teleportation.

How long she might have sat there, lost in the pure wonder of such a possibility, Emily would never know. Ben was calling up the stairs to her. She drew back from what she immediately knew had been temporary madness and hurried down to seek the comfort of his very real company.

After trying one more time to reach Toby, Emily decided to go to his apartment. Ben drove, continuing his gentle harangue about her disregard of her own safety. Emily wondered what he'd say about her *sanity* if she told him what she'd been thinking a few moments ago.

The mailbox in the downstairs hallway listed Toby as the sole occupant of apartment three in the converted Victorian house. Emily knocked on the door, then pounded loudly when there was no response.

"Toby! It's Professor Carr!"

At last she heard sounds inside, and a moment later a still-pale Toby opened the door.

"Toby, thank goodness you're all right! I tried to call you. That man who frightened you—he's the one who stole my book. Who is he, Toby?"

"I don't know who you mean, Dr. Carr," the boy said with a blank look.

Emily stared at him in disbelief. "The tall, dark-haired man in the back of the room. Isn't he the reason you ran out?"

He shook his head. "No, I got sick. I think it was something I ate." He flashed that quick smile. "I ate in the Barfeteria."

Emily didn't believe him. Even his use of the students' nickname for the cafeteria in the Barr Student Center didn't ring true. She'd never heard Toby use student slang for anything before.

Ben stepped forward and Emily distractedly introduced him. Why would Toby lie?

"Look, Toby," Ben said forcefully, "that man could be dangerous. He might want to harm Dr. Carr."

For one brief moment, Emily saw something flicker in Toby's pale eyes, but it was gone too quickly for her to read. Then he quickly shook his head.

"I don't know who you mean. I didn't see him."

Emily knew they would get nothing more. "Okay, Toby, I'm sorry we bothered you—but I *was* worried about you. Are you sure you're okay now?"

He nodded. "I'm fine. But thank you for checking on me."

They both remained silent until they were back in Ben's car, and then Emily burst out, "He's lying, Ben! I know it!"

She half-expected Ben to tell her she was being foolish, but he nodded solemnly. "I think so, too. But why?"

The next day Emily went to the registrar's office to see what she could learn about Toby Shaw's background. It was the only way she could think of to ease the frustration that gnawed at her and disturbed her sleep.

Toby, she discovered, was a U.S. citizen, but his home address was listed as Geneva, Switzerland, and he'd graduated from a private school there. His father's occupation was listed as "international financier." No occupation was given for his mother.

His grades were excellent—a perfect 4.0, and there had been no disciplinary actions against him.

She flipped through his file to the interview conducted with all prospective students and their parents. The interviewer said that both parents and son were very formal in their demeanor and speech, and she'd found the parents to be quite charming. As for Toby, she found him to be rather shy, but eager to come to Wellsford. The school had been recommended to him by a distant relative who'd graduated from Wellsford before Emily's time.

The interviewer had recommended he be accepted, although she expressed doubts that he would take part in extracurricular activities. He seemed, she said, to be a loner.

After returning the file, Emily left the building deep in thought. His father could have enemies, she supposed. Financial wheelers and dealers could get themselves into all sorts of trouble. But she couldn't see the stranger as a "hit man." And neither did that explain his interest in *her*, or in Neville's book.

By the time she reached her office, Emily had been forced to the conclusion that Toby had been telling the truth, after all. So she was back to square one with the dark stranger.

That afternoon a locksmith came to add second

locks to her doors—sliding bolts that could only be used when she was at home. Ben had persuaded her to take this precaution after she'd refused his suggestion that she stay with him for a while.

Emily appreciated Ben's concern, but although she *was* uneasy about this man, she still wasn't truly frightened of him. She was also determined not to let him rearrange her life.

Besides, although she hadn't told Ben about it, she not only owned a gun, she also knew how to use it. Her father collected handguns and had bought her an expensive little German-made automatic. Then he'd taken her to his private club and taught her how to use it. Periodically she went to a range near New Haven and maintained her skills, more to satisfy her father than out of any fear.

Last night, after Ben had reluctantly taken his leave, Emily had gotten out the gun and stared at it. The cold steel felt very reassuring in her hand—which probably meant that she was more afraid of the stranger than she was willing to admit.

Alec leaned back in the warm, swirling waters. A Berlioz symphony filled the big, glass-walled room. Beyond the windows lay his ever-evolving gardens, shadowed now in the late afternoon. He picked up a crystal wineglass and sipped at its contents, lost in thought.

He didn't like this situation. From the moment he'd spotted that kid, Alec had felt the situation grow more urgent. The thought of one of them— even a boy—near her was very troubling. It seemed to lend credence to their speculations.

On the other hand, from what he'd seen, Wellsford was an excellent school, and it was certainly possible the boy was there simply for an education.

But whatever the reason for his being there, the Mevoshee would quickly become curious, thanks to Alec's appearance. His damnable curiosity meant that some action would now be required.

Menda, the Council Leader, was not happy with him. She knew— as he did himself—that he'd had no business being there.

Emily Carr's face swam before his eyes. He saw her as she'd been at the lecture: beautiful, vibrant, sure of herself. She was a wonderful lecturer, and she knew her subject. But she was also quite possibly very dangerous.

At last the soothing waters and the soaring music began to do their work. His concerns about Emily Carr slipped deeper into his mind. But the woman herself remained very much there, tormenting him and sending his thoughts in a direction they hadn't gone for more than a year—not since he'd lost Janna.

Emily unfolded the map eagerly, then traced a finger over it until she located the area: the extreme northern part of New York State, not far from the Canadian border. The Adirondack region. She bent to examine it closely.

Something had hardened in Emily after that episode during her talk. She had an intense dislike of mysteries, stemming, no doubt, from the mystery of her own birth. Mysteries *had* to be solved; that's all there was to it.

Two weeks had passed and the stranger had not reappeared. Some instinct that certainly didn't bear close scrutiny was telling her that the next move had to be hers. Unfortunately, he'd left no trail for her to follow—except for the book.

The map she was studying, which she had acquired from the New York State Historical Society, was a copy of one drawn in 1882, only eight years after Neville had visited the area.

Her slowly moving finger stopped suddenly. "Aha!"

There it was: Traverton's Mill. The name was written in tiny script, blurred with age. This was the "hamlet" described by Neville, the closest settlement to the place where he'd met the old woman.

She checked the names of surrounding towns —very few—then looked at the current map of the area she'd spread out next to it. After comparing the two for some time, she picked up a Magic Marker and drew a circle in what seemed to be the appropriate spot on the new map. Traverton's Mill, if indeed it still existed, had to be there.

The 1882 map showed a road leading to it from the nearest town, but that road wasn't shown on the current map. However, that didn't mean a road couldn't be there; it could simply be an old gravel road too unimportant to be on the map.

She was going to go up there. Even before the stranger's appearance, she would probably have done so—but now she was determined. The book was her only connection to the stranger, and the story in the book led to that place.

Still, despite what Ben called her obsession

with Neville's book, Emily knew that the chances of unearthing any similar tales up there were slim. After all, Neville's cronies had found nothing. And the chances of tracking down the stranger were probably no greater.

But she was going anyway.

That evening she fixed a farewell dinner for Ben, who was leaving for Europe the next day. She still hadn't agreed to join him in Rumania, although she had gone so far as to apply for a visa just to please him.

The evening was uncomfortable for Emily. Ben was behaving as though they were about to be separated forever, while Emily's thoughts kept straying to her journey to the Adirondacks, about which she'd said nothing to him.

When he finally took his leave, Emily stood in the open doorway with the imprint of his kiss on her lips and watched his car disappear down the dark street. And with a sudden, chilling premonition, she knew that by the time she saw Ben again, her world would have changed irrevocably.

She closed the door and hugged herself against that terrible certainty. What was happening to her?

The subject of Emily Carr had been debated for two weeks, both within the Council and among the people. Alec did not take part in any of these debates, chiefly because he was preoccupied with an internal debate on that same subject.

Many people (and a part of Alec as well) thought that no action should be taken. After all, they reasoned, even if their suspicions regarding her were correct, there was no indication that she had any understanding of her heritage. She was a Tiyazh.

But many more (and the other part of Alec) saw danger in inaction. In all likelihood, the Mevoshee by now would have become interested in her—and who knew where that could lead? No one accused Alec of indiscretion, but that wasn't necessary. He knew he'd been foolish to have indulged his curiosity about her, thereby undoubtedly bringing her to the attention of the other side.

The debate was, however, thoroughly enjoyed by all, despite the possible danger to them this woman posed. No one could remember a time when they'd faced such a momentous decision.

Or perhaps it would be more accurate to say that the debate was enjoyed by all but Alec. For his part, he wished he'd never laid eyes on Emily Carr. Most of the time, anyway.

Finally the Council summoned Alec to its chambers. He sat there before them, listening as they reiterated every point made during the past two weeks, then announced their decision.

"While a strong case can certainly be made for taking no action at all, we believe that the possible risk posed by Emily Carr requires that we take action. She is to be brought here so that we can determine the truth about her."

Menda, the Leader, paused, her pale eyes boring into Alec. "You will do this, Alyeka?"

Alec recognized that he was being given a choice. Did they know of his ambivalence where Emily Carr was concerned? While it was true that they never probed each other's thoughts, regarding that as an unforgivable invasion of privacy among themselves, if not with the Tiyazh, it was also true that some thoughts were too obvious to be ignored.

He hesitated for only a second before nodding.

Emily stowed her bags in the rear of the Wagoneer, then backed off to stare at it ruefully. She'd decided to rent it because she knew she might be traveling back roads, or perhaps even leaving the road entirely, but her innate thriftiness was offended by the thought of wasting so much money on a foolish whim.

And that's precisely what this is, she told herself for the umpteenth time. Make no mistake about it, Emily Carr.

As she stood there berating herself, her neighbor Peggy came through the hedges. Emily had already asked her to feed Chaucer, but she hadn't told her where she was going.

"Good heavens! Did you trade in your Honda?" Peggy stared in shock at the dark blue vehicle with its faux wood panels.

Emily shook her head. "No, it's in the garage. I rented this. I'm going to a very rural area of upstate New York and I thought I might need four-wheel drive."

She immediately regretted her admission. She didn't want anyone to know her destination, lest the stranger show up and find out from them. She thought about telling Peggy that, but decided it sounded overly melodramatic. Besides, he could easily guess that she'd gone up there.

"I should be back within a week, but if I'm not, I'll call. Thanks again for being willing to feed

Chaucer and water the plants."

Fortunately, Peggy was on her way to work and didn't press for any more details. Emily went back into the house one last time. Her briefcase sat in the small foyer. In it was the copy of Neville's book and both maps, as well as a small cassette recorder and the usual supply of notepads. She'd made a copy from the copy and had taken the precaution of storing it in her safe deposit box at the bank.

She picked up the briefcase, then set it down again, gnawing at her lower lip as she raised her eyes to the second floor. She'd decided last night not to take the gun, and she should get out of here before she changed her mind. She was sure it was against the law to carry a handgun with her.

But in the end, caution won out over the legalities. She got the gun and put it too into her briefcase.

"I really am being ridiculous," she said aloud. "He's gone, the book was nothing more than a drug-induced dream, and I'm wasting a lot of time and money."

She was still remonstrating with herself as she began the long drive north.

Using the cover of darkness, Alec moved quietly through the narrow strip of woods behind Emily's house. He'd parked his car a few blocks away in a dark, secluded spot.

He stopped within the protection of the trees at the back edge of her yard. One dim light shone from somewhere on the first floor. The upstairs was in total darkness. It was three a.m. and she would surely be asleep. He reached out, probing delicately for her—then frowned. Nothing.

A moment later he was once more in her house, at the top of the stairs. He heard a soft thud and the cat reappeared, its back once again arched threateningly until he soothed it. Then he picked it up and stroked its thick, soft fur.

"Dammit, where is she?"

Unfortunately, the cat could provide no answers. He set it down again, then began to check the house. It appeared that some luggage might be missing, though not all of it. Her briefcase was gone as well—but not her passport. A suspicion began to form, but he wanted proof.

A quick check of the garage revealed that she hadn't taken her car. He returned to the house. The cat was here, and a watering can and plant food sat on the kitchen counter. So someone was taking care of things for her—and that person would know where she'd gone.

Alec returned to his car, then drove to a nearby motel and checked in for what remained of the night. Late the next morning he drove to her house, parked boldly in the driveway, and went up to knock on her door. He could sense someone watching from the house next door.

After knocking several times and contriving to appear disappointed, he walked to the house from which he was being watched. He barely had time to knock before the door was opened by an older woman.

"Good morning," he said and smiled, while at the same time sending out the slightest possible suggestion of harmlessness. "I wonder if you could tell me whether Emily might have gone away for the summer. We're old friends—

colleagues, actually—and I'd hoped to see her while I'm in the area."

"Oh dear, well, I'm afraid you've missed her. She left yesterday morning. I saw her drive away about ten o'clock."

"Drive away?" he echoed. "But her car is in the garage."

"Yes, she had another car—well, not a car exactly. One of those big station wagon sorts of things, the ones they always advertise on TV for driving into the mountains, you know."

Alec picked up a clear image of the vehicle. He asked where she'd gone, even though at this point the question was superfluous.

"I really don't know where she went or how long she intends to be away, but you could ask Peggy. She lives on the other side of Emily and always takes care of Chaucer. That's Emily's cat."

Alec thanked her, at the same time making sure she wouldn't remember him. Then he crossed the yard to the other house—just on the unlikely chance that he could be wrong. The door was opened by an attractive, dark-haired woman. The moment she saw him, her eyes widened in shocked recognition and she began to close the door again.

Alec reacted with his usual lightning speed, even though he didn't at first understand the cause for her fear. He stepped into the house and closed the door behind him, scanning quickly to see if anyone else was home. But the only other occupant of the house was a baby, sound asleep in his playpen in the living room.

The woman stood perfectly still, her face devoid of all expression. Within moments, he had confirmed his suspicions and was gone from the house.

Peggy walked toward her son's playpen, then paused. Why had she come in here? He was sound asleep, and she'd been busy making stew for dinner tonight. She wandered back to the kitchen, shaking off a strange, disoriented feeling.

Alec drove his car back to Danbury Airport, turned it in, then filed a flight plan for Plattsburgh and climbed into his Cessna. His task was certainly going to be much easier now.

Instead of landing at Plattsburgh, he flew over the airport, then headed west. A short time later, his plane dipped low over the Adirondacks—and vanished.

Chapter Three

With the unpleasant memory of more than three hundred miles behind her, Emily left the motel in Plattsburgh the next morning and climbed into the Wagoneer once again. She decided that if anyone even mentioned the New York State Thruway in her presence in the future, she'd become violently ill.

Why couldn't New York be a more manageable size, like Connecticut? Or more to the point, why hadn't Neville encountered the old woman in the Catskills instead of the Adirondacks?

Nevertheless, she was eager to be on her way again and drove off to the accompaniment of Creedence Clearwater Revival's "Bad Moon Rising," a song guaranteed to drive away any lingering sleepiness. As she sang along, it occurred to her that the line about the "devil on the loose" might be uniquely appropriate. *Something* was surely on the loose. How else to explain the compulsion she'd felt to undertake this absurd trip?

Despite her attempts to make light of it, Emily was uneasy. She'd often felt the urge to follow certain tales to their origins, but nothing had ever felt quite like this. And never before had she heard a quiet voice within her urging her to forget about it and go home.

Two hours and only two wrong turns later, she reached Thomasville, the town the old map showed to be closest to Traverton's Mill. She drove slowly along the main street, then let out an appreciative sound when she saw the small library. Three elderly women were standing on the front porch, books in hand. Emily parked the Wagoneer and went up to them.

She was informed that the library would be opening in a few minutes, then discovered to her delight that one of the women owned a small bed-and-breakfast and would be happy to provide her with accommodations.

A cheerful young librarian unlocked the door, and it was only as the women trooped inside that Emily noticed a sign proclaiming that the library was also the site of the local historical society. Fortune was surely smiling upon her this day.

She wandered about the rows of bookshelves while the women turned in their books and chatted with the librarian. Then, when they had taken themselves off to find new reading material, Emily approached the young woman herself.

She introduced herself as a professor of folklore who happened to be visiting the area, and inquired if it might be possible to speak with someone from the historical society.

"Well, there's no one actually here. They have some displays upstairs and you're welcome to look at them—but if you could tell me what you want, I might be able to steer you to the right person."

So Emily explained about Neville's book and Traverton's Mill, then asked if the village still existed.

"Well," the librarian laughed, "I guess that depends on your definition of existence. There's not much left of the mill itself. In fact, there might be nothing at all left anymore. I haven't been over that way for years. But I'm pretty sure there are still a few houses there.

"I've never heard any tales about magic people around here, but if there ever was such a story, the person most likely to know about it would be my grandmother. She's eighty-five and still as sharp as a tack, believe me. She's a retired schoolteacher. She actually taught in a one-room school, and she lives in it now. She bought it when the county abandoned it."

Emily smiled. "That's what I call dedication. Do you think she'd be willing to talk to me?"

The librarian laughed. "You may regret asking. She does love to talk. I'll call her. Would you like to go out there now?"

"I'd love it—if it's convenient for her, of course."

The woman went into her office, then returned a moment later to inform Emily that she was invited to lunch and a "nice long chat."

"You may be there for dinner as well," she

grinned. "But at least she's a great cook."

Emily thanked her, then paused. "I have one more question. Has there by chance been anyone else in here asking about Traverton's Mill—a tall, dark-haired man?"

The librarian shook her head, but she seemed puzzled and Emily decided to enlist her help just in case he should follow her. If she had chosen the library, so, in all likelihood, would he.

"You see, the discovery of this book is something of a find in my field, and I have this colleague who knows about it and is very jealous. I have reason to believe that he actually stole the book from me, though fortunately I'd already made a copy. He's one of those classic male chauvinists who just can't stand the thought of being beaten by a woman. You know the type." She grimaced very effectively. "And it's possible that he could be coming up here, too."

The librarian rolled her eyes commiseratingly. "I know the type, believe me. If he shows up, I won't tell him you were here—and I won't tell him about Gram, either."

Emily gave her a more detailed description, then added for good measure: "He's very arrogant—and a real bully, too."

"I never heard of you, I never heard of Traverton's Mill—and I don't even *have* a grandmother." She grinned. "Good luck. I hope Gram can help you."

After getting the directions to Mabel Smithers' home and telling Mrs. Davison she would definitely take a room, Emily drove through the town. She didn't know whether to be disappointed or relieved that the dark stranger hadn't shown up here. What other reason could he have had for stealing the book? On the other hand, having already gotten what he wanted, why had he then put himself at risk by showing up at her lecture?

Emily had to admit that his behavior thus far certainly lent some credence to the theory espoused by Ben and the police: that he was some sort of weirdo, possibly even a psychopath. She rather wished that she knew more about that most frightening of all criminals.

Despite the librarian's description of her grandmother, Emily was unprepared for the woman who opened the door to the bright red schoolhouse. She would have guessed her to be no more than sixty-five—twenty years younger than her actual age. And she looked like every kid's favorite teacher: a pleasant, slightly plump, round-faced woman whose bright blue eyes wouldn't miss anything—but just might overlook a few things.

Mabel Smithers led Emily into her charming, old-fashioned kitchen and sat her down to a huge bowl of homemade ham and bean soup and crusty, fresh-baked bread, then listened carefully as Emily explained about Neville's book between bites.

"How fascinating," the woman exclaimed. "I'd never heard of it, but you just might have solved an old mystery for me—even though it's one I hadn't thought about in years. When you reach my age, you learn to live with a lot of mysteries."

"What mystery?" Emily asked, after praising the delicious food.

"When I was a little girl, I used to hear my father and grandfather mention Traverton's Mill from time to time. I don't remember now exactly what they said about it, but it left me with the impression that there was something not quite right about that place."

"What do you mean?" Emily asked eagerly.

"Well, that's just it—I don't remember. Perhaps I never really knew what it was. Just one of those times when you make a certain association and then never quite forget it."

She paused to butter some bread, then continued. "But I *do* know that whatever it was, it kept them from hunting over around there."

"Do you know if anyone lives over there now?"

"I believe so. It seems there are a couple of families living over there—not local people, though. At one time, there were probably ten or twelve families, including the Travertons—but that was years ago, when the mill was still operating."

She went on to talk about the history of the area in general. "There used to be Indians around here, of course, and I suppose the old stories might have come from them. They often told tales of 'magic places,' you know. They pretty much kept to themselves, but my granddad knew them. He was a circuit-riding preacher and their church was part of his circuit."

She pressed Emily to accept some more soup, and just as she got up to refill the bowls, they heard a car drive up. For one brief moment, Emily nearly panicked, certain it must be the stranger. But it quickly became obvious that her hostess knew who it was.

"That'll be Frank, my oldest son. Ever since his Ruthie died, he's taken to dropping by around mealtime." Her blue eyes twinkled. "Of course, if I invited him, he'd say I'm too old to be cooking for him."

A moment later, the front door opened, and she called out, "I'm in the kitchen, Frank."

Frank appeared in the kitchen doorway, and Emily was shocked to see that he actually looked older than his mother. Mabel Smithers introduced them and invited Frank to sit down. True to her prediction, he protested that he hadn't come for her to feed him—but it was a weak protest.

"Maybe you can help Emily, dear. Did Daddy ever say anything about Traverton's Mill that you remember?"

Frank's craggy face grew thoughtful. "I know he never wanted to hunt over there. No one did, as far as I know. He used to say you could get lost too easy in those woods. Never could understand that, though. Dad never got lost in the woods."

He tucked into his lunch as Emily and Mabel returned to the general history of the area. When he had finished, he leaned back in his chair and cleared his throat, drawing their attention.

"I just remembered something Dad told me once—a story *his* daddy had told him when he was a boy. Something about a guy who went hunting over there and didn't come home 'til the next day. I remember it was supposed to have been below zero that night, but the guy was okay even so. I think there might have been more to the story, but that's all I remember."

He shook his head. "Don't expect that's much help."

"Oh, but it *is* helpful," Emily assured him. "It's

just the kind of thing I was looking for. A story like that could easily have accounted for a local belief that the place was haunted—or filled with magicians."

"Could be," Frank agreed. "But it seems to me there was more, that whatever it is that bothers folks about that area goes back even further. Probably old Indian stories, like Mother said."

"If I wanted to go hiking over there, is there anyone who could act as a guide for me? I'd be happy to pay whatever he or she wanted."

"Well," Frank drawled with a quick glance at his mother, "Stevie'd probably be glad to help you out and earn some money. He's my grandson. He's fifteen and he knows the woods—been hunting and fishing since he was ten. One of those kids who just naturally has a knack for knowing where he is. We tease him that he's got a compass for a brain. Sometimes seems like there isn't much else up there."

He chuckled, then looked at her consideringly. "That's pretty rugged country, though. You done much hiking?"

"I've hiked part of the Appalachian Trail and I do some hiking in Harriman State Park every summer," Emily told him. "I've even done a little rock climbing—but I'm far from expert at that."

"Well, then, it'll probably work out. You should be able to get that Wagoneer into some of the old logging roads, so you might not have to walk all that far. There's logging roads all over the place —some in better shape than others."

Then he gave her a mischievous grin. "But I wouldn't count on running into any magic people

69

over there. They probably took off long ago for the Sunbelt, like everybody else."

It was just past midnight when the nondescript pickup truck cruised slowly past Mary Davison's big old Victorian home. The porch light had been turned out, but a small spotlight illuminated the "Bed and Breakfast" sign out front, and two others mounted on the side porch roof lit the parking lot. A dark blue, wood-sided Wagoneer was parked beneath one of them.

Alec drove to the next cross-street, turned around, and drove slowly past the house again. A light was on in one of the second-floor rooms, and just as he approached the house, a silhouetted figure appeared in the long window. She pulled back the semisheer curtain for a moment and seemed to be peering out into the darkness, then dropped the curtain and drew the drapes. Alec caught only a quick glimpse of her—but there was no mistaking that pale gold hair.

He thought it was strange that she should have looked out at that moment—but then a lot of strange things seemed to be happening lately. Too many coincidences for his comfort. It made him wonder about their talents. How much was innate and how much was learned? They'd never really questioned that before. Unlike the Tiyazh, who were always questioning everything about themselves, his people simply accepted who and what they were.

When he was in college and living among them, he'd always been amused by their eternal self-doubting and self-analysis. Now, thanks to

Emily Carr, he was beginning to do the same thing.

He drove on, then slowed again as he approached the town library. Then he swung the pickup to the curb and got out to check the sign affixed to the door.

After that, he drove out of town, then turned onto the road to Traverton's Mill. Halfway there, he turned again, onto a smooth, faintly luminous road, and was quickly swallowed up by the darkness. Behind him, the thick forest closed up, obliterating the road.

The next morning, Sharon, the librarian, had just unlocked the door and returned to the desk when the bell indicated that she had a customer. Wednesday was early-opening day, since the library closed at noon. This early in the morning, she was expecting the usual elderly crowd. But the man who approached the desk was a stranger —and clearly not elderly.

Perhaps it was because he was rather roughly dressed in faded jeans and an old plaid flannel shirt that she didn't immediately associate him with the man the beautiful blonde professor had warned her about. But the warning came back quickly when he greeted her pleasantly, then launched into a story about a change in plans that allowed him to come here to meet a faculty colleague who was doing some research in the area.

"No, I haven't seen her," Sharon lied, feeling decidedly uncomfortable under the scrutiny of those very black eyes. "I'm sure I would have remembered her, because we don't get many strangers up here this early in the season."

Alec thanked her and said she would probably turn up later, then left the library just as two elderly women were approaching the door. He stood aside and held the door for them, his smile just as charming as the one he'd given the librarian. None of them would remember him.

He chuckled as he slid behind the wheel of the pickup. So he was an arrogant male chauvinist who was trying to steal her work? And a bully as well? He laughed aloud, amused by Emily Carr's subterfuge, even though it indicated that she expected to be followed. He wondered who she really thought he was.

The ways of the Tiyazh never failed to amaze him, no matter how much time he spent among them. Half of them seemed to spend a considerable amount of time and energy trying to keep the other half in a state of bondage—failing completely to recognize that they were really two parts of the same whole.

It was beginning to change now, of course—but he recalled quite clearly from his college days the beginning of the women's movement. Out of necessity, he'd remained on the sidelines, but he'd never doubted that the women would succeed one day. As far as he was concerned, the world of the Tiyazh could only be better for it when they finally did.

A sharp and powerful longing for Janna washed over him as he once again approached the Bed and Breakfast. She'd gotten caught up in the women's movement at her college and they'd spent long hours during vacations discussing it.

Janna was on his mind quite a lot these days, he thought as he spotted the Wagoneer still parked in the same spot. Perhaps his sister Leesa was right: it was a final flare-up before the flame died. A good sign, she'd said—a sign that he was finally letting go.

But what he hadn't told Leesa—or anyone else—was that he suspected that Emily Carr was the real reason for this sudden onslaught of memories.

Emily awoke to the knowledge that she hadn't slept well, even though she'd been in bed for nearly eight hours—two more than she usually slept.

Vague memories of strange and terrifying dreams dogged her as she showered and dressed. None of them would come back clearly, and that seemed somehow worse than being forced to relive them.

She opened the drapes and pulled back the lacy curtains and stared out at a bright, sunny day, remembering that strange moment last night when she'd suddenly become convinced he was out there. There'd been an old pickup cruising slowly down the street, but she couldn't see the driver, and in any event it was an unlikely vehicle for him to be driving.

She laughed at that thought now, wondering just what she thought he *should* be driving—a broomstick, perhaps? Or maybe he simply flew through the air under his own power.

But her laughter died away quickly, and she shivered. Who was he? An ordinary weirdo? A psychopath? A Shekaz?

There was too much strangeness in her life at the moment—too much nibbling away at her reasoning, too much that didn't make sense. And now she was going to a place that people seemed to think might be haunted.

I should get out of here right now, she thought: go home and work on my book.

But Neville's book had taken too great a hold on her. She had to see this through. She hadn't the faintest idea what she hoped to accomplish by hiking through the woods today—but she would still do it. Then she would go home and put all this behind her—and put the stranger from her mind as well.

She went downstairs to enjoy a huge breakfast, the likes of which she never bothered to prepare for herself. Considering how reasonable Mrs. Davison's rates were, Emily hadn't expected anything more than donuts and coffee—her usual fare. But there were eggs and home fries and thick slabs of country ham and fresh blueberry muffins, and the excellent coffee came with real cream. Her hostess surely couldn't be getting rich from this business.

The only other guest at the moment was a middle-aged man who was visiting an elderly aunt in a local nursing home. Over breakfast, he inquired about her reason for being here and she told both him and their hostess about her profession and Neville's book.

"Sounds like fun," he said with a grin. "A lot more interesting than selling insurance."

"It *is* fun." Emily smiled, even though that didn't quite describe this particular quest. "When I talked with Mrs. Smithers yesterday, she pointed out one of the most interesting aspects of folk mythology. People often 'know' things without giving a second thought to the origins of that knowledge. It's just passed on from generation to generation without anyone's ever considering the truth behind it."

"Mabel was right." Mrs. Davison nodded. "I've heard many people speak of Traverton's Mill as a place to be avoided—and I never really questioned it, either."

"Do you recall anything specific?" Emily asked.

Mrs. Davison shook her silvered head. "No, nothing more than Mabel told you. I just remember my mother saying it was a 'bad place,' and I suppose I just assumed there were some unpleasant people living over there."

"Do you know who lives there now?"

She frowned. "Two families, I think. They're not local people, but they come here to shop. Welfare types, by the look of them, with poor, half-starved-looking children. Someone said they're living there illegally and those houses aren't fit to live in."

"Doesn't sound much like your 'magic people,'" the other guest chuckled. "Unless they've fallen on hard times."

Emily laughed. "I don't think that would be possible. According to the book, they could turn anything into gold anytime they chose."

"So *that's* the real reason for your search," he teased.

They moved on to a discussion of the supernatural, and once more Emily was confronted with evidence of how willing most people are to believe in the unbelievable. Mrs. Davison told of her grandmother who had visions that had often come true, and her fellow guest spoke of attending a faith-healing when he was little.

Emily said that while few people would believe that stones could be turned into gold, surveys had shown that nearly 70 percent of the population believed in ghosts—and most people accepted all sorts of psychic phenomena as being genuine.

It was, as she had so often said during her lectures, as though we are all aware at some subconscious level of the existence of other worlds just beyond our reach.

Stevie Smithers showed up just as Emily was finishing her breakfast. He was a tall blond boy with a mild case of acne and an engaging smile. While Emily went upstairs to collect her gear, Mrs. Davison persuaded him to have some muffins.

Emily picked up her backpack, then set it down again and opened it. She frowned at the gun. It bothered her to carry it—but she suspected it might bother her still more if she *didn't* take it. She justified it to herself because they would be hiking in wild country, although she knew perfectly well that a handgun provided little protection against bears or whatever else lived in those woods. And it didn't seem likely that it could be any help against sorcerers, either.

When she came back downstairs, she noticed a rifle leaning against the wall in the foyer next to Stevie's backpack. So he had come armed as well. That made her feel somewhat better.

They climbed into the Wagoneer and Emily said she would stop at the grocery store to pick up some lunch for them, although she couldn't imagine herself being hungry after that breakfast.

Stevie patted his well-filled backpack. "Grammie Mabel sent some sandwiches and a thermos of iced tea. There's plenty for both of us."

So Emily picked up fruit and cookies to add to their cache. Then, as she drove past the library, she noticed someone coming out. She hadn't expected it to be open this early and made a quick decision to check with the librarian again—just in case her feeling last night had been accurate.

She found Sharon, the librarian, with her head bent over a computer printout. The young woman looked up and smiled a greeting. Emily asked if the man she'd mentioned had shown up. Sharon shook her curly head.

Emily thanked her and left the library in a state of confusion. Why did she have such a strong feeling that Sharon had been lying—that he *had* been there? It made no sense.

She paused on the library steps and scanned the quiet street, seeking either the man or that pickup she'd seen last night. Then, seeing neither, she got back into the Wagoneer. Of course Sharon hadn't seen him. Why would she lie? It reminded her of the Toby Shaw episode. Her behavior was beginning to seem very paranoid.

Some ten miles out of town, Emily saw the first actual evidence of the existence of Traverton's Mill when they came upon an old signpost that marked a gravel road. Emily turned onto it, then asked Stevie if he knew anything about the people who lived there now.

He merely echoed Mrs. Davison's statement about their being "welfare types" and not local people. Obviously the inhabitants of Traverton's Mill were at the bottom of the local social strata.

They were driving along a straight stretch of road when Emily suddenly saw something shimmer faintly off to the left. In the brief moment before it disappeared, Emily thought that it looked like a path or road.

She didn't realize that she had automatically slowed down until Stevie asked if something was wrong. She shook her head and sped up again just as they passed the spot. There was nothing there now but an unbroken stretch of thick forest. Emily decided that it must have been some sort of weird optical illusion, like those "wet" spots one sometimes saw on roads during the summer.

Still, she felt a faint prickling sensation along the back of her neck, and it hadn't quite vanished by the time Stevie pointed out that they were coming into Traverton's Mill. All that remained of the old sawmill were piles of rotting lumber and some large chunks of metal covered by weeds.

Beyond that was a short row of houses on either side of the narrow road. A few were still more or less standing, with caved-in roofs and empty windows framed by shards of broken glass, but most were little more than stone foundations filled with weeds and debris. Emily had counted nine of them by the time they rounded a sharp bend in the road and came to two more houses, one on either side of the road, that were larger and in somewhat better repair.

An old truck set up on cement blocks and a rusty refrigerator provided yard ornamentation in front of one house, while two grubby-looking children chased some squawking chickens around in front of the other.

Emily slowed to a crawl out of fear that either the children or the chickens would run out into the road. Just as they passed the house, a sallow-faced and very pregnant woman of indeterminate age came to the door and peered out at them.

She thought about stopping to ask the woman some questions, but decided she wasn't likely to be of much help. She looked both frightened and feeble-minded.

"Jeez," said Stevie as they left the sad scene behind. "How can people live like that?"

"Sometimes they don't have much of a choice," Emily pointed out.

"Yeah, that's what Mom says. But Dad says it's because they're lazy and keep on having kids they can't afford because they know everybody else will support them."

Emily made a noncommittal sound. She guessed that there must be some interesting political discussions in the Smithers household.

About five miles past the village, Stevie told her to slow down, and a few minutes later she saw an old, deeply rutted dirt road that made her glad for the first time that she'd rented the Wagoneer. Stevie advised her to switch to four-wheel drive as soon as they turned.

"I don't know how far we'll be able to go," he went on. "These roads are all in pretty bad shape and we had some really heavy rains this spring, so some of them could be washed out."

In fact they were able to drive quite a distance, although both Emily's driving skills and the Wagoneer's talents were put to some severe tests as they encountered several bad washouts. Then, finally, they came to a spot where a hillside had caved in and buried what road there was.

"Looks like this is it," Stevie said, reaching for his backpack. "But we got farther than I thought we would."

He took out some maps and spread them out on the hood. Emily peered at them and frowned. They weren't like any maps she'd ever seen before. Stevie saw her expression and explained.

"They're topo maps—for topography. The U.S. Geological Survey does them." He pointed to a spot near the center of one map that featured swirls of irregularly drawn lines, close together in some places, farther apart in others.

"This is that hill ahead of us. See how the lines are closer on the far side than they are on this side? That means it's steeper on the other side. And these numbers show the elevation."

Emily studied it, comparing it with other features of the land around them, and decided that the maps really weren't all that difficult to read, although she wasn't sure she'd like having to rely on them.

"How big is the area that people avoid?" she asked, staring at the vast empty space around them.

His finger traced roughly a third of the one map and a portion of another. "Most of this, I guess. It's sort of hard to say."

Then he stared off into the distance. "There *is* something weird about it, you know. Me and a couple of guys came over here last summer. Mom and Dad didn't know about it."

He threw her a look that seemed to anticipate a lecture. Then, when none came, he went on.

"Jerry had just got his license and we borrowed his dad's Cherokee. Our folks thought we were going fishing. But, see, we wanted to check this place out. We figured that if no one ever went hunting over here, there might be some bucks with big racks."

"What did you mean when you said there's something 'weird' about it?" Emily asked, stifling her revulsion at the thought of killing deer at all, let alone the absurdity of taking the biggest and strongest.

"You've done some hiking, right?"

She nodded.

"Have you ever been out in the woods where there wasn't a sound—no birds, no animals?"

Emily thought about it and shook her head.

"That's what I mean. Anytime you're in the woods, there are birds and squirrels and chipmunks and other things in the underbrush. You can always hear something, even if you can't see them."

"But there was nothing there?"

"Right. I don't know how long it'd been that way before we noticed it, 'cause we were making noise ourselves. But we all started noticing it when we were climbing this hill. There was this little valley on the other side—and it sure was quiet."

"Can you find that spot?"

"Sure. That's where I was going to take you." He pointed to a spot on the map. "Here it is—see? It's not a bad climb up from this side, but it's a real sheer drop into the valley."

Emily studied it and noticed a thin line meandering not far from the spot he'd indicated.

"What's that?"

"Another logging road. We could have gone that way, but I think it's in worse shape than this one—and besides, you wanted to see the mill."

Emily continued to study the map. The county road that led to Traverton's Mill was shown, and she saw that the other road that led to this mysterious valley came rather close to the county road at a point about halfway between the turnoff and Traverton's Mill—approximately the spot where she'd seen that strange shimmering illusion.

Keeping her tone casual, Emily pointed out the proximity of the two roads at that spot.

"Yeah, but they don't connect. Those old logging roads wander all over the place."

She thought about asking if they'd ever connected, then realized the foolishness of the question. The forest there had been old growth, thick and impenetrable.

"How long will it take to hike there?" she asked instead.

"Maybe about two hours." He shot her a grin. "But that depends on how good you are."

She lifted her chin in mock challenge. "As good as you are, even if I don't know these woods the way you do."

He laughed as he carefully refolded the maps and put them back into his backpack. Then he took his rifle out of the Wagoneer, and Emily stared pointedly at it.

"I hope you don't intend to shoot anything."

"Nope. It's just for protection. There are snakes around here, you know. Bears, too."

Emily tried to ignore the remark about snakes.

"But I thought that bears were supposed to be harmless?"

"They usually are, but this time of year you can run into a mother with cubs, and then things can get pretty hairy."

"Well, let's hope Mom chooses another spot for a stroll today," she replied as she strapped on her backpack. Then she gestured extravagantly. "Lead on."

For the most part, the way was relatively easy. Stevie seemed to be avoiding the steepest climbs, whether for his own benefit or hers she couldn't guess. The weather was perfect: warm sun and a light, coolish breeze.

Because of their earlier discussion, Emily paid more attention than usual to the sounds around them. They saw almost no animals, but there was scarcely a moment when the woods weren't filled with their furtive sounds. And anytime she looked up, she saw a bird or two circling above them.

At one point, something large and dark slithered across in front of them. Emily gasped, and they both stopped. Then Stevie began to move forward, circling away from the snake.

"It's only a blacksnake," he said over his shoulder. "They're harmless."

As far as Emily was concerned, "harmless snake" was an oxymoron. But she followed after Stevie, holding her breath until they were well past the spot.

Then, abruptly, the trek became more difficult, and she forgot to pay attention to sounds as they struggled up steep hills, then all but slid down the other sides. Stevie finally called a halt when they had reached the top of the steepest hill yet.

"That's it, I think," he said, pointing to the next hill barely visible through the trees. "Let me check the map again."

While he studied the map, Emily turned in a slow circle, her ears straining to pick up any sound. Somewhere far behind them she heard a crow calling, but that was all. The forest was silent.

Stevie put away the map. "Yep, that's it all right." Then he saw her expression. "See how quiet it is?"

Emily nodded. They stood there for several minutes, waiting for a sound. The silence was so complete that it almost seemed to be an entity itself. She wasn't displeased when Stevie finally suggested that they get moving again.

The climb up the next hill wasn't all that steep, but it was very long. Emily discovered to her surprise that she was hungry, and Stevie declared that he was *always* hungry. Both of them kept up a steady chatter to dispel the great silence.

Then they emerged from the forest at the very edge of a steep cliff, beyond which lay the valley Stevie had told her about.

It was an incredibly beautiful spot: a long, narrow valley enclosed on all sides by steep hills covered thickly with evergreens. A small stream wandered about the valley floor, visible in spots as it reflected the sunlight.

But somehow it seemed strangely forbidding as well—although Emily had to admit she might be prejudiced by Stevie's description.

They stood there side by side, staring down into the depths of the valley. The silence seemed even greater here, although she wasn't sure how that could be possible. Not a single bird circled in the deep blue sky.

"Can you *feel* the silence?" she asked him after a few moments. "I know that sounds strange, but . . ."

"Yeah, I can feel it. We all felt it—like a sort of pressure or something."

Emily cast a quick look behind them and Stevie laughed. "Yeah, we kept doing that, too. I figure it's like in the movies. When things get real quiet, you know something bad's going to happen."

"Are you trying to scare us both?" She laughed —but she still turned to look again.

They settled down to their lunch. Emily asked Stevie about his career plans and discovered that he wanted to become a marine biologist. She commented that that was a rather unusual choice for someone who'd lived all his life in the mountains.

"Well, I'd like to be an explorer, and Mr. Hardy, my biology teacher, says the ocean's about the only thing left to explore. I took scuba lessons this winter in the pool at the 'Y' and we're going to Florida this summer, so I thought I'd take a look at the University of Miami. My teacher says they've got a good program."

"So you're going to leave all this." She gestured around them.

"Yeah. I would no matter what I decided to do. There's nothing here."

They lapsed into silence again and Stevie's last words echoed in her mind as she continued to stare off into the valley. *Was* there nothing here?

She actually found herself shaking her head in denial. No, there was something here; she was sure of it. But what was it?

When they had finished their lunch and put the remains back into their backpacks, Stevie plunged into the forest again, while Emily paused for one last look at the valley. That sensation of being watched was more powerful than ever—and yet it felt strangely benign.

Suddenly something shifted briefly in the scene before her! For one incredible moment, she saw strange shadows superimposed over the valley—forms she couldn't quite make out. Houses? A place that was far larger than the narrow valley?

It was gone as quickly as it had come.

A deep, powerful sense of loss washed over her—as though she'd been given a teasing glimpse of something she'd sought all her life, only to have it snatched away again before she could truly see it.

Panicked, she turned toward Stevie, to find him just turning to see why she hadn't followed him. She wanted to tell him what she'd seen, but the words stuck in her throat. So after one quick glance back at the now-normal valley, she hurried after him.

By the time she dropped Stevie off at his house several hours later, Emily knew she had to go back to that valley—alone. She wasn't conscious of having made any decision, of having any choice in the matter. She *had* to go; it was as simple as that.

Stevie protested about the money she offered him, but when she insisted, he thanked her and said he would add it to the money he was saving for a car.

Then she asked if she could borrow his topo

maps overnight, not at all sure what explanation she could give for wanting them. But he merely handed them over and told her she could get copies if she wanted at the library, then leave them with his cousin Sharon, the librarian.

Alec saw the silent tears streaming down old Tapha's face and the beginnings of a smile curve her lips—and like the others, he knew even before she spoke.

"Yes," the old woman said in a soft voice the moment her eyes flew open. "She *is* Susurra's daughter. I felt the blood-bond."

"Tapha," one of the other Elders said gently, "are you sure that you are not feeling only your *hopes*?"

Tapha stared at the questioner steadily, but without rancor. "I am not so feeble that I cannot recognize the blood-bond, even at such a distance. She is my daughter's daughter."

The discussion began immediately. Once again a guest at their deliberations, Alec sat slightly apart from the Council, thinking his own thoughts.

From various places of concealment, he'd watched Emily Carr and the boy as they made their way steadily to the valley. Then, when he was certain where they were headed, he'd returned here to inform the others.

So Emily Carr was half-Azonyee. What remained to be discovered was what other blood flowed in her veins.

He realized only now how very much he'd been hoping that she was only Tiyazh. Then he could set aside his thoughts of her. Now, not only could he not forget about her, he knew he would be forced to deal with her. And what if their suspicions proved to be correct, and she was half-Mevoshee as well?

He had doubted that, since he couldn't imagine how he could be so attracted to her if that were the case—but then he realized that if it were true, it meant that another of their race had once been attracted to them: Emily's mother, Susurra.

"Alyeka, explain yourself, please. You appear to be even more disturbed than we are at this news."

He came out of his thoughts to meet the sharp gaze of the Leader. He heaved a sigh and nodded.

"I find her very . . . disturbing."

"Is it possible that you have chosen the wrong word, my son?" His father smiled.

Alec waved a hand in a gesture of surrender. "Very well. I find her attractive."

"So she is," her father agreed. "Except for that pale hair and those blue eyes, she looks very much like her mother—and Susurra was, as we all know, a very lovely woman."

"In that case, Alyeka, we are all glad that you are a Shekaz and therefore trained to a greater degree of self-control." The Leader's dark eyes bored into him.

"Perhaps it is time you find another mate, Alyeka," one of the others suggested gently.

"Yes, I know." He smiled. "But all things come in their time."

"If you wish, someone else can take over from here," Menda, the Leader, stated.

"No, I'll do it. But I won't tolerate any . . . abuse of her."

The others looked at him in surprise, and Alec

immediately regretted his outburst. He was made aware once more of the fact that he'd picked up some bad habits from the Tiyazh. But he also knew that he'd meant what he'd said.

"Alyeka," the Leader said reprovingly, "we have no intention of abusing her. But we must know the truth about her origins."

"And if she *is* half-Mevoshee?" he asked challengingly.

"Then we will decide what to do."

Chapter Four

Alec stood quietly beside her bed, staring at the delicate face and the pale hair fanned out across the pillow. She slept on her back, with the covers drawn up to her throat.

His outburst at the Council meeting came back to him, and he wondered what had prompted it. He didn't even know this woman—not yet, anyway—so why had he felt compelled to rise to her defense? Besides, he'd been among the first to proclaim that she could represent a great danger to them all—and he believed that now more than ever.

He pushed those thoughts away impatiently and reached out with his mind, probing hers with great care. He couldn't be sure that somewhere in her there might be the capacity to recognize his intrusion—even in sleep.

But he found out what he needed to know at this point without her moving at all. He withdrew and was gone from her room.

A short time later he drove the old pickup out of town, heading home. When he came to the luminous road, he thought about the brief vision she'd had of it. He hadn't expected that. But it hadn't surprised him to discover that she'd also briefly glimpsed his home. Tapha's skills had become less precise with age, and Emily Carr had obviously picked up something while the old woman probed for the blood-bond.

He'd gone to Emily with the intention of planting a suggestion that she return to the valley, only to discover that she had already decided to do just that. The valley itself was drawing her, without any help from him.

Emily devoured her breakfast, thinking ruefully that two days here might well change her eating habits. Then, after paying her bill and thanking Mrs. Davison profusely, she stowed her things in the Wagoneer and drove downtown. She stopped at a camping supply store and bought a compass, gased up the Wagoneer, and reached the library just as it was opening for the day.

Sharon greeted her pleasantly and inquired about her trip into the woods.

"Unfortunately, we didn't come across any magic people," Emily replied with a grin. "But it was an interesting hike, and there *does* seem to be something unusual about the place."

She showed Sharon the topo maps and explained that she'd borrowed them from Stevie and wanted to make some copies. Sharon showed her where the copier was, and Emily managed to copy the portions of the maps she needed. Then she went back to pay Sharon and to hand over the original maps.

"So your colleague lost, after all. And don't worry, if he shows up after you've gone, I still won't tell him anything."

Emily thanked her and said good-bye. As she drove out of town, she thought about Sharon's last remark. This time, she'd had no sense at all that she was lying. So obviously she hadn't been lying yesterday, either.

What I need, she told herself, is to get back home and into a familiar routine. I've really let myself get carried away this time.

But she reminded herself that even if she'd overreacted to the mysterious valley, the dark stranger was quite definitely real, and not the result of an overworked imagination. Furthermore, she had awakened with the certainty that he was around here somewhere.

She kept an eye on the rearview mirror as she approached the turnoff to Traverton's Mill. Was it really such a good idea to go back there alone, even if she did have a gun?

But she continued to drive even as she gave herself numerous reasons why she should go home instead. She was going back because she *had* to go back; it was as simple—or as complex —as that.

Emily had been so caught up in her internal debate that she failed to realize she was once again approaching the spot where she'd seen that strange mirage the day before. In fact, she'd very nearly succeeded in putting it from her mind entirely, ascribing it to some obscure scientific phenomenon she couldn't have understood even if it had been explained to her. A trick of the light and weather conditions, no doubt.

So she gasped in amazement when she saw it again! But this time she kept her eyes on it, slowing down only slightly as she approached the spot where, against all reason, a road shimmered faintly in the darkness of the forest.

She rolled to a stop a few yards from the place where it intersected with the road to Traverton's Mill. And this time it not only continued to exist, it even seemed brighter, more defined.

She backed up slightly and pulled the Wagoneer off the road, then peered cautiously all around her and opened the door. Her eyes never left that luminous path that seemed to be glowing with an inner light, rather than merely reflecting the sun. Then, as if to prove her point, the sun dipped behind a cloud—and the path seemed to grow even brighter.

Still holding onto the door and poised to jump back in, Emily turned slowly to check her surroundings once more. No one was in sight.

Taking a deep, steadying breath, she walked the few yards to the mirage, certain it would vanish upon such close inspection. But even when she tentatively put out a foot to touch it, it remained very much there.

She bent to examine the surface more closely. It almost appeared to be crushed glass, but when she touched it, it was smooth, not sharp. She withdrew her hand and stared down the length of the road. It was visible for about a quarter-mile, after which it made a sharp bend and apparently turned downhill.

Then she returned to the Wagoneer and got out Stevie's maps. Each time she looked up from them to the road, it seemed to be both beckoning her and taunting her.

From a hillside about a half-mile away, Alec watched her through powerful glasses. He knew she would return to the valley in any event, but he was curious about whether she would choose this route. It would be, he thought, a measure of the pull exerted by the valley. If she chose to venture onto a road she knew didn't exist, then the lure of the valley was powerful indeed.

He waited patiently as she bent over some maps, then stared for a long time at the road, and finally got into the Wagoneer and drove forward onto the shining path.

From the moment she drove onto the strange road, the voice of reason that had been urging her not to do this subsided. Something else took over in its stead—something very deep and primitive. At one level, she knew she had just taken the first step out of reality, and she feared that greatly—but just as she'd known she *had* to return to the valley, so now she knew she had to take this road to get there.

The road was perfectly smooth and seemed to be running straight through the forest, dipping and rising with the contours of the land. She'd gone nearly a mile before she looked into the rearview mirror.

Despite her certainty that she should take this road, a wave of terror rushed through her. Behind her she saw nothing but thick forest!

She stopped and turned around to stare out the rear window, but all she saw was that same unbroken stretch of forest. The road was literally vanishing the moment she had passed!

That gave her some pause, and she sat there for a moment. She hadn't gone far. Should she turn around, hoping it would then reappear and carry her back to the *real* road?

But that deep certainty soon gained the upper hand and she drove forward again, this time keeping an eye on the odometer. According to the maps, she should soon reach an intersection with one of those old logging roads.

In fact, she reached it more quickly than she'd expected, but her relief was tempered by the realization that the shimmering path she was on merely crossed the intersection and continued on its way.

She stopped in the middle of the intersection and, after once again checking her surroundings, got out and spread the maps on the hood, then checked her compass as well. Then she got back into the Wagoneer and continued along the nonexistent road. There was no doubt in her mind that it would lead her directly to the mysterious valley, although if she were correct, she would approach it from the opposite end.

Less than a half-hour later, Emily saw the shining road come to an abrupt end. When she glanced again in the rearview mirror, it had ceased to exist behind her as well. The Wagoneer sat in a small clearing totally surrounded by forest, as though it had been dropped there from the sky.

She got out, once again holding onto the door and poised to jump back in at the slightest sign of . . . what? What on earth did she expect to find out here? Some other intrepid explorer who had followed the now-vanished road? The dark stranger perhaps?

Thoughts of him made her reach quickly into the back of the Wagoneer to grab her backpack. Inside it she felt the reassuring hardness of the gun.

Ahead of her was a thick fringe of trees around what appeared to be a cliff. She strapped on the backpack and started in that direction, knowing even before she came out of the forest what she would find.

And there it was: the valley. Just as she'd expected, she was seeing it from the opposite end, but there was no doubting that it was the same deep, narrow valley. For some distance on both sides, a rocky ledge jutted out into the valley. She walked along it for some time, studying the valley from various angles.

Shadows once again moved across the valley floor, but this time there was a perfectly obvious explanation for them: clouds that were from time to time obscuring the sun. Yesterday, though, the sky had been perfectly clear.

It took some moments before she noticed that absolute silence, and when she did, she began to cast nervous glances around her. The feeling of being watched grew ever stronger, but she ignored it and removed her backpack, then drew out a thermos of iced tea.

She sat down and considered the situation. She'd come here on a road that didn't exist—a road that had led her directly to a valley avoided by all living things. A valley where she'd seen strange shadows.

Now what was she to do—having taken leave of her senses to come here? Should she attempt to find a spot where she could descend into the valley itself? Or should she simply wait here to see what would happen next?

Of all the emotions she felt at this moment, fear was unquestionably the least of them, although the rational part of her knew it should be uppermost.

She drank some more iced tea and thought about Neville's book. Would she, like him, suddenly discover an old woman wandering about where she had no right to be?

Even as she thought this, another thought crept from her subconscious into the forefront of her mind: Neville's story hadn't been the result of a drug-induced dream. It had been true! And somewhere down there in that valley lay the proof.

But if Neville's story was true, then what about the dark stranger? Where did he fit into all this? Because she was quite certain that he did.

"If you meet one, you will know." The old woman's statement about the Shekaz came back again. Emily shivered. If he *was* one of them, why was she interested in her? Had their first meeting in the bookstore been accidental, or part of some unknowable plan?

She reached for her backpack, intending to take out an apple. But she suddenly had the strongest sensation of something touching the back of her head lightly, and her hand moved quickly to the spot. At the same time, she turned around.

He was about thirty feet away, leaning casually against a tree, arms folded across his sweater-clad chest and one long denim-clad leg propped against the trunk.

And he was smiling slightly—a lazy sort of smile that suggested he'd been there for some time.

Emily pulled herself quickly into a crouch, then grabbed the backpack and pulled out the gun. He remained where he was, and that slightly amused expression didn't waver.

"Hello, Emily Carr," he said in that low, pleasant voice she'd been hearing in her dreams. "I'm Alec."

"You're a thief," she stated succinctly, rising and leveling the gun on him with both hands.

"Guilty as charged," he acknowledged pleasantly. "But I *do* resent being called an arrogant male chauvinist."

Then he shrugged. "Well, I suppose 'arrogant' is fair enough, but not the rest of it."

Emily frowned. How could he have known about that—unless Sharon had been lying, after all? But that question was far less important at the moment than another: why wasn't he reacting to the gun?

His dark brows drew together. "Who was it

who was supposed to be 'faster than a speeding bullet'? I can't seem to recall." Then he shrugged his wide shoulders again.

"Well, it doesn't matter. He wasn't—but *I* am."

"You're what?" she asked in confusion. This conversation was rapidly becoming surreal. She was aiming a gun at him—and he was chatting pleasantly.

"I'm faster than a speeding bullet. But it's hard work, so I wish you wouldn't pull the trigger."

Emily chose to ignore that. "Who are you and what are you doing here?" she demanded, still aiming the gun, even though her arms were becoming more tired by the moment.

"I told you my name. As for why I'm here—well, you could think of me as being an updated version of Neville's old woman."

"Are you trying to tell me that you're Azonyee?" she scoffed, her fear having propelled her out of her earlier fantasy.

He merely nodded, still smiling.

"And I suppose you're a Shekaz as well?"

Another nod. Then he pushed himself away from the tree and began to walk casually toward her. She tensed and cocked the gun. He stopped, now less than twenty feet away.

"Well, this is as far as I come. Any closer and I wouldn't be able to stop the bullet if you get foolish. We used to practice with rubber pellets."

He's insane, she thought. He might even be a psychopath.

"I'm perfectly sane—and psychopaths don't exist among us."

The unbelievable arrogance of this man made

her angry—so angry she didn't bother to question how he'd read her mind. But she *had* started to think again about that aura of invincibility that had drawn her attention from the very beginning.

"So you picked up on that from the beginning, did you?" he asked with a low chuckle. "I'm not really invincible, but rather close to it, I guess."

Emily said nothing. At this point, she was even afraid to *think* anything. But she managed to hold the gun steady even so.

"Emily Carr, you disappoint me. You're not ready to face the truth even now. Very well. What about the road that brought you here—the same one you saw yesterday, too? Then there are those shadows you saw down in the valley yesterday." He gestured behind her toward the valley.

In her shock, Emily actually began to lower the gun. But then she brought it up quickly again, as though the cold, hard steel were her last remaining link to reality.

He *couldn't* know about those visions. She hadn't told *anyone*.

"Did you sleep well last night?" he asked with that damnable smile.

"Wh . . . what do you mean?"

"Just that you must have awakened feeling more refreshed this morning. Deep sleep will do that. You can thank me for it if you like."

She *had* felt exceptionally well rested this morning. Confusion began to swarm over her—but she still kept the gun aimed at him.

He stared at it. "That gun is beginning to bother me, and you can't hold it like that much longer in any event."

The gun suddenly jerked itself from her grasp and went sailing off behind her. She automatically whirled around to stare after it. Then, unbelievably, it reappeared, moving slowly through the air to his outstretched hand just as she turned to find him beside her. He held it pointed away from her and examined it.

"Very nice. Perfect for someone your size. Can you actually shoot it straight?"

Emily began to back slowly away from him, then tripped over her backpack and landed on the rocky ground. He dropped the gun and hurried to her, crouching down just as she tried to scramble to her feet. He halted her by catching hold of her wrist.

"Calm down. Are you hurt?"

She pulled her wrist from his grasp, and winced. Her hand hurt from having the gun wrenched away. He took her wrist again, then slid his hand gently over hers.

"I didn't mean to hurt you," he said with what sounded like genuine regret.

Her hand grew very warm as he covered it completely with his. She tried to tell herself to pull away, but her arm wouldn't obey. Then suddenly he released it and the strange warmth was gone. So too was the pain. He sat back on his heels and smiled at her again.

"Well, Emily Carr, I suggest we get going."

"Where?"

He waved a hand toward the valley. "To my home."

"You live down there?" she asked, her eyes darting about the valley floor even though she knew there was nothing down there.

"In a manner of speaking. There but not there. You know. You read the book."

She edged away from him, then scrambled to her feet, eyeing the gun on the ground behind him. "Now listen, Alec, I'm not coming with you. I'm going back to my car."

"It isn't there."

"What did you do with it?"

"I didn't do anything with it. It just isn't there. Neither is the road."

She had continued to move slowly around him as he spoke. Then she flung herself at the gun—but just as she did, it rose once more into the air and hung there, suspended just beyond her reach. She heard him getting to his feet. Then the gun moved to him and he plucked it from the air. After removing the clip, he handed it back to her.

"There. Since you seem to want it so badly, you can have it." He turned and bent to pick up her backpack.

Emily took off, running at top speed into the forest. She no longer doubted that he was exactly what he said he was, and her fear lent her even greater speed.

But she'd gotten no more than a hundred yards before she was abruptly stopped. Her heart was pounding in her throat and her lungs were heaving—but her feet would not move.

He came up behind her and reached around to pry the gun from her paralyzed fingers. "I'll put it in your backpack."

Then he lifted her into his arms. "Now listen to me. In a moment, everything is going to go black.

You'll be conscious, but you still won't be able to move. I know you're scared, but I promise you'll be safe."

And her world did indeed go black.

But no sooner had the light gone out of the world than it returned: a different light in a different place. Her head began to throb and she felt dizzy. He lowered her onto soft, smooth cushions and knelt down before her.

"It's over. Just rest for a few minutes. You'll be all right."

He withdrew, and she risked opening her eyes again. The room was spinning around her, so she closed them again and fell back against the cushions.

Then she opened them again as she heard him speaking. At first she thought her hearing must be affected as well, because she couldn't understand him. But then, as the room spun less violently, she saw that he was standing with his back to her, speaking in some strange language. A faint bluish glow emanated from something in front of him that she couldn't see. Then the glow vanished and he turned back to her.

"Jeyah will help. I'll get some for you."

He disappeared through a curved doorway and Emily pushed herself up straighter, trying to take in the details of the room even as she sought a means of escape.

The room wasn't large, but she thought it might well be the most luxurious room she'd ever seen. It was impossible to assimilate all that she saw with a quick scan: paintings, various objects of art, a richly hued Oriental rug that covered much of the floor. And gold—a lot of gold. Where the walls met the ceiling there were bands of gold filigree, and more of the same along the mantel and sides of the marble fireplace.

The sofa she sat on and several chairs were covered by some sort of hide that felt like velvet, but both richer and softer to the touch. The wooden tables were a mellow amber color, and glowed with a rich patina that made the intricate carvings in them even more striking.

Across from her was a row of long, narrow windows framed by shutters in that same wood. The shutters were open, and through them she could see an endless stretch of woods.

She shifted her position, fighting down the accompanying wave of dizziness, and saw that behind her was a set of glass doors that were open to a stone terrace and a garden beyond that she could just glimpse.

She pushed herself to her feet, staggered, then fell back again. She knew now why he'd left her a means of escape.

But escape to where? she asked herself. If she were truly in a place that wasn't real, how could she hope to get back to a place that was? Her head throbbed, and she stopped thinking about it for the moment.

When the latest wave of dizziness had passed, Emily's gaze fell on three small jeweled flowers on the table before her. Their stems were gold and the bases appeared to be crystal, or perhaps quartz.

She recalled an exhibit at the Cooper-Hewitt Museum in New York where she'd seen similar ones. Fabergé. She picked up the closest one and saw marks along the stem. But when she tried to read them, her eyes refused to focus and she set it down again—just as he walked back into the room.

"They're Fabergé," he said. "He was a Frenchman who worked for the Russian czars. His most famous creations were the Imperial Easter Eggs —like the one on the shelf there." He indicated a set of free-standing wooden shelves in one corner, supported by thin rods of gold.

Emily followed his gaze briefly, but she'd lost interest in Fabergé. Instead, she stared at the gold tea service he set down on the table between them. The tray and the teapot were banded in precious gems, as were the bases of the gold cups.

He knelt down opposite her and began to pour something into the cups. A strange but enticing aroma filled the air. She was about to ask what it was when he told her.

"This is called jeyah. It's an herbal tea. It will help the dizziness and the headache."

He handed her a cup, and she had it almost to her lips before it occurred to her that she shouldn't be drinking anything this man gave her.

"I want to go home—*now*," she stated, setting down her cup.

"I'm afraid that's impossible," he replied equably. "Drink your tea."

Then, as if to prove it wasn't tainted, he poured himself a cup and began to drink as he watched her with those dark, dark eyes.

She picked up her cup again and sipped at it tentatively. It tasted even better than it smelled.

When she looked at him again, she saw his face more clearly and rather wished that she hadn't.

It was a compelling face; she had to admit that. Not handsome in the classical sense, but boldly masculine. A thoroughly absurd rush of heat shot through her. How could she possibly be attracted to this man?

He raised his eyes to hers briefly, then abruptly got up and moved away to a chair. She thought she detected a certain annoyance in the movement, but she couldn't be sure. Nevertheless, some inner voice suggested that she might have the upper hand at the moment.

"I assume this is your home and I'd like to know why you've brought me here," she said, adopting a frosty, imperious tone.

He stretched out his long legs and continued to sip tea as he watched her. "Before we get to that, are you prepared now to accept that I am what I said I was?"

"At the moment, all you are is a thief who has now kidnapped me," she replied in the same tone.

"So none of this," he gestured around them, "is sufficient proof for you?"

"All this proves is that you're either very rich or a highly accomplished thief."

She finished the tea and set the cup down on the table. But even before she released it, the gold teapot rose from the tray and tipped to pour some more tea. She was too stunned to back away, and just sat there, her eyes traveling from the teapot to him.

"One of the least appealing qualities about you

Tiyazh is your unwillingness to ignore what is self-evident," he said with a slight frown. "I am Azonyee. I'm also a Shekaz. And you know that's the truth."

The teapot returned to its place. Tiyazh. She remembered that word from Neville's book: the Azonyee term for all the rest of the world's population.

"Well, perhaps in your case Tiyazh isn't quite right. I would like to know what you know of your origins, Emily Carr."

Her origins? An uneasiness took root in her. What did her origins have to do with anything?

"Mmm, I thought you must have been adopted when I saw that picture of your family. So you know nothing of your real parents?"

She stared at him. "What picture?"

"The photograph I saw in your house. Please answer my question."

It was an order, not a request, and Emily bristled. "My origins are none of your business."

"On the contrary, they're very much my business. They're the reason you're here. Now please tell me what you know. You must realize that I can find out anyway."

Her anger transformed itself into cold fear.

"Don't be ridiculous," he said, but with surprising gentleness. "I won't hurt you. I merely meant that I can find out for myself, the same way I found out about the visions."

"How could you have known about them?" she asked. "I told no one."

"I read your mind—which is exactly what I'll do again unless you tell me what you know about

107

your real parents."

Emily felt the dizziness return, but this time his words were the cause. She tried to find another explanation, but there was none. Final acceptance of what he was came now—and with it a fear beyond anything she'd ever known.

He got to his feet with a sound of disgust, strode across the room, then turned suddenly to face her again.

"I am *not* some sort of monster, Emily Carr. How could you be more afraid of me now than when you thought I might be a psychopathic killer? And I've done nothing at all to hurt you, despite the fact that I could easily do so.

"If you were an ordinary Tiyazh, I could forgive this attitude of yours. But you aren't—and furthermore, you have studied folklore and magic. You should be more *understanding*."

To her amazement, Emily felt her fear recede, despite his obvious anger. She actually had to restrain herself to keep from laughing. Or was she becoming hysterical?

"No, you're not hysterical. I don't frighten you. It was all pretense on your part—and I dislike pretense."

He returned to his seat again. "Now tell me what you know."

So she told him everything. "But I don't understand why this is important," she finished. Then she put up a hand to stifle a yawn.

He got up and drew her to her feet. "You will have your answers from the Council. For now, you need to rest."

"There must have been something in that tea,

after all," she muttered, more to herself than to him.

"It contains a mild sedative. It's often used by novices after 'porting—or even by experts like me if it's been a particularly difficult 'port."

She frowned, but before she could speak, he explained.

"Teleporting—the way I brought you here. The same way I got into your house and into your room last night."

She just stared at him, trying unsuccessfully to think of something to say. But before she could, he lifted her off her feet and carried her from the room. She was asleep even before he deposited her onto the bed. He drew a cover over her and then stood there staring down at her for a long time.

Alec sat on a cushion at the edge of the terrace, staring out at his garden, his thoughts on the woman sleeping in his bed.

He was displeased with himself for having become annoyed with her. Of course she feared him; why shouldn't she? Azonyee blood might be flowing in her veins, but her thoughts were Tiyazh thoughts. And she couldn't read *his* mind, after all, which he ruefully admitted was just as well.

He felt himself caught in the grip of surpassingly strange emotions. Her beauty touched him deeply. So too did her spirit, and even her vulnerability.

Alec was very uncomfortable with these feelings, so he pushed them away and concentrated instead on his garden.

The garden covered nearly an acre of hilly land. It was actually a collection of many small gardens, each separated from the others by narrow walkways and small bridges, or by fountains and waterfalls. A botanist would have seen immediately that it was also an impossible garden, containing species that couldn't possibly survive here. Lush jungle foliage coexisted with specimens from the frozen tundra and arid deserts.

He emptied out his mind, then let it fill up with the sounds of the fountains and waterfalls and the little brook that flowed over rounded stones. After a while, he began to make some minor adjustments. A waterfall shifted its path slightly. Rocks moved about.

Emily opened her eyes to darkness—and fear. She very nearly screamed, stifling it at the last possible moment as the dim shapes of furniture appeared. She sat up and saw pale moonlight streaming in through the windows. And then she remembered it all.

Suddenly the darkness became threatening once more, and she fumbled for a switch on the carved wooden bedside lamp, then gave up.

"He probably just *thinks* it on," she muttered, then shivered as the knowledge of all he could do flooded her mind.

A Shekaz—the most powerful of all in a race of incredible sorcerers. How laughably inadequate her first descriptions of him to herself now seemed.

And he still hadn't told her why she'd been brought here.

Then she frowned, searching her memory for something he'd said that now seemed important. "If you were an ordinary Tiyazh . . ." Then he'd said she wasn't. What on earth had he meant? He'd made some reference to her profession, but she didn't think he'd meant that. And why was he so fascinated with her origins?

For one moment, Emily found herself edging close to the unthinkable, but she backed off quickly and got out of bed. She was pleased to discover that both the dizziness and the headache were completely gone. In fact, she felt quite good—apart from being ravenously hungry.

The gleam of gold in a carved doorway caught her attention, and she discovered it led to a bathroom. She stopped to stare at the huge tub set before a wall of glass. She walked to it and put out a hand to touch the rim and felt the eternal coolness of real marble.

She found the toilet in a separate cubicle, then turned on the gold taps and splashed some water over her face. After that, she studied her face as best she could in the mirror. There was a ceiling light fixture—gold, of course—and more gold lamps around the mirror, but she couldn't find the means to turn them on.

She looked terrible: pale and disheveled, her long braid partially undone. She tugged at it and freed it the rest of the way, then combed her hair with her fingers.

Her stomach began to rumble in protest of who knew how many missed meals. So she left the bathroom, found the door into the hall, and crept along it quietly until she reached the living room.

The light was better there because of the bright moonlight pouring through the windows and the glass doors. And so she saw him immediately.

He was sleeping on the long sofa, lying on his back with one arm flung out to touch the floor. A blanket covered him from the waist down, but his chest was bare.

Emily stood there for a moment staring at him and fighting that treacherous warmth that was spreading rapidly through her. Did he know about it? If he could read her thoughts . . .

She turned away, following the direction he'd taken when he'd gone to get the tea.

The kitchen was reassuringly normal. No gold anywhere. Just a very modern, well-equipped kitchen. She opened the refrigerator and saw that its light, at least, didn't seem to require magic to operate.

It was well stocked with fruits and an assortment of cheeses and other things in plastic bowls. Tupperware in the home of a sorcerer? She stifled a giggle.

After rummaging about some more, she made herself a meal of fruits and cheeses and crackers, assembling it all on a wooden tray. She started to carry it to the small table set in a glass-walled corner filled with plants, then stopped, remembering that garden she'd glimpsed.

So she crept back through the living room, taking a circuitous route that kept her as far from his sleeping form as possible.

Even in the color-draining moonlight, the garden was breathtaking. She set the tray down beside some cushions, then dropped onto one, her need for food temporarily set aside as she stared at the scene before her. There were waterfalls and fountains and she could see the gleaming silvery ribbon of a small stream. In the silence of the night, their combined sounds were wonderfully musical, and the light breeze brought subtle, exotic scents.

She devoured the food, then stretched out on the cushions as she continued to stare at the garden. The breeze was cool, but not cool enough to drive her back inside.

She must have dozed off, because when she opened her eyes again, the sky was beginning to lighten and the breeze was chilling her. She got to her feet, then stopped as she saw the dark figure in the doorway.

He came toward her, clad only in loose-fitting white shorts that emphasized his lean, muscular body and bronzed skin. He sank down onto a cushion and yawned as he ran a hand through his disheveled black hair. He looked almost unbearably sexy, and when he suddenly looked up at her, she was certain he must have read her thoughts.

She cried out as something settled over her shoulders. Then she saw it was a blanket and drew it about herself.

"Thank you," she said, trying not to be astonished at this latest bit of magic.

He merely nodded and turned away from her to stare off into the garden. She sank down again, keeping a careful distance from him.

Overhead, the sky grew lighter still, and streaks of pale gold and pink appeared. Then she heard a slight change in the sounds of the water and peered out into the garden. She drew in her breath audibly as she saw movement out there. The course of a nearby waterfall altered. A fountain suddenly rose to greater heights. She turned back to him to find him still staring fixedly at the scene.

He's doing that, she thought, then wondered that she had any capacity for amazement left.

"It's my hobby," he said without turning to her.

They both sat there silently as the sky grew brighter. From time to time, Emily cast a quick sidelong glance at him. Despite her fears, she was thoroughly fascinated by him, and she knew he must know that. She wondered just how good he was at reading her thoughts. Could she conceal *anything* from him?

He turned to stare at her, his expression neutral. "No, you can't."

Then he stood up with one fluid movement that made her think of a ballet dancer, and not the athlete she'd likened him to previously.

He extended a hand to her. "Come. It's light enough now for me to show you the garden."

"You created all this yourself?" she asked as they walked along the path.

"Yes." He began to explain about the different habitats, naming plants she didn't recognize— which were many.

"But where did you get them—and how can they live here?" she asked, unable to understand how desert plants could thrive next to species from rain forests.

"I went to these places and brought them back. They survive because I told them to."

There was no hint of humor in his tone, and Emily stared at him. His face was turned in the other direction, but when he turned back to her, he was smiling.

"We're walking in a place that doesn't exist," he pointed out. "So it shouldn't seem strange that this can happen, too."

They came to the end of one path, where a steep, rocky incline lay ahead of them.

"This is where I plan to extend it next, but I haven't decided what to do with it yet."

She could see that creating a garden on that barren slope would be difficult. "And you'll do it all with magic?"

"Only if I feel lazy—or if it's beyond my physical abilities."

They retraced their steps, and when they came to an intersecting path, he stopped. "I'm going for a run. I'll stop to pick up some clothes for you as well."

Before she could reply, he jogged off into the woods. Emily started back toward the house, then stopped with a startled cry as his voice came to her—*inside her head.*

"Use the tub if you like. I've turned it on for you."

She pressed shaking fingers to her temples. Telepathy. Did that mean he could read her thoughts at a distance as well? She held her breath, half-expecting an answer—but none came.

When she walked into the bathroom a few moments later, she saw that the tub had been filled and the water was churning lazily. She began to strip off her clothes, then stopped. Was it possible that he could see her as well as speak to her across the distance?

After a moment, she finished undressing and slipped gratefully into the tub, determined not to let her paranoia get out of hand—justified as it might be in this case.

Chapter Five

He walked in unannounced just as she was drying herself with a big, thick towel. Emily knew that she had probably lingered too long in the tub, but that certainly didn't excuse his intrusion. She wrapped the towel tightly around herself and glared at him.

He handed her a pile of clothes and turned to leave the bathroom. "Is seeing your body any more intimate than reading your thoughts?" he asked just before he closed the door with careful emphasis.

His question had just the effect on her that she assumed he'd intended. She simply stood there for a time, staring at the closed door. Then, wanting to deny him the pleasure of her confusion, she picked up the clothes he'd left for her.

There were several sets of soft cotton trousers and matching tops, underwear and a pair of beautifully made moccasins. And it all fit perfectly. Perhaps he'd read her mind to determine her sizes.

How could these people possibly live with each other? Surely no society where people spied on each other's thoughts all the time could have survived so long. It was "Big Brother" on a scale that even Orwell couldn't have envisioned.

She dressed and rebraided her hair, then walked out of the bathroom to find him waiting for her.

"Do you always listen in to each other's thoughts?"

He actually looked surprised. "No, of course not."

"But you find it perfectly acceptable to do that to *me*?"

He said nothing as he walked past her into the bathroom, but she would have sworn that he'd looked just the tiniest bit chagrined.

Emily went back out to the garden to await what she regarded as being the next round in this strange battle. She sat down on a cushion and thought about her situation, knowing that he might well be listening into her thoughts. Since he seemed at the moment to be reluctant to answer her questions, perhaps he might feel moved to comment on her thoughts.

Was it Neville's book? Was that the reason she'd been brought here? Was there something in it— something she'd overlooked—that could pose a threat to them? If so, bringing her here wouldn't serve their purpose. Others now knew about the book as well.

"We're not concerned about the book," said that low voice inside her head.

Once again, her hands flew automatically to her temples, but she persisted. "All right, if it wasn't the book, then what is it?"

But the only sounds she heard were the songs of birds that had come into the garden and the light, pleasant music of the waters.

When she decided that she wasn't going to get an answer, she tried to absorb the tranquil beauty of the day. The sun had by now climbed high enough to be warm on her face, and a feather-light breeze drifted down from the pine forest, bringing its own scent to add to that of the garden.

Sometime later, she heard a sound and turned to see him emerge from the house, wearing nothing but a towel wrapped about his trim waist. His bronzed skin and black hair still glistened with moisture. If tranquillity had been eluding her before his arrival, it vanished altogether now.

He walked over to the cushions where she sat, flung the towel aside, and stretched out beside her. Emily quickly averted her gaze—but not before she felt the impact of that magnificent male body.

He knows, she thought with acute embarrassment. He must know the effect he has upon me. Perhaps he's even toying with me—or maybe this is intended to be some form of reparations for his having barged into the bathroom.

On the other hand, who knew what their customs were? Emily had traveled enough to know that behavior that is outrageous in one culture can be quite acceptable in another. And she was certainly in his world now.

She waited for him to say something, but he remained infuriatingly silent. Did that mean she had shamed him into not listening in to her thoughts? She decided to test that theory and chose to think about Ben.

No one would really be missing her yet, but even though he was in Europe, Ben would be among the first to become concerned if he couldn't reach her. He'd been more worried than she had about Alec.

"Who is he?" Alec asked suddenly—aloud this time.

Emily said nothing, having decided that two could play this game. She simply kept an image of Ben in her mind.

"Why are you thinking about him? You haven't thought about him before."

She maintained her silence, and the image.

"If you don't want me reading your mind, then answer my questions. I can read minds on many levels, and I've only just touched the surface of yours."

Emily knew a threat when she heard one, no matter how softly it was delivered. She whirled to face him, forgetting entirely about his nakedness until it was too late. So she kept her eyes carefully on his.

"The term 'arrogant' doesn't begin to do you justice, Alec. You're like a child who enjoys showing off."

He met her gaze for a long moment, then

abruptly broke into laughter. "You're right—at least from your point of view. So this Ben thinks I'm some sort of psychopath who's got an obsession with you?"

"From *his* point of view," she said mockingly, "it makes sense."

"Then he doesn't know you came up here?"

She thought about lying, then quickly realized the futility of that. "No—but he knows about the book, and I'm sure he'll guess if he can't reach me."

"Your neighbor is expecting you to be gone for at least a week," he pointed out.

"How did you . . . ? You read her mind, too." She answered her own question disgustedly. "Alec, I want to know why I'm here—and I want to know *now*."

He cocked his head and smiled at her—that same lazy smile she'd seen when she'd met him at the edge of the valley.

"I don't frighten you at all, do I, despite all the 'childish' displays of my powers?"

"No, you don't—and stop changing the subject."

"Interesting," he said, then got to his feet. "Let me get dressed and I'll explain it to you on the way. They'll be waiting for us."

"Who'll be waiting for us?"

"The Council of Elders," he replied as he disappeared into the house.

Emily had just enough time to begin getting nervous before he returned, dressed in the same loose garments that she was wearing. But apparently he was making some concession to the occasion. Around his neck, suspended on a heavy gold chain, was a large gold medallion bearing a beautiful intricate design. He saw her staring at it.

"It is an ancient symbol for my work as a Shekaz: the balancing of the earth forces."

Then he motioned for her to follow as he started down the path he'd taken earlier. Curious as she was about his work, she decided to deal with the more immediate issue. She'd thought he hadn't sounded happy about this upcoming meeting.

"You don't like the Council, do you?"

A smile flickered briefly. "So you read minds a bit yourself, do you? It isn't that I don't like them; my parents are both on the Council. But sometimes I disagree with them."

"Like now?"

"That remains to be seen," he responded cryptically. "Now, if you've finished asking questions, I'll explain the situation to you."

She remained silent—but so did he, for so long that she turned to him as they walked along the forest path. He glanced at her briefly, then, to her surprise, reached out to take her hand.

"Emily, this will be difficult for you. That's why I've decided to explain it to you myself, rather than wait for the Council to do it.

"The reason you were brought here is that we have discovered that you are at least partly one of us."

She made only a soft sound as her mind began to race back over the past few weeks: her unwarranted fascination with Neville's book, her obsessive need to come up here, then to return to the valley. It now fell into a pattern she should have seen—and perhaps *had* seen on some level.

"So you'd already guessed that?"

"Maybe. I . . . I don't know. It doesn't shock me as much as it should, so, yes, I guess I might have thought of it subconsciously."

She knew she was rambling, but couldn't stop herself. "When I was a baby, my parents—my adoptive parents, that is—used to call me their 'fairy child.' There's an old tale about fairies leaving babies . . ." She paused, drew in a shaky breath, then went on in a choked voice:

"They were more right than they knew, weren't they?"

But then his exact words came back to her. "You said I'm *partly* one of you. Which part? What did you mean?"

"Your mother was Azonyee. We don't know yet about your father, except that he wasn't one of us."

Her hopes of at last finding her parents had soared—only to plummet again as she absorbed his words.

"You said my mother *was* Azonyee? Is she dead?"

His warm grip on her hand tightened slightly. "Yes. She died a long time ago—shortly after you were born. But you will meet your grandmother. She's a member of the Council. It was she who identified you as being of her blood when you first came to the edge of the valley."

There were so many questions hidden in his words, but Emily's dazed mind had fixed on an image that was always there: a newborn baby in a big wicker basket on a darkened doorstep.

"Why did she abandon me?" she asked, unable

to keep the pain and anger out of her voice.

They had continued to walk, but Alec now brought them both to a halt, and when Emily looked up at him, she both saw and felt his gentle understanding. Although she was too distraught to know it now, it was a moment that would always remain with her.

"I think that she didn't have a choice—especially if we are right about your father."

"My father?" she echoed, mentally bracing herself for yet another shock.

"We have some reason to believe that your father might have been Mevoshee."

"I . . . I don't understand."

"It is possible that he was Tiyazh, of course, although that too is forbidden. But for him to have been Mevoshee would be . . . far worse."

"Because you're enemies," she said dully.

"No, Neville didn't get that quite right. We're not enemies in the Tiyazh sense. We're opponents, as we have always been down through the ages. We have always lived separately; that is how it must be. And there has never been a union between Azonyee and Mevoshee."

"Then what makes you think my father could be Mevoshee?"

"There is something in you, Emily—something I sensed that first time I saw you in the bookstore. But it would have been risky for me to have probed more deeply."

"I don't understand—risky for whom?"

"For me—and perhaps for you as well. We each have different talents, Emily, and that is why I brought you here—so that those who possess such talents can find out if there is Mevoshee blood in you."

"And if there is?"

He shrugged. "Then the Council will decide what to do."

But Emily had heard that same dislike in his tone she'd heard before when he mentioned the Council, and she shuddered.

He stopped again, just as they were coming out of the forest into a village.

"Emily," he said, taking both her hands in his this time, "I will not allow any harm to come to you."

"Then you think they might want to . . . to harm me?"

"I don't know—but I will protect you."

He dropped her hands and started to walk toward the village, but she grasped his arm and brought him to a halt.

"What happened to my mother, Alec? Did they . . . kill her?"

He shook his head sadly. "She killed herself. I was very young at the time, but I remember it. Such a thing had never happened before."

Because of me, she thought. She killed herself because of me.

Alec grasped her shoulders almost roughly. "No, Emily, she killed herself because she had betrayed her people—broken a rule we live by. You were only the result of that betrayal—not the cause of it."

So many emotions were engulfing her, dragging at her. The one that rose to the surface was anger. "Why did no one know how she felt? If you can read each other's minds, why wasn't she stopped?"

"No one knew. She had been outside, studying art. And when she came home that last time, she 'ported herself into the valley—and then took her life.

"There was much debate after that about the wisdom of sending anyone but Shekaz outside to be educated. Now the rules are stricter. Students must come home regularly, and they're visited while they're outside. It was a terrible time for everyone, Emily—and for your grandmother most of all."

But Emily didn't hear him. The image of a baby in a basket had been replaced by that of a terrified woman, returning here to die in shame and guilt.

She knew at some level that Alec was right: her mother's death wasn't her fault. But that didn't lessen the pain.

Alec led her onward into the village, but Emily paid scant attention to her surroundings. She was thinking now of all the melodramas she'd constructed over the years to explain her mother's desertion. Would it not have been better to have gone on believing one of them might be true— that her mother was still alive and had found happiness despite what must have been a terrible time for her?

She was only vaguely aware of the curious stares she received as they made their way along the main street of the village. People spoke to Alec, but since she couldn't understand the language, even that failed to draw her out of her haze of pain and regret.

Then they reached a lovely park, where Alec led her down a flower-bordered path to a large building—stone with a red-tiled roof, like his own home and the other buildings she'd seen.

"This is the Council building," he said as he pushed open the handsomely carved wooden door inlaid with gold designs.

Emily stopped, remembering suddenly that he'd said her grandmother would be there.

"Her name is Tapha," he said before she could speak. "You will know her, I think."

But Emily wasn't at all sure that her grandmother would want to know *her*. What memories would she bring to someone who had suffered so? Her eyes filled up with tears, and as a result the scene before her very nearly blinded her.

Gold! It was everywhere! The walls and floor were gold-veined marble, and the high ceiling was made entirely of hammered gold. Huge discs of intricately designed gold studded with precious gems hung on the walls, interspersed with gold and crystal sconces.

At the far end of the room, beneath a huge gold disc, sat a group of men and women, all wearing robes that appeared to be made of spun gold, decorated with rubies, emeralds, and other precious stones.

Emily was so bedazzled by all this that Alec took her hand once more and led her to the ornate gold chairs that had been placed before the assemblage. She sank down into one of them, then began to search the faces of the women members fearfully.

When her eyes met those of a woman near the far end of the group, Emily knew this was her grandmother. How she knew she couldn't have said. She saw no resemblance, but there was still no doubt. They stared at each other for a long moment, but Emily could see no emotion on the older woman's handsome face.

Alec had remained standing, one hand resting lightly on her shoulder. Then her attention was torn away from her grandmother by an imperious female voice.

"Be seated, Alyeka."

Emily looked up, realizing that must be his real name. She saw him bow slightly—very slightly—then trace a sign in the air before seating himself next to her. Her eyes went involuntarily back to her grandmother, who now averted her gaze.

She hates me, Emily thought. She hates me for the pain I must be bringing her.

No, she does not hate you, said that quiet voice in her head. You will meet with her later.

"Alyeka!" that same woman said again, her tone sharp with annoyance. "You have told her."

"Yes."

Emily heard the challenge in his voice and stared from one to the other. It was obvious they didn't like each other. Even she could feel the tension in the air.

The silver-haired woman's pale eyes dismissed him and turned instead to Emily. "Emily Carr, do you have any reason to believe that your father could be Mevoshee?"

"No, of course not. Until a few minutes ago, I knew nothing of either of my parents." Her own tone was sharper than she'd intended. Already she didn't like this woman, who was obviously the leader.

"You have never been contacted in any way by one of them?"

"No—or at least not that I'm aware of."

"What about this boy—this student of yours?"

"Student?" Emily echoed in confusion.

"I hadn't told her about him, Menda," Alec interjected, then turned to Emily.

"There was a Mevoshee boy among the students at your lecture. He ran from the room when he saw me."

"Toby?" Emily stared at him.

Then she turned back to the Leader. "Toby Shaw *was* one of my students, but he never approached me in any way, although he *is* greatly interested in folklore."

The woman's eyes bored into her, but Emily's gaze never wavered.

"You are wise not to lie to us, Emily Carr—but no doubt Alyeka warned you against that. You must be tested. We must know if there is Mevoshee blood in you."

Emily was rapidly running out of patience with this woman's cold, imperious tone. Did she care nothing for the fact that Emily had only just learned of her parentage—and her mother's tragic death?

"Why should it matter?" Emily challenged. "I have no talents, and I want only to return to my home and my work."

"It matters to *us*," was the frosty reply.

"And what if I don't want to submit to your 'test'?" Emily asked, refusing to let the woman's piercing gaze affect her. "You have no right to treat me this way—kidnapping me and then making such demands."

One of the male members, seated just to the left of the Leader, intervened. "Emily Carr, we apologize for frightening you. But we too have fears. This has never happened in all our history."

Emily shifted her gaze to him, realizing instantly that he must be Alec's father. The resemblance was striking. His next words confirmed it.

"My son was instructed to bring you here without causing you any more fear than was necessary, but we realize that all this must seem very strange to you. We ask only for your cooperation."

Emily was grateful for his gentler tone and words, but her reply was still firm. "That depends upon what it is you intend to do. I don't like having my thoughts read any more than I like being kidnapped—however carefully."

"The test is not painful," he said. "There are those among us who can look deeply into you and know if there is Mevoshee blood in you."

"And if there is?" she asked, her gaze now scanning them all.

"Then we will decide what action to take," replied the cold voice of the Leader. "You are both dismissed."

Alec got up immediately, but Emily remained seated, her gaze locked onto the Leader until, finally, the older woman broke it. Then Emily got up and walked out, with Alec trailing along after her.

"I don't like her," Emily stated the moment they were outside.

"Neither do I," he responded, "But she *is* the Leader."

"How can someone like that have such a position? Is it because she's the most powerful?"

He laughed. "Hardly. She wasn't even a

Shekaz. But how can you even ask such a question? Look at the people you elect to office."

He certainly had a point. "But I thought it would be different here."

"Well, it isn't. Menda was elected as a compromise candidate. Our politics are often as strange as yours."

"She doesn't much care for you, either," Emily observed.

"No, she doesn't—but then Leaders usually feel that way toward Shekaz—and especially toward the most powerful ones. Besides, the rivalry between our families goes back for generations."

"My grandmother seemed so . . . cold," Emily said, her voice dropping lower with sadness.

"She has suffered greatly," he pointed out gently. "Besides, any show of emotion there would have been inappropriate. She wants very much to see you."

As they walked back through the village, Alec forced himself *not* to listen in to her thoughts. Emily Carr was a rather remarkable person. Because of her delicate beauty, he'd assumed she was a fragile creature, one who would require his protection to see her through this ordeal. She still might need that, of course—but he now knew that she had considerable reserves of strength.

He smiled to himself as he thought about the way she'd challenged Menda, the Council Leader. Even he would not have dared to behave that way, and it was well known among them that he skirted the edges of propriety where Menda was concerned.

On the other hand, she had done herself little

good—especially if she proved to have Mevoshee blood in her. Menda could be a very formidable opponent.

He glanced down at her as she walked along beside him, lost in her thoughts. The promise he'd made to her had not been an idle one. He would not allow harm to come to her. But he was now beginning to think about the cost of that promise.

And beneath it all was still that sense he'd had from the very beginning: that Emily Carr represented a very great danger to them.

"The Azonyee and the Mevoshee have existed since the beginning of time. We believe ourselves to be the descendants of the Old Gods who created the world. Our legends hold that they argued down through the centuries it took them to accomplish that task.

"We are opposing forces—as they were. Not Good and Evil, as Neville's book might have led you to believe, though. Good and evil are Tiyazh inventions. We are simply opposites."

He paused and smiled at her as they walked through the woods toward his house. "You could think of us as being opponents in some sort of Super Bowl. Neither team is good or bad. And we Shekaz are the team members.

"Neville defined 'Shekaz' as meaning 'Warrior,' but that isn't really true, either. The word is difficult to translate, but I suppose the best translation would be 'Balancer': the ones who fight each other to maintain that balance of the earth forces.

"Both sides select the most gifted of their

132

people to train as Shekaz. The battles must take place in the Outer World, since neither side can penetrate the other's home. Those who determine when and where the battles take place are called Nastranos. They too are selected for their special talents—in their case, the ability to 'read' the earth forces.

"Tiyazh have always been aware of those earth forces, although their understanding of them is limited. As I'm sure you know, the mythology of many peoples are filled with references to places where these forces seem strongest."

"Ley lines, you mean," Emily asked.

"Yes, that is the best-known name for them. When the nastranos determine that these forces are in danger of becoming unbalanced, the Shekaz go to that place and fight to restore the balance."

"Are you talking about physical battles?"

"No. There is never any physical contact. We fight by calling on those powers, drawing them into ourselves, and using them against our opponents."

The folklorist in Emily found all this utterly fascinating. He was certainly correct that the concept was not a unique one. These mysterious forces within the earth had been a part of folk mythology since the beginning of recorded thought.

She was also, finally, beginning to accept his earlier statement that no previous union between the Azonyee and Mevoshee had occurred. This belief in the separateness of the two groups was at the very core of their whole belief system—the most powerful of taboos.

And yet she might be living proof that that taboo had been broken.

Then she thought about his revelation concerning Toby Shaw. They'd had no opportunity to discuss that.

"Why was Toby Shaw so afraid of you? Do you kill each other any time you meet?"

"No—never. The point is that we simply aren't supposed to meet at all, except in battle. I hadn't noticed him, to tell you the truth. He is young and his powers are still unformed. If he'd been older, I would have known immediately, of course.

"He ran because he sensed my presence—and that is exactly what he's supposed to do: get away from me. If he seemed unduly upset, it was probably because he knew who I am. The most powerful Shekaz are always well known to the other side."

"But if you all move freely between your world and ours, such chance meetings must occur regularly," she said.

"Not all that often. There aren't very many of us—and only a few actually go outside to be educated: Shekaz, of course, and some others who choose to do so. Many never leave this land at all.

"Still, the chance meetings *do* occur more often than in the past. More and more, the young do choose to go outside to be educated. It's a topic of much discussion among the Elders.

"The world of the Tiyazh once held little to interest us, since we lived far better than they did. But now there is much to interest us out there, although there is much we dislike as well: crime, pollution, wars, all the inequality."

She certainly couldn't blame them for that, but she felt compelled to defend her world nevertheless. "So you take what you want—microwaves, VCRs, stereos. Most of what you have in your home came from outside, from that world you despise—from the creativity of people you consider to be your inferiors."

"We don't *take* things," he replied, apparently choosing to ignore the rest of it. "We buy what we want."

"With what?"

"Gold. We can create all of it that we need. And we have Swiss bank accounts just like wealthy Tiyazh. We have advanced, you see." He smiled at her. "We even have credit cards."

They walked into the impossible garden he had created by "telling" it to grow. Emily shook her head ruefully. What had the world come to when the modern version of Merlin used American Express?

When they entered his house, Emily saw that the crystal globe in its gold base that she now knew was their version of a phone system was glowing softly. Alec went over and put his hand on it and the globe brightened. After a few moments, he turned back to her, smiling.

"Your grandmother wishes me to bring you to her."

Tapha reached out to place a hand on either side of Emily's face as she stared into her granddaughter's eyes. Emily gasped as an image grew in her mind—dim at first, then startlingly clear.

"My mother," she breathed, holding to the image of the lovely woman who was obviously younger than Emily herself was now.

"Yes," her grandmother said softly. "Her name was Sussura. She is in you—in your face."

Emily nodded. Except for the black hair and dark eyes, it could have been her a few years ago. Then the image began to fade as Tapha lowered her hands.

Emily brushed away her tears, then kissed the old woman on her cheek impulsively. "Thank you. Now I can remember her."

Alec had stayed with her at Tapha's little house, because her grandmother's English was very limited. He'd explained that they all studied English in school since it was the language of their unwitting "host country," but those like Tapha who rarely went outside spoke it only haltingly.

But Tapha seemed more interested in hearing about her life than in talking about Emily's mother, and while Emily could understand that reluctance, there was much she wanted to know.

After a while it became obvious that the old woman was growing tired, and they took their leave. As they walked back to Alec's, Emily voiced her frustration.

"There's so much I wanted to learn about my mother—and about any other family I have here."

"It is difficult for her, Emily, but I think she will tell you more. And you really haven't any other close relatives. Susurra was an only child. There are a few cousins and I will see that you meet them, but they too still feel the shame that your grandmother feels."

Emily felt a keen disappointment. Having finally discovered (at least in part) who she was, she'd been hoping to find a whole group of relatives.

She asked Alec about his family and learned that he had a sister and a young niece. Uncertain about their customs, she asked if he had anyone "special" in his life.

"A wife, you mean. We have marriage just as you do—although our marriages last." He grew silent for a long time, so long that she thought she wasn't going to answer her question. Then, when he did speak, his voice was carefully controlled.

"Her name was Janna. She died more than a year ago. We had no children."

Sensing that he didn't want to discuss it further, Emily didn't push. But she was increasingly curious about this man who had come so suddenly to occupy such an important place in her very confused life.

Emily was trying very hard to approach the meeting with the nastrano with the stoicism of one going to the dentist or the gynecologist. But it just wasn't working. However much those others might poke at her body, they didn't probe her mind.

Alec, perhaps in an attempt to calm her, was talking about the various duties of the nastranos, whom Emily learned were second in importance to their society only to the Shekaz—and in many ways perhaps even more important.

In addition to monitoring the earth forces, they were the healers. Their intimate and intricate relationship with those powerful forces allowed them to effect cures for anything and everything.

All of the Azonyee were capable of psychic healing to some extent (Emily recalled how he'd eliminated that pain in her hand). But only the nastranos could perform major healing, and nothing was beyond their abilities.

"Nothing?" Emily frowned. "But you're not immortal?"

"No, although our lifespan is somewhat longer than most Tiyazh, at some point the body simply runs down—like the machine it is. And that even the nastranos can't cure."

He indicated a path that led uphill into the forest. "Ledee lives up here. All the nastranos live apart from others, and apart from each other as well. If they lived too closely with the rest of us, the combined psychic emanations would interfere with their monitoring and using the earth forces."

Emily walked up the steep path with him, but she was wondering if she really wanted the information this Ledee could give her. What good would it do for her to discover that her father was or wasn't Mevoshee? Either way, she would still know nothing of value.

Furthermore, she was irritated at Alec's unwillingness or inability to explain to her why they were all so worried that she might be half-Mevoshee. She didn't doubt that their fear was real, but she needed to understand it.

Strangely enough, though, one thing that *didn't* bother her was the consequences of such a revelation. She wasn't sure why she felt no fear of these people; she only knew that she didn't. Alec had sworn to protect her if necessary—but how could he protect her if the Council decreed her death? Surely he couldn't go against them. And yet, she was not afraid.

Perhaps, she thought, it is just that I still don't truly accept that all this is *real*.

Finally they reached a small cottage. Alec walked up to the door, but didn't knock. He simply stood there waiting, and a moment later the door opened and a very tall and quite beautiful woman stood before them, her strange, pale eyes passing quickly over Alec and coming to rest on Emily.

Emily was struck by her beauty, but even more startled by her youth. She appeared to be not much older than Emily herself. Somehow she'd expected that this most powerful of the nastranos would be much older.

Ledee smiled at her. "We are much like the Shekaz, Emily Carr. Our powers are strongest at a young age, then begin to fade as we grow older. Come in, please."

She stood back, and Emily stepped into her house, then turned to see Alec walking away. She hadn't expected him to leave and must have made a sound of protest. Or perhaps Ledee had merely read her mind again.

"Alyeka could not stay. His presence is too disturbing." Ledee closed the door and gestured her into the small living room. "Shekaz and nastranos always avoid each other unless it becomes necessary for a Shekaz to be healed. You could say that our powers clash, creating disturbances in us both.

"It is worst of all for Alyeka and me, because he is the most powerful of Shekaz while I am the most powerful nastrano." She gestured Emily to a chair, then took another across from her.

"You have grown fond of Alyeka," she said,

139

making it a statement, not a question.

"Well, I'm not sure 'fond' is the proper word." Emily smiled. "He fascinates me—and he is very attractive."

"Indeed he is. Shekaz always are, for some reason. His mate Janna was also a very attractive woman."

"He said she died a year ago. What happened?"

"Janna died in a plane crash. She was returning from a successful battle against a very difficult opponent. It was what I think you call an irony—that she should have accomplished an ages-old mission only to die as a result of modern technology."

"Will he marry again?" Emily was thinking about his unwillingness to talk to her about Janna.

"Perhaps—perhaps not. Such things are decided in their own time."

"There is something in him I can't quite put into words—something very . . . peaceful."

Ledee nodded. "Yes. All Shekaz have that. It is the quality we seek when choosing Shekaz, and Alyeka may just be the most powerful our people have ever produced."

"I'm afraid that I just don't understand their battles, even though he tried to explain it to me."

"It is difficult—perhaps impossible—to explain to one not born among us. That peacefulness you spoke of is really a perfect harmony with certain of the earth forces. We nastranos can monitor them and draw upon them to heal, but only the Shekaz have that harmony with them. We merely *use* the earth forces, while the Shekaz can become one with them."

Ledee leaned back against the chair and regarded Emily thoughtfully. "Tell me, Emily, have you felt any different since you came here?"

"Well, I'm not sure. This has all been so strange for me. *Should* I be feeling different?"

The nastrano shrugged. "Who could know? You are unique. But one could assume you would at some point. This place is where all our powers are concentrated, where the earth forces are friendliest to us, one could say. The part of you that is Azonyee should be responding to that."

"But if the other part of me is Mevoshee?"

"Ahh, that is the problem. No Mevoshee could come here, you see—just as we cannot go to their home."

"What would happen?"

"Death, in all likelihood. Permanent damage to the brain, certainly—the kind that can happen to a Shekaz in battle."

"Brain damage?" Emily echoed, thinking of Alec.

"Usually it can be healed. But I think you need not worry about Alyeka. He has never come close to losing a battle."

Emily did not want to think any further about that; it was a part of Alec she discovered she didn't want to know about. Instead, she returned to her own situation.

"But since nothing bad has happened to me, wouldn't that prove that there's no Mevoshee blood in me?"

"Not necessarily. Instead of being unable to visit either of our homes, you might be comfortable in both."

Emily sighed. "The only home I want is the one I have in Connecticut. I can understand everyone's curiosity about my heritage, but I don't understand their fear."

"The unknown is always frightening, and perhaps even more so to a people who haven't changed through the ages."

"But how can I pose a threat to all of you? Every one of you has more power than I have—since I have none."

"I personally don't believe that you do pose a threat, even if there is Mevoshee blood in you. But I also think you may signal a change for us—and for many people, change alone is threatening, as I said."

Emily sighed. "Well, I suppose we had better get on with it. Will you be able to see who my father is—see his face or know his name, I mean?"

Ledee shook her head sympathetically. "No—only that he is or isn't Mevoshee. I am sorry, Emily. I know how much you must want that information. To not know your parents is a terrible burden to carry through your life."

Emily nodded. She liked this woman, and consequently felt far less apprehensive than she had. If there was a deep peacefulness in Alec, what existed in this woman was perhaps the opposite: an almost electric force. Even if she weren't beautiful, in the Tiyazh world, such a woman would not go unnoticed—just as Shekaz did not pass unnoticed.

Ledee drew her chair closer to Emily's so that

their knees were touching. Much as Emily's grandmother had done, she pressed a hand lightly against either side of Emily's head.

"Try to empty your mind of all thought, or at least of any resistance. You will feel my presence, but no pain."

Emily closed her eyes and did as told. Then she began to feel strange sensations inside her head: warmth and coldness and a tingling sensation. But that lasted for no more than a second or two—and then she felt nothing but the light pressure of Ledee's hands against her head.

Suddenly something leapt within her. It went from a mild irritation to a feeling of uncontrollable rage within the span of a second.

What happened next would be forever unclear to Emily. She heard her own voice shout "No!", although she wasn't sure she had actually spoken. She began to spiral away into a terrible blackness and grasped wildly for the arms of the chair.

When the blackness had subsided to a faint gray mist, Emily stared in utter horror at Ledee's still body. Her chair had toppled and she lay in a crumpled heap on the far side of the room, against a wall.

Emily clutched her head. It hurt badly and sharp pains stabbed her everywhere. She lowered a hand and saw that it was shaking uncontrollably.

Something has gone wrong, she thought with horror. But whatever it was, it had obviously done more damage to Ledee than to her.

She stumbled over to the nastrano and knelt beside her. Her hand was trembling so much that she had difficulty grasping the woman's wrist, but she finally located her pulse. It seemed very weak.

Emily ran from the house, ignoring her own pain in her urgency to find help. She stumbled and fell as she tried to hurry on the steep path—and then Alec was there, materializing right in front of her. Before she could begin to explain, three others appeared as well: two men and a woman.

"She's hurt—badly, I think. I don't know what happened."

The other three simply vanished again, and Alec reached down to gather her into his arms. Everything went black again, and then the two of them were in his bedroom and he was laying her on the bed.

"Will she die? I don't understand what happened."

Alec sat down beside her and took her hand. "Tell me what you remember."

So she did, saying that she'd really liked Ledee and then describing the sensations she'd felt.

"It . . . it felt like an uncontrollable rage. It came and went so fast—and then I blacked out. And when I came to, Ledee was . . ." Emily stopped, seeing the woman's broken body again.

"I *couldn't* have done that to her, Alec. I *liked* her."

His dark eyes had been focused intently upon her as she spoke, but they now drifted off, and he sat there silently.

"You know what happened, don't you?" she asked fearfully.

He nodded. "I think so. I think the Mevoshee

144

blood is there, Emily—and that part of you lashed out at her."

Emily stared at him in horror. What he described sounded like insanity.

"I think you should get some rest now," he said as he got up. "I will get you some jeyah."

Chapter Six

Emily awoke to a warm, pleasant morning, but one with the promise of heat to come. She felt well rested, and her headache and other pains were gone, thanks, no doubt, to her having slept for nearly eighteen hours.

She went immediately in search of Alec, to find out about Ledee. He had assured her that the nastrano would be all right, but she thought she'd detected an uncertainty in his voice.

But Alec was nowhere to be found. A blanket lay neatly folded on the sofa where he must have spent the night, and the garden was empty.

She made some coffee and nibbled at some fruit and a piece of fresh-baked bread, expecting him to return at any moment. Then, when he didn't, she gave in to an urge to do some exploring.

The day before, Emily had noticed another path that intersected with the path they'd taken to the village. Since it seemed to lead off into the vast forest, she took it. This was not the time to explore the village, where she feared her presence wouldn't be welcome. Everyone would surely know by now what had happened to Ledee.

Besides, she decided that it was time she tested the boundaries of this enchanted land. She had no idea how close she might be to the edge and it seemed important now to try to find out.

After a short time, she began to wish she'd brought her compass, but she tried to keep track of her whereabouts by the sun's position. The path seemed remarkably straight, which gave her some hope that it might lead her to the boundary.

Her thoughts were divided between horror at what she'd done to Ledee and a fear that the Council—especially Menda, the Leader—would decide to punish her for that, and for being part-Mevoshee.

How could such a thing have happened? She had certainly borne no ill will toward Ledee; she liked the woman. And yet, something in her—the Mevoshee blood, if Alec was correct—had lashed out anyway. What if it happened again? What if she lashed out at Alec next?

Alec. How she wished that she had time and the opportunity to consider him dispassionately. She was powerfully attracted to him, but she also feared him. Ledee had said he might well be the most powerful Shekaz of all.

And what did he truly think of her? He had no compunction whatsoever about listening in to and commenting upon her thoughts—and yet

147

he'd not said a word about her attraction to him. Tactful silence because he didn't share her feelings? Or did he in fact share them, but was unwilling to act upon them because of who and what she was?

After walking for what she judged to be several miles, Emily came to a small, rushing brook at the bottom of a steep ravine. The path continued on the far side, still running in a nearly straight line, and she'd encountered no dwellings of any kind.

She stared at the little stream. It was fairly deep and the bottom consisted of mud and slippery, moss-covered rocks. No doubt everyone else here simply 'ported themselves across.

Then she recalled Ledee's asking her if she'd felt any different since she came here. The nastrano had seemed to think that just being here might awaken some latent powers conferred upon her by her mother.

It was intended to be no more than a mind-game. Not for one minute did Emily believe that she could have magical talents of her own. She'd attended yoga classes some years ago as a concession to a friend who had proclaimed their usefulness in reducing stress or preparing one's mind for serious work. So she sat down on the bank of the little stream and went through the exercises designed to empty out the mind and set it free. Then she opened her eyes and stared hard at the far bank, imagining herself there.

And she *was* there, tottering slightly with a mild dizziness! She sank down quickly, staring at the spot where she'd been, half-expecting to find herself still there where the laws of nature as she'd always understood them told her she *should* be.

Powerful emotions tore at her: awe, terror, exhilaration. I did it, she thought; I really did it. I *thought* myself here.

Then she began to laugh uncontrollably, until the laughter began to take on a near-hysterical note. She sobered quickly.

Perhaps she hadn't 'ported herself. Perhaps there was some special magic to this spot that allowed anyone to do what she had done. But in the next instant, she decided that made no sense (not that *anything* made sense in this land). Why would they bother casting a spell when they all had the ability to 'port themselves across?

The dizziness passed, and she got up and began to climb up the hill. When she reached the top, she saw only endless forest, marching up and down steep hills. Here and there the path was still visible, moving in its straight line to somewhere.

She simply couldn't resist the temptation. She stared hard at a point about a half-mile ahead, where the path went up a slight incline. Could she do it again?

An instant later, she had her answer as she put out a hand to steady herself against a tree trunk. But the dizziness was definitely worse this time, and she suddenly recalled Alec's remark that novices used the herbal tea, jeyah, to eliminate the effects of 'porting. So she was obviously suffering no more than any of them did when they learned to 'port.

She sank down against the tree trunk with a smile and waited for the dizziness to pass. She might not have found the boundary, but she had discovered something very important. And if she could 'port, then wasn't it just a matter of time before she could 'port herself out of the valley?

Would she be able to conceal her discovery from Alec? He had said that he was only skimming the surface of her mind, so perhaps if she avoided thinking consciously about this in his presence, she could keep it her secret for the time being.

She got up and began to walk back toward his house, using imaging techniques she'd read about somewhere to turn her discovery into a tiny package that she then concealed in the darkest corner of the labyrinth of her mind.

Alec 'ported himself back across the village, then began to jog along the path that led to his home. Emily would be pleased to know that Ledee was recovering from the attack, and that she had sent a message that she didn't blame Emily for what had happened.

But he was shaken nevertheless. Ledee had been hurled across the room with sufficient force to have broken three ribs, separated her shoulder, and fractured an arm in two places. Not to mention a mild concussion. She was already healing, of course, thanks to the ministrations of the other nastranos and her ability to call upon the healing powers herself. And her mind had been unaffected.

Alec had spoken to her only briefly, since his presence disturbed her, but she'd made it clear to him and the others that she blamed only herself, for not having shielded herself adequately.

And there was now no doubt—if in fact there

had ever been—that Emily Carr was half-Mevoshee.

Menda had told Alec that he alone was responsible for her while the Council debated what to do about her. She'd said that he should have no problem controlling her—as though Emily were some sort of unpredictable wild animal.

He'd replied that they could debate all they wanted, but his position remained the same. He would countenance no attempt to harm her.

He slowed to a walk for the last half-mile to his garden, his thoughts once again on Emily Carr. Menda's parting sarcastic remark haunted him: "You speak as though you would take her as a mate, Alyeka."

He pushed the image of Emily Carr from his mind and replaced it with one of Janna. But he was shocked to discover that the golden-haired Emily kept intruding.

Alec found himself caught in the confusion of the different ways of the Azonyee and the Tiyazh. Tiyazh made love without meaning it. They'd invented a number of ugly words for it, though they just as often deluded themselves into believing that they *were* making love. And in any event, no Tiyazh could truly know what love is, since they lacked that additional element given to the Azonyee because of their talents.

Lust, or mere physical attraction, was totally unknown among the Azonyee. Only when two minds were in harmony could they feel what the Tiyazh claimed to feel.

And yet, there was no doubt that he felt *something* toward Emily Carr, despite the fact that there was no harmony of thought, and probably never could be, given her heritage.

He didn't understand this protective feeling he had toward her, either. In a society where men and women were equally capable of protecting themselves (not that that need ever arose here in any event), it was a surpassingly strange feeling. A Tiyazh feeling, he thought derisively. Another indication that he spent too much time outside.

Alec felt that deep inner core of peace that Emily had seen in him rippling with uneasiness. As he reached the edge of his garden, he reached also for the memory of his beloved Janna—and found it blurred and distant, part of the past.

He walked into the garden to discover his parents waiting for him. Emily was nowhere to be seen. After greeting them and noting their concern, he sent his mind out, seeking Emily. The link between them wasn't that strong yet, but he found her nonetheless, about a mile from the house, returning from a walk in the forest. He withdrew and faced his parents.

"Emily cannot be blamed for this," he told them. "Even Ledee does not blame her."

"We understand that, Alyeka," his mother said gently. "But now we know she has Mevoshee blood and we must decide what to do about her."

"And her powers have now been awakened," his father put in gravely. "Who can know what she's capable of?"

"We could take away her memories of this place," his mother went on. "But if her powers have been awakened . . ." She shrugged eloquently.

"What exactly do you fear?" he asked, having already debated that question with himself without having received any satisfactory answer.

"Some believe that she could be a powerful destabilizing force, that she could disrupt the earth forces in terrible ways—especially if she should go to the Mevoshees. And she will surely do that if she is allowed to return to the outside. She will want to seek out her father—and the Mevoshee will want to see her."

"But we don't know that," Alec protested. "We don't know that she would be a destabilizing force. Given the mixture of bloods, she might well be neutral in her effect upon them."

"Yes, that is so. But she could also have powers beyond our imagining—even beyond yours, Alyeka. You could be in danger."

He shook his head. "No, I cannot believe that. I promised I would protect her, and I will not break that promise."

"Such a promise was unwise, my son," his mother said gently.

"Unwise or not, I have made it. If the Council decides she should die, then I will be put into a position of either breaking my promise to her or breaking my vow of obedience to the Council."

They both stared at him in shock. "Surely you wouldn't . . ." "Your vows are . . ."

He cut them off with a gesture. "I do not want to be put into such a position because I cannot say which I would choose. You must tell them that." He stopped, then gestured toward the forest.

"Emily Carr has become . . . very important to me."

Then, before they could speak again, he hurried on. "Menda has made me responsible for her and I want that to continue. I want the Council to give me a chance to teach her what she must know to control her powers."

"But can you do that, Alyeka? You could certainly teach her if she were Azonyee, but how can you deal with the other part?"

"Who better than me? I have fought and defeated the best they can send against me."

"And you would risk this for her?"

He nodded.

"You speak as though you love her, Alyeka. But how could that be?"

He shrugged. "I do not feel the way I felt with Janna. This is very different."

"Tiyazh love," his father said scornfully.

"Perhaps. And perhaps it is as unique as Emily herself."

The moment she awoke, Emily felt the weight of the day upon her. Today, perhaps even now, the Council would decide her future. Alec had told her they were debating the matter.

Strangely enough, she felt little fear for herself. Was it still a lack of acceptance that any of this was real, or was it some sort of precognition? Alec had told her that precognition was not one of their talents—but then she wasn't truly one of them. Who knew what talents her unique mixture could be bringing forth?

What she *did* feel was fear for Alec. He'd repeated his promise that he would allow no harm to come to her, but when she'd asked how he could go against the Council, he'd simply said it again. And he'd been quiet and withdrawn the remainder of the day and evening, even while they'd both tried to interest each other in a game of chess.

He'd told her about his proposal to teach her what she needed to know to control her talents. She'd said she had no talents to control (guarding her secret carefully), and he'd pointed out that she'd demonstrated considerable talent in her reaction to Ledee's probing. If he'd suspected anything else, he'd given no indication.

She got up, and this time found him in the garden, down at the far end. At first she was sure that one of them had gone mad. Either she was seeing things, or he had gone totally insane.

He leapt high into the air, far higher than an ordinary human being could have done. Then he twisted, somersaulted, touched the ground briefly, and leapt up again.

After a moment, she realized that he was performing some sort of exercises, and her shock gave way to amazement. She'd seen demonstrations of his grace and agility before, but never like this. No human being could possess such talents.

That thought struck her hard. How much she'd been trying to think of him as being just an ordinary man with some extraordinary talents. It had seemed very important to believe that. But he wasn't—and now, neither was she.

A wave of pure horror washed over her and she grabbed hold of the doorway for support. He stopped—in mid-air—and turned toward her. Then he was standing in front of her, his dark brows knitted with concern.

"What has frightened you?"

"Noth . . . *You* did. What you were doing isn't . . . *human.*"

He searched her face, then smiled slowly. "By a Tiyazh definition, I'm not. But you already knew that."

"I knew it, but I guess I hadn't really accepted it."

"It isn't me that has frightened you, Emily. It is your knowledge that *you* aren't human, either."

She nodded slowly.

His expression remained serious, but a gleam of amusement flashed in his dark eyes. "I don't suppose this would be an appropriate time to point out that you're superior to the Tiyazh—perhaps even superior in some way to both of us: the Azonyee and the Mevoshee."

"Is that why the Council may well decide that I must die?" she asked, refusing to be teased.

"That will not happen."

"Strangely enough, I've never really thought that it would. I'm not sure just why I believe that, but I do."

As it turned out, they were both right. They were summoned before the Council early in the afternoon.

As she walked into the glittering Council chamber, no less impressed than she'd been the first time, Emily looked at them all carefully—and knew.

Her grandmother, although she strove to maintain a facade of neutrality, was smiling. Alec's parents seemed to feel somewhat less constrained; their smiles were welcoming. And Menda's earlier frostiness had hardened into a glacial expression.

"We have reached a decision," Menda stated in an ominous tone, once the formalities had been dispensed with.

Deciding that it was time to show the Leader some degree of respect, Emily contrived to look concerned—although she knew that if Menda were reading her thoughts, she would surely know the truth.

"Since you are new to our ways, Emily Carr, I think you should be told that condemning you to death would have been very difficult for us. We have no crime here, and the only time in our history that anyone has ever broken the rules by which we live, she took her own life."

Emily's eyes went involuntarily to meet those of her grandmother, and for just a moment she saw the old woman's composure slip. Emily looked quickly back at Menda, her own eyes telegraphing the very clear message that she regarded the Leader's words as an unnecessary affront to her grandmother—and to her as well.

You would have voted to kill her, she thought, hoping that the Leader heard that thought. She felt Alec stir slightly beside her and knew that he at least had heard her.

If she heard, Menda chose to ignore it. "Alyeka has said that he will assume responsibility for you and will teach you what you must know. Therefore, we give you over to his charge."

"And when I have learned what I must know?" Emily challenged. "Will I then be permitted to return to my own world?"

Once again she felt Alec's uneasiness communicate itself to her, although this time he hadn't moved.

It was Alec's father who responded. "Perhaps you will not want to return, Emily Carr. You may find that you will like it here."

"That decision must await the end of your training," Menda stated in an end-of-discussion tone.

As soon as they left the Council building, Alec turned to her. "Emily, no good will come of your behavior toward Menda."

"I don't like her. If she'd had her way, I'd be dead."

"I think not. She may have contemplated that solution, but I do not believe she would have carried it through. As she said, such a thing has never happened here, and I do not think she would have wanted to be the first to issue such a decree."

Emily was far less certain, but she let the matter drop.

"I cannot just remain here indefinitely, Alec. There are people who will be concerned about me. And I have other obligations."

"We will return to your home tomorrow," he replied, "So that you can assure everyone you are well and explain your absence."

"Since you say 'we,' I assume that I'm going to have to explain you as well. That may be difficult, since there are those who know you stole Neville's book from me."

"Ahh, but I did that only to attract your attention—and in any event no harm was done, since you have another copy."

"That sounds like a rather far-fetched explanation to me," she said doubtfully.

"Not if we appear to be very fond of each other. To a Tiyazh mind, that might seem quite romantic."

She ignored his sarcasm. "Well, I suppose it's the best possible explanation."

"And you will tell them that we have now decided to join forces to track down the source of this myth."

She said nothing as they walked through the park outside the Council building. He too remained silent, but then suddenly turned to her.

"You have become . . . very important to me, Emily. I'm very much attracted to you, although I don't understand it. Perhaps it is nothing more than your uniqueness. It is certainly very different from the way I felt about Janna."

Emily was stunned by his confession—and by his obvious confusion. She realized that she'd grown accustomed to thinking of him as being supremely self-assured.

"I . . . I don't know what to say, Alec. I can't deny that I've been attracted to you as well. I'm sure you already know that. But it's very difficult for me to concentrate on such feelings with everything else that has happened. Sometimes this still seems like nothing more than a very vivid dream to me."

"I understand."

"Tell me about Janna," she said as they began to stroll through the village.

She thought he would refuse, but to her surprise he began to talk about her quite freely. They'd known each other all their lives, of course. She was two years older than he was and their families were quite close. It became obvious to Emily that neither of them had ever had eyes for anyone else—and that such a thing was quite normal in this small, closed society.

His descriptions of her created an impression of a strong, vibrant woman—a powerful Shekaz herself. She asked if he could create a picture of Janna in her mind as her grandmother had done with her mother, and he obliged. In her mind's eye, she saw a strong face that was handsome rather than conventionally beautiful: wide-spaced gray-green eyes and short, curly brown hair with a reddish tint.

"She made the furniture you have admired. Working with Ierwood was her hobby, as mine is gardening. And we both liked to play Tiyazh as well—which didn't please our families much."

"Play Tiyazh? What do you mean?"

"Travel—play tourist all over the world. Our families thought we spent far too much time outside. Janna truly liked the Tiyazh, for all their many faults. What she liked best was their science. She had an engineering degree from M.I.T. —one of only a few women in her class at that time. And she was fascinated by the women's movement that was just beginning at that time.

"But in the end, it was Tiyazh science that killed her. She died in a plane crash when she was returning from a battle. Although the cause of the crash was never determined, I am sure there must have been a bomb on board. Otherwise she would have had time to 'port to safety."

"And you have no children?"

"No. We had planned to begin a family. We both wanted children, but it would have been difficult for Janna. She would have been forced to give up her profession during her pregnancy."

He led her to a small cafe where tables were placed on a terrace overlooking the village shopping area. There, as they dined on food that would have been served proudly at the best of the outside world's restaurants, Emily watched the life of the village.

There were numerous small shops housed in the ancient stone buildings with their red tile roofs. People came and went on their errands, all of them dressed in the same loose, comfortable garments she and Alec wore. Most were on foot, but occasionally a small electric golf cart made its way along the cobbled street. And a shop just across the way displayed the latest videos, including, she noticed, a large collection of Nintendos. The clash of ancient and modern brought a smile to her face.

After lunch, they walked through the rest of the shopping district. Although there were many shops displaying small appliances, Emily noted aloud that there were no furniture stores or shops selling major appliances. Was there a mall somewhere? she asked with a grin.

"No, such things are stored in warehouses outside town, and furniture is often made by craftspeople here, who get their wood from the ler forests."

But Emily had lost interest in his words. They had come to a shop that displayed the most beautiful gold jewelry she'd ever seen: delicate strands of gold wire woven in intricate designs and studded with tiny gems. She noted that there were no credit card signs in the shop's window and asked him what they used for money.

"We don't have money. There's no need for it."

She frowned. "But how do these shopkeepers get paid?"

"They don't. They have no need for money, either." He smiled.

"I don't understand this, Alec."

"It's quite simple, really. We can create wealth —gold—any time we choose. So why bother? We use it to pay for what we want from outside, then distribute it here."

"I just don't see how such a system could work. There must be people who take advantage of it—that is, take more than they produce."

"Of course: children and the elderly. But they have their own value. Children are our future, and the elderly represent our collective wisdom."

"And everyone else works?" she asked doubtfully.

"What else would they do? None of us works very hard—at least not by Tiyazh standards. There is no need."

Emily was fascinated by such an unlikely system—but she was more fascinated by the exquisite gold jewelry. "Could *I* acquire some of that?" she asked.

"Come inside and ask," he replied, ushering her into the shop. "I wanted you to meet my sister in any event."

Alec's sister was named Leesa, and although she was much smaller and more delicately made than Alec, the family resemblance was strong. Emily liked her immediately, and Leesa was delighted with her interest in the jewelry. When they left a short time later, Emily was wearing two bracelets and a lovely neck chain.

The day had grown quite warm, and when they reached the edge of the village and set out on the path that led to his home, Alec stopped and turned to her.

"I'll 'port us home."

Before she could reply, he had circled her waist with his long arms—and they were there in his living room. This time, she felt none of the dizziness she'd experienced before, and that seemed to surprise him as well, since he held onto her for a moment before dropping his arms.

"Have you by chance been discovering your talents?" he inquired with an arched brow.

Emily hesitated, then finally nodded. She told him about her experience out in the woods.

"It was so *easy*. I didn't expect that."

He chuckled. "Just in case you're beginning to think you might be Superwoman, I'd better tell you that any child of twelve or thirteen can do what you did. But 'porting yourself out of the valley is a different matter altogether. Don't try that, Emily. I will tell you when you're ready for that."

"Exactly what is it that you need to teach me?" she asked, slightly miffed at his easy dismissal of her abilities.

"Humility, for one thing," he responded, and chuckled. "Of course, I'm not exactly the best one to teach you that, am I?"

"No, but you certainly are a master of understatement." She smiled.

"First it will be necessary for us to determine what talents you possess. And that requires your trusting me enough to let me probe your mind."

"You've already been doing that, whether I trusted you or not," she pointed out archly.

"Not in the way I mean. As I told you, I've only skimmed the surface, picked up thoughts that are most important to you at any moment. Do you trust me?"

"Well, since my life appears to have been given over to your control, I guess I'd better, hadn't I?"

"I think you do—more than that Tiyazh mind of yours will admit. The kind of trust I'm speaking of is completely alien to Tiyazh. In a sense, that's what I meant when I teased you about being embarrassed at my seeing you naked. Intimacy means something different to us, Emily. For us, true intimacy is the blending of minds and thoughts—not just surface thoughts, but the very essence of our beings. What you Tiyazh would call 'soul' or 'spirit.' And for that to happen, there must be trust."

Emily found that notion profoundly disturbing, although she didn't tell him that. But then she probably didn't have to.

"We will begin your training as soon as we return—but now I have a surprise for you."

She let him lead her off into the garden, then along yet another path into the woods, one she hadn't noticed before. Within moments they emerged into a clearing, and she gasped with pleasure at the scene before them.

"You wanted to go swimming," he said, gesturing to the pond.

So she had. She'd been thinking about it as they'd walked back from the village. "But I don't have a swimsuit with me," she protested.

"This is my private spot—and I've already seen you naked," he replied as he began to strip off his shirt.

Emily hesitated. She sensed that this was some sort of test of her willingness to trust him. When he had flung his shirt aside and was reaching for the waistband of his trousers, she turned away and stared instead at the idyllic scene.

The pond was perfectly circular and surrounded on all sides by the thick forest. The water was so clear she could see the pebbly bottom. They stood on a large, flat rock that jutted out over the water, creating a perfect diving place. On the far side was a steep hill, and a small stream of water rushed down over moss-covered rocks.

As she still stood there hesitating, he stepped up beside her, then executed a perfect dive off the rock. The water that splashed over her felt surprisingly warm.

He surfaced and then began to swim toward the other side, and Emily found herself reaching for the buttons on her shirt even before she'd decided to accept his implicit challenge.

She stripped off her clothes quickly and plunged into the water. The temperature was perfect—too perfect. She began to wonder if he'd created this place with his magic the way he'd created his garden.

She loved the freedom of swimming naked, something she'd done only once in her life in a friend's pool years ago. The feel of the water slipping over her warm flesh was decidedly erotic —even without the knowledge that another naked body was sharing this pond.

When she had come close—or as close as she dared—to where he was treading water, she asked about the pond, and he told her that he had indeed created it, and the warmth came from his having tapped into an underground thermal spring. The cold water streaming down from the mountain kept it from becoming too warm.

They swam about for some time, and then he suddenly 'ported himself back up to the rock. Emily stared at him, realizing only then that it would be impossible to get back up there by normal means.

"'Port yourself up here," he challenged.

But Emily suddenly wasn't at all sure that she could. It was impossible to concentrate with him standing there, unself-consciously displaying his bronzed body. Still, she closed her eyes, trying to block out that image and imagine herself there at the same time.

And then she was there, swaying slightly on her feet until he reached out to catch her. Damp flesh met damp flesh, and Emily felt the heat of desire flare up within her. She pushed out of his arms quickly.

They both stretched out on the rock, keeping a discreet distance between them as they dried off in the sun. The water evaporated quickly, but the memory of slick muscles pressed against soft, wet curves lingered to torment her. She was almost painfully aware of his presence.

Was he reading her mind even now? Did he know exactly what she was feeling? She thought about the age-old games that men and women play, denying with words and actions what they felt inside. It began to seem absurd.

"It is," he muttered lazily. "Tiyazh nonsense. But since they're incapable of true intimacy, I suppose it's just as well they play those games."

"But I'm one of them, despite my genetic heritage," she reminded him.

"For the time being, you are. But you will learn."

"And am I going to learn to read *your* mind?" she asked. "Things are awfully one-sided now."

He raised himself up on one elbow and looked over at her lazily. "You will learn."

Then he slowly ran his dark eyes over the length of her before lying back down again. It was the first blatantly sexual thing he'd done, and the effect on Emily was such that for a moment she simply stopped breathing. Then she let out her breath with an involuntary sound and he chuckled.

"Perhaps you'll have some incentive to learn."

Then, belatedly, she understood why he seemed so unaffected by her. Emily wasn't vain, but she *was* accustomed to men wanting her. But she realized now that what he wanted was different: that true intimacy he'd spoken of that can only come from a union of minds.

"I'm not really so different," he said in that same lazy tone. "I just have better self-control. I can wait."

Emily stood at the edge of the cliff, staring down into the valley and listening to the preternatural quiet. Was it possible that only three days had passed since she'd stood here the last time, fascinated by this mysterious place?

"It's the silence here that everyone notices," she said without turning to him. "There aren't any animals or birds."

"Yes. They sense the forces better than most people do. Now let's get back to your car."

He wrapped his arms around her, and in a blink they were standing beside the Wagoneer. She drove it over the nonexistent road to the real road that led to Traverton's Mill. They would then drive to Plattsburgh, where she could turn in the rented vehicle. Alec, she discovered, was a licensed pilot, as were most of the other Shekaz. There was a small landing strip in the valley, but 'porting a plane in there was a difficult feat, so most of the time their small fleet remained at Plattsburgh.

Emily wasn't keen on flying in a small plane, even though Alec pointed out to her that she was perfectly safe, since even if something happened to the plane, he could always 'port them to safety.

With each passing mile, her interlude in the valley began to seem more like a dream, despite his very real presence beside her. She also felt something else, something she couldn't quite describe.

"All of us feel that," he said without being asked. "The valley is situated on a very powerful intersection of the earth forces, and although we don't notice it when we're there, we feel its absence when we leave."

Despite his statement about the safety of flying, Emily was nervous as they flew south. They had been in the air for only a short time when she felt a gentle, soothing touch in her mind.

"Stop it!" she ordered. "I don't want a tranquilizer—in whatever form."

He withdrew immediately, but shook his head

in disgust at what he obviously considered to be the foolish ways of the Tiyazh.

They landed at Danbury Airport and rented a car to drive to Wellsford. The closer they came to her home, the more eager Emily became to actually get there. The valley had begun to recede into the realm of dreams, despite Alec's presence, and Emily wanted desperately to return to her real life.

But then she recalled that moment before she'd set out on her journey when she'd been certain that nothing would ever be the same again. The thought chilled her. She didn't want to let go of the life she had here—not for all the magical talents in the world.

Just as they pulled into her driveway, the front door opened and her neighbor Peggy walked out.

"Are you sure she won't recognize you?" Emily asked as Peggy started toward them.

"I'm sure," was his calm reply.

Emily believed him—but she was horrified to think that he was able to do such a thing. She got out of the car quickly and greeted Peggy.

Alec got out, too, and Peggy stared at him. But Emily saw no look of recognition on her neighbor's face. She introduced the two of them, saying only that Alec was a colleague she'd unexpectedly run into. She thanked Peggy for taking care of Chaucer, but didn't mention that she'd be needing her services again. She knew Peggy wouldn't mind, but Emily was resisting any thought of returning to the valley. She belonged here, where life made sense and people didn't fly through the air and get into each other's minds.

As soon as she could decently break off the conversation, Emily led Alec into her house. Never in her life had it felt so good to be home, despite the luxury she'd just left behind. She called Chaucer and he came running, complaining in his distinctive voice about her absence.

She picked him up and hugged him until his complaints turned to a low, rumbling purr. Then she turned to Alec, who put out a hand to the cat. Chaucer rubbed his head against Alec and continued to purr loudly. Emily stared from one to the other.

"He doesn't usually like strangers," she said in surprise.

"I'm not exactly a stranger," he reminded her.

She didn't want to be reminded that he'd been in her home twice before. She didn't even want him here now. She set Chaucer down.

"Emily," he said gently. "I'm here because you must return to the valley with me—and because my presence will prevent any of the Mevoshee from coming here for you."

"And what if I want them to come?" she challenged. "After all, it's only from them that I can hope to learn about my father."

"Everything in its time," he said patiently. It was an expression she was quickly learning to dislike.

He brought in their luggage, and she went upstairs to check her answering machine. The first message was from her mother, and as Emily stood there listening to that dear, familiar voice, she was horrified to feel a small but important gap open up between this woman who had raised her and her new self.

Toby had called and left a message that he would fly directly to Baton Rouge to meet her for their research trip into the bayou country. She realized that she hadn't mentioned that to Alec. Nor did she want to. When the time came, she would find a way to be there. Not only did she have to fulfill a commitment to a colleague, but she would also possibly be able to use Toby as a means of contacting his people.

She heard Alec coming upstairs as two messages from friends played, neither of any consequence. And then Ben's voice came on.

"Em, I can't shake the feeling that you're going to follow that crazy book of yours. Maybe you already have. And I'm worried about that nut who stole it. If I don't hear from you in the next day, I'm going to call your parents. And by the way, I miss you—a lot."

"That is Ben?" Alec asked with amusement.

"Yes. I'll have to call him. He's in Dublin."

"A good place for him," he replied. "But I agree that you'd better call him so he doesn't upset your parents."

Emily calculated the time difference and decided it might be a good time to reach Ben. How easy it would be to lie to him, she thought guiltily as his phone began to ring. He answered just as she was about to give up.

"Ben, it's Emily."

"Em? God, I'm glad to hear from you. Are you all right? Has that guy been bothering you?"

"No, I haven't seen him. But I've made some discoveries about Neville's book and I'm going back up there." She took a deep breath. "Ben, I won't be able to join you. It's going to be a very busy summer. I'm sorry."

"So am I," he replied with far more feeling than she'd shown. "But I know how you are when you get hold of something."

They talked for a few minutes more, then hung up. Emily sat there, awash in guilt and regret. Ben deserved better treatment than this. Furthermore, *she* didn't deserve what was happening to her, either.

Finally she got up and went downstairs, deciding to wait until later to call her mother. She was hoping she could persuade Alec to stop playing watchdog long enough for her to meet them for lunch or dinner tomorrow, although she knew that was unlikely.

He was in the living room, examining an antique table. She picked up her purse. "I have to do some grocery shopping and run some other errands. There's nothing in the house to eat."

He straightened up and turned toward her. "I'll come with you."

"But I'm only going shopping," she protested.

She thought about arguing the point with him, about trying to make him understand that she needed some space. But she was sure he already knew that. So she gave in—ungraciously.

They went to the supermarket. She thought perhaps he might at least remain in the car, but he followed her inside. She assiduously ignored him, pretending that she was shopping alone. But the only result of that was that she noticed the looks he received from others—particularly women, though men seemed to notice him, too.

She began to wonder if something of his uniqueness—his otherworldliness, as it were—communicated itself to everyone.

"If you see one, you will know." The words of the old woman, quoted to Neville, came back to her again. So perhaps she hadn't been unique in her initial reaction to him, although she might have been somewhat more fanciful in her description to herself.

And he certainly was master of all he surveyed, wasn't he? She had as yet no real knowledge of the limits of his powers, but decided that perhaps she didn't *want* to know.

On the other hand, as she took a cart and began to make her way through the aisles, she began to imagine the havoc he could wreak upon the place. Just imagine items flying off the shelves, or people frozen in the act of reaching for a container of milk, the way he'd "frozen" her when she'd tried to escape. Or perhaps he could perform some of his gravity-defying exercises and vault himself from one aisle to another.

In spite of her present mood, Emily began to smile. There *was* a certain pleasure to be had from such secret knowledge. She wondered if they felt like that when they were "outside."

But she too could do at least one of those impossible things. She could 'port herself to the far end of the store, though she'd probably have to leave her cart behind. She enjoyed that thought for a few seconds before the horror of being *different* overtook her.

Then she felt that increasingly familiar gentle

touch against her mind, like soft, soothing fingers, and whirled about, seeking him.

But he wasn't even looking her way. He was busy examining the produce, picking out some grapefruit. The absurdity of it drove away the lingering traces of her terror. There stood the world's most powerful sorcerer—picking out grapefruit. And calmly reading her thoughts at the same time.

He turned toward her then, with that lazy, sexy smile, and for just a moment she saw him as other women must see him: darkly handsome in an uncompromisingly masculine way. If she didn't know who and what he truly was, she might be flirting with him herself.

He came toward her and she saw that those very dark eyes were glittering with amusement.

"I think it might be very nice to have you flirt with me," he said in a low voice.

She returned to the pretense of ignoring him.

The line at the checkout counter was rather long, and when a toddler in the cart ahead of them began to whimper, then move quickly to a full howl, Emily wished they could just 'port themselves and the groceries out to the parking lot.

Then the howl subsided to a whimper and was gone. Emily saw the child staring at Alec and turned quickly to him herself. He feigned a look of total innocence. When she looked back at the child, his mother was fussing over him, clearly wondering why he'd stopped crying.

A few moments later, when they were piling their purchases on the belt, she heard the child start up again as his mother wheeled her cart out of the store.

"A very handy talent," Emily muttered. He merely chuckled.

Then they drove onto campus so she could stop by her office to check for mail or messages. Since the summer term hadn't started, there were few people about, but Emily suddenly recalled his dramatic appearance at her lecture.

"You wait here. There could be some people around who'll remember that lecture."

"We have a story to cover that—remember?"

She shook her head. "It's too far-fetched. Who's going to believe that you'd steal a book just to attract my attention? And even if they *did* believe it, they certainly wouldn't believe that I'd become . . . involved with you after that."

She got out of the car, then turned to see him following her.

"Don't worry about it," he said calmly as he fell into step with her. "If anyone *does* remember, I'll take care of it."

"Alec, there's something *immoral* about stealing people's memories."

"The only memory I would be stealing is of no consequence," he replied equably.

"I know that, but what bothers me is the fact that you can do it. It's *wrong*!"

He shrugged. "We do what we must do in order to live among the Tiyazh. You'll understand that in time."

"I really dislike your attitude toward them— toward *us*," she added. "You feel nothing but contempt."

"That's not true, Emily. What I feel is a sort of indulgence. The Tiyazh are like children. Sometimes they're amusing, often they are annoying—and occasionally they are very destructive."

"I am one of them," she reminded him angrily, "despite my heritage."

"I know that—and you have all their qualities as well."

He reached over and seized her hand, caressing it gently.

"You are merely seeking reasons to dislike me. It won't work."

Their table was set in a small, private alcove, softly lit by candles and covered with fine damask. On the far side of the dining room, a pianist played romantic ballads that mingled with the tinkling of crystal and silver.

"How did you know about this place?" Emily asked for the second time. He'd insisted they go out to dinner, even though she'd bought food.

"It's well known," he said with a shrug. "And it's your favorite place."

"You couldn't have had a reservation," she persisted. "You didn't make any calls, and this place is always booked well in advance." She'd seen that momentary look of confusion on the face of the maitre d', followed by quick agreement that, yes, there was indeed a reservation.

" 'Well in advance' in this case was about two seconds," he replied, then turned his attention to the approaching waiter.

"Why did you insist upon going out?" she asked when the waiter had left. "I don't think it's such a good idea for us to be seen in public so much."

"Why not? I think we make an attractive couple." He leaned toward her and took her hand. "Maybe I brought you here to seduce you—just as Ben did. But of course it didn't work for him."

She jerked her hand free. "Stop it, Alec, or I'm going to leave right now!"

"Now *that* would draw some attention," he replied as the waiter returned with their drinks and the menus.

She tried to ignore him, turning her head this way and that to see if there was anyone there she knew. In the far corner she saw her department head with her husband and another couple. Thank heavens she hadn't been in the audience during the lecture.

Although she steadfastly avoided looking at him, Emily felt the heat of his gaze upon her. Curls of sensuous warmth spread through her. Then she saw an image—unbelievably clear—of the two of them naked on the cushions in front of his fireplace.

For a moment she thought that the images were of her own creation and she struggled to keep them from him. But then, seemingly against her will, she met his eyes—and she knew where that image had come from.

He chuckled softly, sending more ripples of heat coursing through her.

"Perhaps there *is* something to be said for seduction, after all." He smiled. "I've never tried it before."

Then he deftly moved the conversation to more impersonal matters as their dinner began to arrive—as if, she thought, he were determined to prove that he could be a charming companion.

He asked about her work and quickly showed himself to be rather knowledgeable about mythology and folklore. But then perhaps they all were; some of it, at least, had been written about them.

She recounted some of the old tales about magic tribes, and he nodded.

"Centuries ago we were less inclined to keep our existence secret. The world was much larger then, in the sense that people of one tribe or state knew little of those in other places. And of course everyone believed in magic. There was so much they couldn't understand.

"We've had to become more secretive in the modern world. To attract attention to ourselves now would be to court problems."

Emily, who had done a lot of thinking about their unique talents, finally asked a question that had been on her mind for some time.

"If you wanted to, you could use your talents to help people, couldn't you? If you can plant suggestions in my mind—or take away memories—you could also put suggestions into the minds of those in power—to urge them to do what is right."

"No, we will not do that. We do not interfere in the Tiyazh world, except when we must for the sake of our work. That issue was settled long ago."

"But why?"

"Because what happens out here has no effect on us—or at least not enough of an effect to justify interference."

She became annoyed. "Did you ever hear of altruism, Alec—of doing good for its own sake?"

"I am familiar with the word," he responded drily. "It is a Tiyazh concept. In a world where people frequently do things deliberately to hurt others, it is necessary to have such a balancing concept. We do nothing to harm each other—and as I said, we do nothing to harm the Tiyazh, either."

"Then perhaps you'd better not teach me anything," she stated. "Because I just might decide to do what the rest of you won't do."

He said nothing, merely smiling at her in that damnably all-knowing way.

When they had returned to her house, he surprised her by saying that he would like to meet her parents. "And you must want to see them before we return to the valley."

"Why should you want to meet them?" she asked curiously. She hadn't yet returned her mother's call, and she *did* want to see them—but not with him.

"Knowing the parent helps one to understand the child. And they *are* your parents—despite what you have learned. I think it is important for you to see them now as well."

Something about his response didn't ring true, although she couldn't say why. In the silence that followed, she saw his expression turn to one of slight puzzlement.

"All right," he said. "I wasn't being totally honest with you because I know how you feel about mind-reading. But it's possible that they know something they haven't told you."

"About Susurra and my father? No, they know nothing."

He drew her into the living room, then seated them both on the sofa. "I've been thinking about your parents—your real parents, that is. Emily, your father must have known about you, at least if our belief that the Mevoshee are like us in every way is correct."

"What do you mean?" She frowned.

"Artificial means of birth control don't exist among us. We have no need for it because we can control our bodies. Men control the production of their sperm and women control their ovulation. So they must have decided to have you."

Emily was stunned. "But you're saying that he *knew*—and yet he let her abandon me, and then kill herself!"

"He could not have prevented her from killing herself because he could not have followed her to the valley. As for why he would have allowed you to be abandoned, what other choice did he have? Neither of them could have brought you back to their people without risking their lives. Death might very well have been the penalty for such a transgression."

"Then why did they let me happen?" she asked, disliking this discussion, but fascinated.

"I don't know the answer, but I still think it's possible that your parents could know something they haven't told you. It may well be something they never connected with your origins. If your father knew of your existence, then I think at some point he would have come to check on you. Certainly in his place, I would have had to assure myself that you were being well cared for."

"But if that's true, then he must not want to see me now. Otherwise he would have contacted me."

"I think he might have decided it would be best for you to live out your life without knowing anything of your true heritage—which might well have happened if I hadn't come along."

Chapter Seven

Emily hated deceiving her parents and she very much resented the living proof of that deception who sat across from her, chatting pleasantly with them. It also did not help that he seemed wholly unaware of her anger—yet another deception, since she knew he was very much aware of it.

Guilt and shame were involved in another way, too. She now knew who her real mother was and had at least a chance of discovering her father as well, and she could not avoid seeing these two wonderful people who'd raised her in a slightly different light.

She should have been able to say that these were her "real" parents because they were the ones who'd made her what she was. But her unique heritage made even that claim less than honest. She no longer was what she had been, even though she clung desperately to the hope that this would be no more than a strange interlude, after which she could go back to being herself again.

She had presented Alec to her parents as a colleague, suggesting that he was independently wealthy and therefore free to devote his time to research—a contemporary Neville, as it were. And to explain why she was bringing him to meet them over lunch, she had further hinted at a romantic interest.

Being normal parents who wanted to see their daughter settle down to marriage, they'd been delighted. And it was obvious that their delight had only increased now that they'd met him.

Emily marveled at the display of charm that flowed so easily from him. He was clearly being every parent's dream of a prospective son-in-law.

Of course, she thought cynically, that's not so hard to do if you can read minds and know exactly what people want to hear.

Then their eyes met and she saw a hurt expression cross his face. Well, maybe she wasn't being fair. He couldn't help it if he had more means at his disposal than ordinary people when it came to social situations. Perhaps what she really felt was envy.

Her mother began to talk about her lifelong love of horror stories, and particularly about Anne Rice's marvelous vampire series. Did Alec have any interest in those old legends? Emily had never found them of much interest.

"I've never made a study of them," Alec replied. "But history is full of tales about people who aren't quite what they seem to be. I suspect it's because we all see a dark mystery in every other human being—something we can't quite understand. Vampires and werewolves are just two manifestations of that."

Emily felt a sudden chill. Although she'd never had any professional interest in that kind of myth, she'd inherited her mother's love of horror stories, and the one thing that stood out now was how they were so often portrayed as creatures of extraordinary charm.

She couldn't bear to look at the man across the table. Could all his charm, his gentleness, everything she liked about him be a sham? How could she know what was real when he could alter reality itself? What if he was really using her to further some evil goals—something involving the Mevoshee, for instance? He'd portrayed them as opponents rather than enemies, as Neville had suggested—but what if Neville was right?

She continued to keep her eyes lowered as she ate her lunch and the talk flowed around her. But after several minutes, her head was literally drawn up, as though by unseen fingers beneath her chin—and she was forced to confront him.

Please trust me, Emily. Perhaps I can compel you to do some things—but I cannot compel trust.

The words were a soft plea inside her head, even as his eyes issued their own appeal. And all of this took place as her father was talking about his year at Oxford, where Alec had also spent a year. No sooner had Alec communicated his message to her than he was back to that conversation. The juxtaposition of the real and the unreal was dizzying.

Her mother asked Emily about the project on which she and Alec were supposed to be collaborating, and Emily began to make up her lies. But she was quickly caught in a wave of self-revulsion over her deception, and Alec stepped in smoothly to explain it all.

When the leisurely lunch was over, Emily and her mother rose to visit the ladies' room. As soon as they were out of earshot, her mother began to talk about Alec.

"Emily, he's *wonderful*! And his feelings for you are so obvious. But you seem a bit uncertain about him."

Emily was seized with an urgency to tell her all of it, but a vision of her mother's expression prevented it. So she said that she'd only just met him, after all, and wasn't about to rush into anything.

"There *is* something about him that's rather unusual," her mother said. "So I think I can understand your hesitation. He's just a bit *different* somehow."

She paused in the act of applying her lipstick and frowned at their reflections in the mirror.

"You know, he reminds me of someone. It's rather strange, because I'd forgotten all about him. It was so many years ago."

Emily struggled not to let her shock—and her eagerness—show. "Oh?" she asked casually. "Was it someone I met?"

"You met him, but you were just a baby. There was a group of writers that I was part of at that time. We used to meet regularly, either at a restaurant or at someone's home. After you were born, I often had them to our house.

"The man Alec reminds me of was part of the group for a short time. I saw him only twice, as I recall. It was an informal sort of group, with people drifting in and out all the time. I think someone said he moved to California."

"What do you mean when you say Alec reminds you of him? Did they look alike?"

"Oh, no, not at all—except for the fact that they're both tall and athletic. No, Doran had very light hair—the color of yours, actually. I can't really explain what I mean, except that they both seem different—in the same sort of way." She paused as she searched through her bag for her brush.

"It's strange that I should have thought of him again after all this time."

"What did you say his name was?" Emily asked, hoping her mother wouldn't find the question strange.

"Doran—or perhaps it was Duran. I'm not sure. But I remember that he was quite taken with you. We even laughed about your having the same shade of hair."

By this time they were leaving the restroom and Emily was forced to pull herself together to face her father and Alec. Somehow she managed to make the appropriate conversation and end the meeting—but the moment she was alone with Alec in the car, she sank against the seat with a dazed expression.

"She told you," Alec said as he watched her.

"Yes. She said you reminded her of someone

she'd met briefly a long time ago, when I was a baby. And she said that he saw me and was 'quite taken' with me, and they laughed about us both having the same hair color. He called himself 'Doran' or 'Duran.' Do you know that name—or one like it?"

He was silent for a moment, then nodded. "I think so. Most of us try to pick Tiyazh names as close to our own as possible. If it's who I think it is, his name is or was Turan."

"Do you know him? I mean, did you ever see him?"

"No, he had retired before I finished training. But I remember the name. He was a very powerful Shekaz, one of the best of his time. Ketta, my mentor, fought him twice—both times to a draw."

"I didn't realize that could happen."

"It doesn't happen often, and Ketta and Turan may be the only ones who've ever done it twice."

"Is Ketta still alive?" Emily asked hopefully. Just to meet someone who had met her father was more than she'd ever hoped for.

"Very much alive. We'll visit him when we get back. I got an image of this man Duran from your mother's mind, so we'll know if it's Turan."

"Alec," she began, knowing she was raising a difficult subject. "If there is any chance he's alive, I must meet him."

"We will talk about it when you're ready."

The trip back to Emily's home was made largely in silence. Alec left her to her thoughts—or so she assumed, since he made no comments.

My father *did* care about me, after all, she

thought, knowing that she sounded like a silly child. But perhaps in a way she was. Something—a very important something—of her childhood had been taken from her, and now she felt that she was regaining it.

She hadn't quite forgotten that moment over lunch when she'd likened Alec to creatures from horror tales, but she was so engrossed in her thoughts about her father and how she could meet him that when he raised the issue after they'd reached her house, she was inclined to brush it off as a temporary silliness—a stray thought not worth discussing. He obviously felt otherwise.

"You don't believe that," he stated categorically.

"No, I don't," she agreed. But a tiny part of her couldn't quite let go of that thought, and he, of course, knew that.

"Emily, you must trust me enough to open your mind completely to me—so that mine can be open to you as well."

"So you can't really read my mind if I don't want you to," she said.

"I could, I suppose—but I won't."

"I don't understand."

"It would be wrong."

"Then why wasn't it wrong for you to read it without my agreement before?" she persisted.

"It was necessary then."

"There's a definite lack of logic, or a double standard, operating here, Alec."

"No, what there is is one Azonyee and one Tiyazh: a very difficult combination."

"So the real object of all this training is to get me to think like an Azonyee?"

"That's part of it, yes," he admitted.

"Maybe I can't."

"You will."

"Why should I? I have no intention of living the rest of my life in your world, Alec."

"I think you will change your mind. Our destinies lie together, Emily. I am sure of that."

She looked up at him, stared into those intense dark eyes and wavered in her resolve. How much of what she felt for this man was real? How could she separate the awe she felt at his power from more normal feelings? Were normal feelings even possible under such circumstances?

He drew her slowly into his arms, giving her every opportunity to resist, even though he must have known she wouldn't. Then he lowered his face to hers, and with his lips just barely touching hers, he said softly:

"Is this real?"

It was and it wasn't. His mouth moved slowly, sensuously, against hers as his hands molded her curves to his hard angles. His tongue probed at hers, sending little tendrils of fire through her, demanding and getting more. Finally she made a sound that could have been either protest or surrender, and he raised his head again, leaving his imprint lingering on her lips.

"Is it real?"

She didn't respond because there was no need. Never in her life had she wanted a man as she wanted him. She hadn't thought it possible to want someone so much, and she wasn't sure it *should* be possible. It felt like a loss of self.

He released her. "When it is right, it will happen."

Right? How could it be more? she asked silently.

You will see, came that soft voice within her head.

"Ketta will be happy to meet you," Alec said as he turned away from the fading light of the taz-crystal. "We can go now."

"Is it far? Can we 'port there?"

He smiled. "It's several miles and we'll walk. 'Porting isn't our usual means of transportation within the valley, and besides, I'll use that time to explain some things to you."

"About Ketta?"

"About Shekaz in general," he answered as they set out toward the village.

"If the man your mother met as Duran is in fact Turan, Ketta will be able to tell you something about him—but not very much. When Shekaz are joined in battle, the only things they learn about their opponents are their strengths and weaknesses as they relate to the battle." He paused with a slight frown.

"It's difficult to find the right words to explain all of this to you, Emily. As you know, in these battles each of us draws upon the earth forces and those forces are then channeled through us and directed at each other. Basically, whoever does a better job of using those forces wins.

"There are about as many theories about how and why this happens as there are Shekaz. Some believe the forces choose us. Others think that certain of us are born with an affinity for those forces. Some think that the force remains constant for any given Shekaz, while others believe that they change from battle to battle.

"But there's more to it than simply harnessing the forces, however important that may be. We play on each other's weaknesses by probing for them during the battles. If a Shekaz becomes impatient, for example, that's a weapon that can be used against him or her. Or if there is anger or some other emotion that is clouding an opponent's judgment at that moment, it too becomes a weapon. The essential quality that makes for the perfect Shekaz—other than his or her ability to harness the earth forces—is the ability to remain totally calm and in control."

"But how can you *not* have any emotions at such a time?" she asked. "I mean, it's a battle—and you could die."

"That's true, but death or permanent psychic damage happens only rarely. What usually happens is that one or the other accepts that the battle is lost and withdraws. It is forbidden to continue attacking an opponent who has withdrawn. And in any event, there is no need."

Emily said that the battles sounded rather genteel, not unlike chess matches. He agreed.

"But to answer your question about emotions, Shekaz are trained to drain themselves of all emotion prior to a battle. One who cannot do that for whatever reason does not go into battle at that time. I did not accept any challenges for nearly six months after Janna's death for that reason.

There was too much pain and anger in me then."

"How are Shekaz selected?"

"The process is long and complicated, lasting many months. Other than an ability to harness the earth forces, which can be determined rather easily, the qualities sought are the ability to achieve an inner calm and a lack of basic character defects."

"I've never met anyone who doesn't have at least *some* character defects," she scoffed.

He laughed. "You have now. I'm perfect. I'm surprised you haven't noticed that by now."

"I see. So you don't consider excessive pride or self-righteousness a flaw."

"Not when it's justified," he retorted with a grin. "But seriously, you're right, of course. Everyone has defects. Shekaz simply have fewer of them, or have them to a lesser degree.

"I think you also have to understand that our lives here are such that the flaws you see in so many Tiyazh just don't exist among us. All our children are loved and wanted and grow up in complete families. We have no poverty, no mental illnesses, and there's no competition to speak of. We all have talents of one sort or another and are always free to pursue them. No one gets stuck in a job he or she doesn't like."

"You make this place sound like Utopia," she said skeptically.

"It is," he replied sincerely.

Emily thought it unlikely. "You implied that there's no such thing as illegitimacy or divorce. Surely that can't be true."

"It is. First of all, our world is very small, and

by the time a man and woman decide to marry, they will have known each other for many years —since childhood. And then there's the fact that communication is never a problem between couples. It's impossible to hide thoughts and feelings from each other."

"But you said that you don't read each other's minds, that you respect each other's privacy."

"We do—until close friendships develop. And mind-reading within families is important. It's part of the intimacy. I know that Tiyazh teenagers would be horrified to think that their parents were reading their minds—but we accept that and no one resents it."

Emily found this both fascinating and terrifying. There was no doubt that lack of communication, whether between parents and children or between husband and wife, was at the root of just about all problems within families, but going to the opposite extreme seemed unthinkable to her.

I don't think I could ever accept that, she thought, not without a certain regret.

"Perhaps you never will."

"But then why are you insisting that you and I belong together?" she asked. "Surely you could find someone here?"

He shook his head. "No, I already know everyone here. What Janna and I had was very special —even among us. What you and I have—or will have—is very different."

Emily was touched by his candor, but still doubtful.

He smiled at her. "There may be something to be said for the powerful physical attraction the

Tiyazh consider to be so important."

He had only to mention it for her to begin feeling that incredible desire again—not that it had been far from her mind in any event. But she was curious about his words.

"Are you saying that physical attraction plays no role in your relationships?"

"It doesn't. Janna was not a beautiful woman. I think you would call her striking, but certainly not beautiful. There are many women here whom I find far more beautiful than she was. But beauty is only pleasing to look at; a mind can be beautiful to *live* with. And unlike beauty, it doesn't fade."

She couldn't help wondering about their standard of beauty—and where she fit.

"I find you exceptionally beautiful. I thought that about you immediately. But if your mind hadn't attracted me, I would have done nothing more than admire you for a moment—much as one admires a fine work of art."

By now they had reached the village, and once again she felt herself the center of attention. No one was rude, but neither did they attempt to hide their interest in her.

As they were passing a shop that sold herbs and spices, a man came out, and Emily immediately recognized him as one of the people who had arrived just after Alec when she'd run from Ledee's house. Presumably he was a nastrano. She stopped, and Alec did, too. Before she could put her question to him, he answered it.

"She is better, but still weak, of course. She will want to see you when she is stronger, Emily—

and be assured that she blames only herself for what happened."

"Please tell her that I will visit whenever she wants to see me," Emily said with relief.

They continued through the village, turning down a side street where the familiar sound of childish laughter drifted toward them. Emily realized that she'd seen few children, except for babies, when they'd been in the village before.

A few moments later they came to a big playground, beyond which was a larger building she assumed was a school. The large grassy area was filled with children playing.

Most of them were gathered around a huge circular pad of bright blue that appeared to be a trampoline of some sort, although it was set flush with the ground.

Children were leaping high into the air and engaging in clumsy imitations of the exercises she'd seen Alec perform in his garden. She watched them for a few seconds before she realized that instead of hunkering down to propel themselves into the air, they were simply leaping to impossible heights. Then one child stopped in mid-air!

Emily came to a halt on the sidewalk and stared in amazement as the boy, who was probably ten or eleven, assumed a cross-legged position and just sat there about six feet above the pad. Then an even younger girl did the same thing, settling down beside him as other children leaped and twirled around them.

"Several of our most promising future dancers," Alec remarked.

"How long can they stay there?" Emily asked. But even as the words left her mouth, both children settled slowly to the mat.

"By the time they become adults, they'll be able to maintain those positions for however long they choose. We'll attend the next performance. It's our version of ballet."

"Can you do that?"

"Only for a few seconds. It's a special gift only a few of us have."

Then she spotted another group of children standing in a large circle as a big red ball bounced back and forth in the air, never touching the ground.

"What are they doing?" She couldn't see any of them touch the ball. Was it a magic ball?

"They're exercising their telekinetic powers. The object of the game is to bring the ball to rest above the very center of the circle. It can only be done through cooperation, not competition. It's a favorite game—like your football or baseball. Even adults play it."

They stood and watched the children for a while longer, and Emily became aware not only of their interest in her, but also of the almost worshipful eyes on Alec. When the game ended, one of the children whose back had been turned suddenly saw him and literally hopped toward him, calling his name. Emily smiled, recognizing what must be the very beginning of the girl's 'porting ability.

She propelled herself into his outstretched arms, then looked at Emily with a shy smile. Her likeness to her mother, Alec's sister Leesa, was so remarkable that she required no introduction.

"This is Tasse, my niece," he said. "Tasse, this is Emily."

The girl smiled and said, "Hello, Emily." Then she began to chatter in her own language.

"Emily doesn't speak our language yet, Tasse. Maybe she'll have to go to school as you do."

A bell sounded at that moment, and the children began to move unhurriedly toward the school building. Alec set down his niece and she scampered off to join them.

"Do they go to school year round?"

"Yes, but not every day. The school year is staggered, with older children going longer hours. We think they learn better at their own pace."

"It sounds like a good system."

"Our children are very important to us, and we don't try to fit them into adult molds. It's a system that works well for us because even as adults we don't work as Tiyazh do. So there's no need for them to be regimented."

On the far side of the school were rows of small houses, each set amidst many trees and broad lawns that afforded privacy. Alec turned into the path that led to one of them.

"This is Ketta's house."

Emily felt a rush of anticipation. She'd been so entranced by the children and by all he'd been telling her that she'd nearly forgotten their destination.

As before, Alec simply approached the door and waited. Within seconds, it was opened by a short, gray-haired woman whose face was wreathed in a wide smile. She stretched out both hands to Alec, a gesture she'd seen them use before, then turned to Emily as Alec introduced her.

"This is Ketta's wife, Nabla."

"Welcome, Emily." Nabla put out her hands and Emily took them.

"Ketta is in his garden," she said in heavily accented English. "Please join him there."

Ketta's garden proved to be even larger than Alec's, although on much flatter ground. The air was filled with beautiful scents and the musical tinkling of waterfalls and fountains. From its depths, a man emerged and walked toward them.

Emily thought that she had never seen a handsomer man, despite his advanced age. He had a full head of pure white hair, worn long in the fashion of men here, and deep-set very blue eyes in a face of classical beauty.

The two men extended their hands to each other and stared for a long moment into each other's eyes. It was an oddly intimate scene that touched Emily deeply, and she recalled what Alec had said about a Shekaz's mentor being another parent. Then Ketta fixed Emily with those sky-blue eyes.

"Welcome, Emily. I see your mother's beauty in you."

Then, before she could reply, he motioned them to the cushions and took a seat himself, betraying no sign of his age, though Alec had told her he was sixty-eight.

Alec explained the meeting with her parents and the man who'd called himself Duran.

"Let me see him," Ketta commanded, staring at Alec.

Emily held her breath—but not for long, because Ketta nodded almost immediately.

"Yes, that was Turan."

"Please," she said. "I want to see him."

Alec deferred to Ketta. "Yours will be the stronger image."

Ketta's eyes met Emily's and the image came instantly, far more quickly and even more clearly than when her grandmother had shown her her mother.

What she saw was a ruggedly handsome man of about forty, with her pale hair and blue eyes. There was a look of strength and nobility to him—and that self-assuredness she was beginning to recognize in all Shekaz.

"Thank you," she murmured, feeling tears begin to sting her eyes.

"Alyeka has already told you that we fought to a draw on two occasions. The second of those times, we fought for nearly three hours, perhaps a record length. In that time, I came to know Turan well—but perhaps not in a way you could understand."

Emily nodded, still holding onto the image. "Alec explained that to me."

"Turan was a very powerful Shekaz, certainly the most powerful I ever fought—though I think less powerful than Alyeka, if only because he could not quite control something within himself."

"What do you mean?"

Ketta paused, obviously seeking the right

words. "There was a darkness within him, a . . . What is the word I seek? My knowledge of English is slipping from disuse. Help me, Alyeka."

The two men stared at each other in silence for a brief moment. "Bleakness, I think," Alec said. "A very deep emptiness."

Then they stared at each other again, and both nodded. Alec turned to Emily.

"I'd not thought of this before, Emily, because I hadn't really known when Ketta's battles with Turan occurred. They were separated by less than a year—twenty-seven years ago. And you are twenty-nine."

Emily nodded, realizing exactly what he meant. She struggled once again with tears.

"He had lost both your mother and you," Ketta said softly. "I think I underestimated him. If he could still fight to a draw under such circumstances, his powers were even greater than I'd thought. He never really lost a battle, you see—and the two with me were his only draws. In my lifetime, only Alyeka has surpassed that record—but of course, he still has battles ahead of him.

"About Turan, I can tell you only this: he had more perfection in him than any Shekaz I have known—except, perhaps, for Alyeka. He retired after our last battle. But it was time. He would have been in his early forties, I think."

"Then he'd be in his late sixties now," Emily murmured.

The two men exchanged glances as Emily sat there thinking about him. Turan. Now at least her father had a name. If only there could be more.

"It is a matter for time and careful consideration, Emily," Ketta said gently.

Then he began to question her about herself as his wife joined them, bringing refreshments with her. She found them both wonderfully easy to talk to, although their English required some assistance from Alec.

As they were taking their leave, Ketta took both of Emily's hands in his and smiled at her. "I hope you have the opportunity one day to meet Turan —and I hope that for him as well. We were opponents, but not enemies."

She thanked him, certain that she *would* meet Turan. Whatever the risk, she was prepared to take it. Her mother was gone from her forever; she could not let that happen to her father as well.

Emily's training began the next day. At first she tried to treat it as an extraordinary opportunity to learn about another culture—a unique sort of fieldwork. But of course that didn't work, since she was too deeply and personally involved, and no good researcher ever allows herself to lose her objectivity.

Furthermore, no culture she had ever studied was as alien as that of the Azonyee. They existed on what was, to all intents and purposes, another planet. It was, she thought, much like studying Martians. There were no frames of reference.

Alec was a very difficult taskmaster. It would be wrong to call him "driven"—though she had accused him of that a few times. He was unfailingly patient and forbearing. But the intensity with which he undertook her training at times astonished her, and at other times angered her.

The first part of the training consisted of determining just what talents she might possess and to what degree. This was very basic education for an Azonyee, something that occurred in childhood.

He seemed loath to make comparisons, however. Instead, there were many "umms" and "aahhs" and shrugs. Could she have been a Shekaz? she asked. A shrug. Well, what about a nastrano, then? "Umm, that's difficult to say." And so on, until she finally stormed out of a session, went off to the woods, and didn't return for hours.

One thing she did know was that she possessed virtually no telekinetic powers. After two days of work, she could manage to make a small ball wobble a bit. He, of course, as he'd amply demonstrated with her gun, had considerable talent. She would spend minutes that seemed more like hours concentrating until her head throbbed and the damned ball would do nothing more than wobble slightly. Then he would merely glance at it and it would fly immediately into his hand. This did not create warm feelings on her part.

But if she had no telekinetic powers, she was a very quick student when it came to controlling her bodily functions. In a very short time, she could engage in strenuous physical exercise, then bring her pulse rate and breathing back to normal in less than a minute.

And she was very good at 'porting, perhaps, he suggested, because it was something she truly enjoyed. She could now 'port herself several miles without difficulty and without any dizziness. When word came from the nastrano Ledee that she would like to see Emily, Emily 'ported herself from Alec's home to Ledee's, a distance of nearly five miles. She enjoyed the visit and left feeling that despite their less than auspicious beginning, the two women could become friends.

One day shortly after her visit with Ledee, Alec sent her to another nastrano to see if she had any aptitude for reading the earth forces. Emily was at first reluctant, after her experience with Ledee, but both Alec and the other nastrano assured her that this was different and involved no attempt to probe deeply into her psyche.

She went through the mind-emptying exercises, then attempted to follow the instructions issued to her by the nastrano in a low, almost hypnotic voice.

She felt . . . something. A sense of being connected to something very powerful. A sense of timelessness. At some point she lost all awareness of her own body.

When the nastrano drew her gently back into herself, she answered his questions as best she could—and got only a slightly puzzled frown.

"Did you not feel *separate* powers?" he asked.

"No—or at least it didn't seem that way. Just one great stream flowing into me. Isn't that what you feel?"

"No, Emily. We sense *two* powers: one in opposition and one for which we have an affinity. It must be because you are both Azonyee and Mevoshee. How extraordinary. I envy you. But of course you could not have been a nastrano, since our craft depends upon our affinity for one power over another."

When she returned to Alec and told him, he said that he'd expected that, and of course she could never have been a Shekaz for the same reason. But he too was clearly fascinated and also a bit envious.

Emily knew that all of this was no more than a preliminary. Telepathy formed the very basis of their society. The other talents were merely conveniences.

Alec talked no more of trust, nor, so far as she could determine, did he continue to read her mind. It was, of course, difficult to tell where normal perceptiveness left off and telepathy began, but she was fairly certain that he had stopped probing her thoughts.

Neither did he touch her, except in the normal course of their work together. In fact, it seemed to her that he often went out of his way to avoid touching her, although she did not confront him about this.

They continued to swim in the pond and take long walks together, and in the evenings they visited with her grandmother or his family or watched videos or played chess. He had turned a small storage room into a bedroom for her, which afforded them both a great deal more privacy. And there was no repetition of that time when he'd walked in on her bathing, even though they continued to swim in the nude.

Emily would lie in her bed at night trying not to think about Alec. During the day she was kept so busy that, except when they were sunning themselves beside the pond, her thoughts managed to stay away from that aching desire. But at night it all poured forth, so powerful in its sensuality that she was sure he must feel it and might even come to her.

But she continued to fall asleep night after night alone in her narrow bed.

Alec sat in his garden after his morning exercises. He always arose long before she did, and it was perhaps the only peace he now had in his life, because when Emily awoke, so did his overwhelming awareness of her. She filled his mind, disturbed his equanimity—and he forced himself to exercise constant, rigorous control over his rampant desire for her.

But he was not exactly unhappy about this state of affairs. He looked forward to each new day with her, each new discovery. He'd been noncommittal about her talents, but he now believed she would be at least as talented as any ordinary Azonyee.

Already her thoughts came to him so clearly that he could not avoid them. Except for his parents and his sister—and, of course, Janna— he'd never read anyone that easily.

He wanted it to be that way for her as well and was confident it would be, as soon as she was ready to trust him totally. Despite the clarity of her surface thoughts, she still hid much from him, whether by design or not he couldn't tell. He ached for that trust as much as he yearned for her body—but not more, which was troubling.

Emily Carr had a sensual hold over him that Janna had never had. With Janna, the physical act had been no more than a very pleasurable part of their love; with Emily, he knew it would be all-encompassing in and of itself. The sheer power of such a thing both intrigued and troubled a man whose previous pleasures had come largely from the mind.

This need to possess her body manifested itself in a total absorption with everything she did, every detail of her appearance.

She usually wore her long hair in a single braid, but sometimes she brushed it out and let it hang nearly to her waist, and on these occasions he imagined its soft silkiness brushing against his skin.

When they had been swimming and then lay on the rock sunning themselves, she always applied a lotion, and he lay there watching her apply it and imagined his hands instead of hers stroking that silken smooth skin.

She had the wonderful grace of a ballet dancer, which he'd learned she'd once been, and when she contorted her body in her exercise routine, he thought about all the other things that body could do, entwined with his own.

In short, he found everything about Emily Carr almost unbearably erotic—and all the more so because he knew there was no intent on her part to arouse those feelings. True, she wanted him, but she was wary nonetheless, knowing he would want more than mere physical union.

Normally, he knew when she had awakened. He could feel it in a heightened awareness of her even before she put in an appearance. But on this morning she succeeded in startling him when she suddenly walked past him into the garden. Then she turned and smiled at him.

"I didn't want to disturb you. I thought you

were meditating."

"I was—and you *always* disturb me," he replied rather recklessly.

Clearly she misunderstood, because she frowned. Having already spoken rashly, he plunged on.

"I meant that I'm always aware of you—too much aware."

She paused, one hand fisted against the swell of her hip. "It doesn't seem that way to me. In fact, I think you avoid me, Alec."

"It's just my way of coping with the situation."

She stared at him for a moment, then turned to walk on into the garden. Then, abruptly, she stopped and turned to him.

"You haven't asked me lately if I'm ready to trust you."

"Are you?"

She nodded, then turned again and hurried along the path deeper into the garden.

The truth was, he knew she was ready to trust him. He'd been aware of it for some days now. Was he actually afraid of what lay ahead for them—afraid of this blazing, all-consuming passion?

He watched as she stopped in the grassy area he'd created for exercising and began her preliminary stretching routine. Then she launched into a series of exercises he'd seen her do before, displaying a supple grace that years of ballet had given her.

Instead of the loose-fitting garments she generally wore now, she exercised in a leotard—a blue one today that matched her eyes. Every muscle of her very fit body was clearly displayed.

Suddenly she began to leap high into the air—too high. He stood up quickly, but by the time he did, she had spun herself around, somersaulted, and settled lightly back to earth. Then she did it again—except that this time she remained in the air, turning slowly until she was facing him and then settling into a cross-legged position about ten feet in the air. She tossed her unbound hair back over her shoulders and gave him a smug smile.

He hurried toward her, then stopped just in front of her and looked up. "Emily, come down. You're too high."

"Are you annoyed, Alec? Perhaps because I can do something you can't do?" She leaned forward slightly to smile down at him.

"I'm not annoyed—I'm worried. It takes practice to settle back down gradually. You're high enough that you could hurt yourself if you fall."

"I can stay up here as long as I want. I've been practicing."

"How long have you stayed up?" he asked doubtfully.

She shrugged. "At least fifteen minutes—but I know I could have stayed longer."

He chuckled. "All right, I'm impressed. Do you have any idea how much training is usually required to achieve that?"

"Quite a lot, from what you said."

Then suddenly she raised herself still higher and swooped down to run her fingers through his hair. He reached up to grab her hand at the same time, and with a startled cry, she came tumbling down into his arms.

"You broke my concentration," she complained.

"Did I?" he asked innocently.

"Could I have prevented that?"

"I hope not," he replied drily.

Then he set her on the ground. "Let's have breakfast and get to work."

Chapter Eight

Emily withdrew. Withdrawal felt to her like a sort of mental shaking, the way a dog shakes its coat to rid itself of water. Then she became aware of the perspiration dripping from her chin and the tip of her nose. She ran her hands over her face, wondering how purely mental effort could be so physically draining.

Alec sat across from her, his dark head lowered as he composed himself. There was certainly no trace of sweat on him, she thought with annoyance.

They had moved beyond the minor games of conjuring up an image for the other to read. That had proved to be remarkably easy. Now, single images had been replaced by whole series: story-telling by thought. He would demand that she tell him—through thought—every detail she was seeing. Then *she* would send the images, and he would constantly remind her to concentrate on details and project them clearly.

When she protested that she failed to see the practical value of all this, he said she should think of it as a way of preparing her mind for more important things: a sort of extended warming-up exercise.

And yet she remained resistant to probing his thoughts, although even without trying she could now pick up some of them. At times she felt confused, uncertain whether or not he had spoken aloud. It was frightening and disorienting, but he told her that was only because of her stubborn persistence in believing that thought-probing was an invasion of privacy.

"How can it be an invasion of privacy when I have invited you to read my thoughts? You're not being logical, Emily."

"If you want logic, then train a computer," she'd snapped before going on one of her frequent walks in the woods.

Still, she knew that her resistance was weakening. She was fascinated by the glimpses into his mind. What interested her most was his preoccupation with her. It seemed that he thought of little else. But then, neither did she think of much besides him.

When she tried to put into words what was happening, the closest she could come was to say that the lines of separation between them, their uniqueness as individuals, was blurring. Sometimes she could scarcely tell where her own thoughts left off and his began.

That was why her walks in the woods had

become so important. They gave her back to herself for a time. When she would announce that she was going off to the woods, she could always feel his regretful acceptance. And although she knew by now that he could reach out to her over at least several miles, she never felt his presence in her mind at those times.

And so, day by day, they concentrated on the mind-reading games—while the *real* mind-reading proceeded at a different level, so subtly that there never really came a moment when Emily knew they had reached that state of ultimate intimacy when neither of them could conceal anything from the other. It simply happened. Layer by layer, their minds were laid bare to each other—until nothing at all remained.

Her first conscious awareness of how far they'd gone came one evening as they walked back through the soft night from a performance by the dance troupe. The night was pure perfection: a brilliant canopy of stars overhead, with a thin sliver of moon hanging just above the horizon and a light, pine-scented breeze flowing down from the hills.

She'd loved the performance: hauntingly beautiful music played on instruments both familiar and strange, graceful dancers performing feats unthinkable to earth-bound performers. And all this amidst the splendor of a park that had been specially planted with evening-blooming flowers.

All of it combined to leave Emily with a languorous, drifting feeling that seemed to hint at still greater pleasures to come. She began to think of a moonlight swim in the pond, of two bodies glistening with beads of water, entwined on the rock.

They were by now at the edge of his garden, and instead of continuing to the house, they started off on the path to the pond. But when the pond itself came into view, Emily stopped abruptly.

"No," she said, softly but distinctly. "I don't want this. I'm not ready for this."

He stopped, too, but said nothing.

She opened her mouth to accuse him of putting thoughts into her mind, then stopped in confusion. Of course he was putting thoughts into her mind; she was doing the same to him. It was all a jumble, impossible to separate now. It wasn't a case of she wanted this and he wanted that. Without conscious thought, they adjusted, accommodated themselves to each other.

"But I can still keep my body to myself," she said aloud. Much of the time now they communicated silently, but when she wanted to assert her individuality, she spoke aloud.

"Yes," he replied. "But you frustrate yourself even more than you do me, because you will never be able to control your emotions as I can because of my Shekaz training."

She could not dispute what was so obviously the truth—another result of their intimacy. Not a day passed that she wasn't made aware of how much people live in lies, or withheld truths. Total candor, she'd decided, is not a natural state for most people, though it was certainly natural to the Azonyee.

She turned and walked back to the house with that truth dogging her steps all the way. Perhaps she couldn't control her emotions—but she could control her actions.

Emily heard the low rumble of thunder as she walked back from a visit to her grandmother. She glanced up to see black clouds gathering along the horizon—the first storm she'd seen here.

These visits to her grandmother left her with a deep, aching sadness. Her great-aunt and a cousin had been there as well, but there was for Emily no sense of family.

She tried to understand, and Alec, ever tuned to her feelings, had explained that they had all suffered greatly as a result of her mother's suicide.

"The Azonyee set great store in the unchangeability of our world, Emily. We've watched as the outside world has undergone change—much of it bad—and we are more than ever determined that such things will not happen to us. Your mother's suicide was a frightening reminder that we cannot keep the outside away completely."

He'd also said that the closeness she sought would come in time, but Emily doubted that. Her grandmother and her few other relatives were always kind to her, but with her telepathic powers growing daily, Emily could feel their restraint ever more clearly.

She saw too the contrast with Alec's family. Their closeness cut through her like a knife, exposing what was so lacking in her own life now. Not even the certainty that her parents loved her could heal that wound. How would they feel if they knew the truth about her? Wouldn't they think of her as some kind of freak?

She walked on, back to the man who offered her what she could not find elsewhere. Did she love him? Normally, such a question would seem all-important. But the usual slow process of getting to know a person and perhaps falling in love had been transformed. They already knew each other better than most couples who had spent a lifetime together.

Alec said that the Tiyazh concept of romantic love was irrelevant to them. It was something the Tiyazh had invented because they could never know true intimacy. She knew he was right, but how could she rid herself of the world she'd grown up in—the world she was still determined to return to?

As she walked and thought, Emily had paid scant attention to the approaching storm. But now a sharp clap of thunder drew her attention. It was still early evening, but the path beneath her feet began to glow as it did in twilight, then faded briefly as a bolt of lightning illuminated the gathering darkness.

She stopped briefly. She was only a mile or so from Alec's house. But just as she considered 'porting herself there, she knew somehow she shouldn't do it. She had no idea *why* she shouldn't; the knowledge was simply there.

She began to walk rapidly, at the same time reaching out to Alec with her mind. But nothing happened. He must be home. When she'd left, he was settling down with a new novel by his favorite science fiction author. He devoured science fiction the way she devoured horror stories and mysteries.

She broke into a jogging pace as yet another bolt of lightning split the heavens, followed closely by a crack of thunder so loud it shook the earth. She continued to seek him out mentally, expecting at any moment to feel that delicate awareness.

By the time she reached the garden, the rain had begun: big fat drops that stung her face and pelted her body through its thin coverings. She ran headlong into the house and called out to him.

Only silence greeted her. A lamp was lit and the book he'd been reading lay beside his favorite chair.

Emily panicked, sending her thoughts out helter-skelter until she began to feel dizzy from the effort. Where was he? And why was she feeling so strange? She took several deep breaths and sat down on a sofa. The storm seemed to be raging directly overhead now. She'd always been afraid of storms, but what she felt now went deeper than that. It felt primitive, the way she supposed animals must feel because they couldn't understand what was happening to their world.

Where was he? Why wasn't he here to calm her? Could something have happened to him? Her thoughts spun with terrifying possibilities that she knew made no sense even as she thought them. Maybe he didn't really exist. Maybe this *was* all a dream, after all—and it was coming to an end.

Then, in the brief silence between claps of thunder, she thought she heard something. A door opening? She got up and ran toward the doorway that connected the house with a small garage where Alec kept a little electric-powered vehicle.

"Emily?"

She cried out and ran to him, colliding with him as he stepped into the kitchen and wrapping her arms about him tightly.

"I went to look for you," he explained, stroking her damp hair. "How did I miss you?"

"I took the long way back," she murmured against his chest. She reached out to that wonderful calmness within him, completely forgetting that it so often annoyed her. But she felt nothing, and even though her body was pressed against his very solid flesh, she was deeply frightened.

"Storms affect us," he said as he continued to hold her. "I should have warned you. They interfere with our powers. I know you must be afraid, but it will pass soon."

"Is that why I knew I shouldn't 'port myself back here?" she asked, recalling that strange certainty. "It wasn't you warning me against it?"

"I couldn't have warned you because I couldn't reach out to you. You may have thought you *shouldn't*—but the truth is you couldn't have done it."

He led her back to the living room and went to start a fire with a battery-operated gadget. It was the first time she'd seen him use it; he'd always started fires with nothing more than a flick of his powers.

As the fire began to blaze, he drew her down beside him. "What you're feeling isn't really fear, even though I know it must feel that way. It's actually a heightened sense of self-awareness because some of the energy of the storm is flowing through you."

He paused and smiled at her. "There's a price for everything, and what you feel now is the price we pay for our talents."

He moved over to sit behind her, his arms circling her and his long legs bent at the knees to either side of her. "I'm sorry I didn't warn you about this," he said again as he pressed his mouth against the top of her head.

She laughed, but the sound was slightly hollow. "Well, at least now I know you're not completely infallible—or totally omnipotent, for that matter."

He chuckled, his breath warm against her scalp. "Storms may be nature's way of forcing us to be grateful, because during them we're no better than Tiyazh."

A few moments later he got up and brought them some wine. They sipped at it mostly in silence, listening to the storm vent its fury. Finally the flashes of lightning grew less frequent and the thunder began to trail off into low, distant rumbles.

Emily was thinking about what he'd said, about how storms reduced them to mere Tiyazh status. It came to her slowly but with total certainty that she no longer wanted to be what she had always been. Even though she'd insisted to herself all the while that she wanted only to return to the life she'd had, something had been changing within her. She could no longer imagine returning to a life bound by the normal senses.

As the storm moved away, she began to feel Alec's thoughts, incoherent at first, like voices heard in the distance, but then growing clearer.

At the same time, she felt a gathering within her, a strongly sensual awareness of herself—and of him.

His arms were crossed in front of her, and where they brushed lightly against the heavy fullness of her breasts, Emily felt an almost unbearable sensitivity. He lowered his head and brushed his lips softly against the curve of her neck, and the sensation traveled through her like a warm flood.

"Yes," he said against her ear, his voice low and husky. "Love-making is always best after a storm. I seem to have forgotten to warn you about that as well."

Emily heard the laughter in his voice, but she could also now feel the joy in him—a pure joy with no sense of conquest within it.

There was, after all, no conquest—only a victory for them both as their thoughts merged and all the reasons she'd once given herself for preventing this melted away. That very carefully drawn line between the intimacy of their minds and the intimacy of their bodies was forgotten.

And yet, she could now feel a slight hesitance on *his* part, a barely perceptible drawing away that vanished even as she focused on it.

"Why?" she asked, not sure whether she'd spoken aloud.

Perhaps she had, because he answered aloud. "It's an awareness of that part of you that is Mevoshee. I can always feel it, but I've hidden it from you in the past."

Uncertainty threaded its way through her, not overwhelming her desire but perhaps holding it in check. His lips and tongue began to toy with her ear, even as his voice in her mind told her that this was a part of her, unique and exciting to him.

Then the uncertainty was gone and that voluptuous warmth began to flow through her, lending a slow magic to their movements as they shifted and fell back against the thick rug and the soft cushions.

He raised himself above her and their eyes met as the firelight played across their faces. Far off in the distance they heard the last low rumbles of the dying storm. She lifted a hand to trace the outline of his jaw and felt the pleasure it brought him. Then their lips met and she could no longer tell whose thoughts she felt.

Urgency built in them both and they savored the feeling even as they moved slowly, languorously—removing clothing piece by piece until the firelight touched two bodies: one pale and luminous, the other bronzed and glowing.

And now she felt those differences between them even as she could feel no distinction between their minds. Her fingers touched smooth, hard muscles as her mind felt his pleasure in her softness.

There was no hesitation between them, no careful seeking for the way to give pleasure. As mind touched mind, they both knew. He knew when that ripe, aching heaviness in her breasts demanded release. She knew how he craved the feather-soft caress of her long hair against his belly and thighs. And both knew when need had reached its wildest, most urgent moment.

He lifted her on top of him and she took him into herself and with each thrust they seemed to rise higher and higher to a place that was pure desire, beyond the reach of mere flesh.

When release came, it shuddered through them both in one long, rippling wave of ecstasy that left tiny echoes of its passage long after it had gone.

They lay still entwined before the dying fire, thoughts mingling lazily as they drifted through a time that was neither sleep nor wakefulness. Emily could feel the depths of his satisfaction and the soft edges of his wonder and knew that it had never been like this for him before, either.

And she could feel his struggle to put what had happened into some recognizable context: not just different from Janna—but more. There was even a brief, sharp resentment and guilt over being forced now to let go of her.

All this should have been painful to her, but it wasn't. She understood this, just as he understood her reluctance to give up her old life. They had not come to each other as blank slates; much had already been written. But that only lent a richness, a wonderfully complex texture to what they now shared.

Emily had begun to learn their language and had quickly discovered that there was actually very little to it. It was a sterile language, utterly lacking in the rich variations of English. They had no writers, no poets—and no words at all for feelings. Now, finally, she fully understood why this was so: the spoken language played so very small a role in their lives.

Alec stirred and propped himself up on one elbow to stare down at her. "You are right, but I think there is still enough Tiyazh in you to want to hear me say that I love you—however inferior the

Tiyazh concept of love might be."

She laughed and nodded. Then, when they had both spoken those words, she agreed that they sounded meaningless.

"As meaningless as Tiyazh wedding ceremonies, but we will have that, too—for your parents if not for us."

"You don't have such a ceremony?" she asked lazily.

"Not a ceremony as such. There will be a celebration. My family will provide that." He smiled at her, a smile that said he knew his next words would bring her out of her slow drifting.

"They know already."

"They know?" she asked even as she felt the truth in his thoughts. "But . . ."

He silenced her with a kiss, telling her through his thoughts how it was with them. His family would know because of the deep, powerful bonds between them.

"They can't *see* us, Emily," he said aloud, amused as he felt her embarrassment. "It's more like a sudden certainty that we have mated."

Then, seeing that she was still doubtful, still thinking in Tiyazh ways, he reached once more into her thoughts to help her see it from their standpoint. We see differently, he told her. We communicate at a different level. There is no prurience involved. We find Tiyazh obsession with sex to be very silly. Sexuality for us is only one form of intimacy—the form we choose to reserve for the one person with whom we have found the greatest union of minds.

He waited patiently as she absorbed all this and began to fit it into the new framework of her new life here. These things were hard for her, but perhaps not as hard as they had been. There were fewer of those dark corners in her mind now, although they were still there: places that even now she unconsciously shielded from him.

Then he drew her to him, knowing that the doubts had been buried as he felt her thoughts return to him. He'd discovered that male-female differences were sharper to her. She felt him as alien, yet craved him all the same. She liked his bigness, his hardness, and therefore made him far more aware of her smallness and softness.

Perhaps this was why their union seemed so much more: that clash of differences, coming together by striking sparks off each other. It was very different from the unbroken flow from mind to body that he'd come to know with Janna.

She stirred beneath him and he felt himself growing hard again with a joyous wonder that brought a satisfied murmur of laughter from her. He lowered his mouth to hers, cutting off her laughter even as he thrust that hardness into her waiting softness.

Emily lingered in bed, watching him as he opened the drapes and became a large dark silhouette against the bright morning sun. Then he stretched, raising his arms into the air and rippling the bronzed muscles along his arms and shoulders. She knew he was both amused and intrigued by her interest in his body, and he apparently wasn't above displaying it, either.

It wasn't really the case that they were turned into each other's thoughts at every moment. To do so required little effort, but it still took some intent and at the moment they remained separate. Nevertheless, when he turned to face her and she could see what was on his mind, desire leapt within her and they slipped into each other's minds even as he returned to the bed.

By the time he left it again, she felt very thoroughly loved—and was also ruefully aware of some aches and pains. He was unfailingly gentle and ever mindful of the difference in their sizes and of his considerable strength, but he was also a very energetic lover. And a very inventive one as well.

He paused in the doorway with a boyish grin. "You haven't even seen the beginning of my inventiveness yet, Emily Carr. Think of the possibilities provided by levitation, for example. I'm very pleased that you have a talent for that."

As he spoke, he filled her mind with a series of erotic images that brought a flush to her fair skin. "But I fell when you touched me," she pointed out.

"Only because your talent isn't fully developed yet," he assured her, then went out to the garden to do his exercises.

Emily hauled her protesting body out of bed and went to the window to watch him. She'd always enjoyed these displays of his athletic grace, but the pleasure now was even greater, since he was naked.

But even as she stood there watching him, even as she felt the aftermath of a night of love-making, little doubts crept into her mind. She didn't want them to be there, but that only made them more apparent.

She and Alec were, to all intents and purposes,

now married—at least as far as he was concerned. He certainly knew that what was to him a natural progression was very different for her. But she'd noticed before that he could conveniently forget that she hadn't been raised among the Azonyee—as though by so doing he could make her too forget that inconvenient fact.

He'd said he was willing to go through a wedding ceremony for her parents' sake. Very generous of him, she thought—but without rancor. It was impossible to become angry with him for any length of time, if for no other reason than that he never became angry himself and was totally incapable of being cruel in any way.

Emily sighed. It was so easy to drift along this way, letting things happen "in their own time," as he so often put it. But it would be a lot easier if that Tiyazh part of her didn't persist in rearing its head to remind her of free will and purpose and too many other things.

He wasn't in her mind at the moment, but she could still feel his bemusement at such thoughts —thoughts he was sure she would shed with the rest of her Tiyazh upbringing.

And some of it was indeed being shed. The longer she remained here, the less she could recall of the details of her life in the outer world. She even thought of it that way now, and in fact was rather nervous about going out there today, though she'd insisted that she call her parents and check in with her neighbor Peggy.

Worse still, in another two weeks she was scheduled to join her colleague in Louisiana. She hadn't discussed it with Alec, but she knew he was aware of those plans—and of the fact that

Toby Shaw would be there. Her link with her father's people.

He finished his exercises and came in to dress for his daily run. "Come with me," he suggested.

"I don't like running, and besides, I could never keep up with you."

"Of course you can. Use your talents."

So she went along, running for short distances, then 'porting on ahead and waiting for him. Once, she hid in some thick foliage and tried to shield her thoughts. But he found her anyway, because it seemed she couldn't quite prevent herself from reacting to his presence.

They returned to the house for breakfast, and she reminded him of the phone calls she needed to make. "It's a pity you can't use your talents to string some phone lines into the valley."

"There are limits, even for us. It isn't that we couldn't run the lines. We actually tried it once. But the barrier interferes with reception."

"But that must mean that you're cut off from your families when you're out there."

"Not really. There are powerful telepaths among us who circulate in and out of the valley. They can pick up distress calls over thousands of miles and identify the source. It's not a perfect system, but it works fairly well.

"And just as a backup, we now have a phone number that is connected to a machine that is monitored every hour."

Emily laughed, as always amused by their combination of magic and technology. Merlin never had it so good.

Then she recalled the emergency phone number in Toby Shaw's file. "I think the Mevoshee may have such a system as well," she said, explaining about the file.

"No doubt they do. We assume they live much as we do."

"Where do they live?" she asked curiously. "You do know, don't you?"

"Of course. In the Scottish Highlands."

He turned away rather abruptly and went off to shower. Emily stared after him and for the first time became aware that he was deliberately shielding his thoughts from her.

She felt a chill. Surely he didn't intend to try to prevent her from seeking out her father. She knew he had some reservations about the wisdom of such an action, but he'd never given her reason to think he would try to stop her.

Try? He *could* stop her. No matter what talents she might have acquired, she was no match for a Shekaz—and certainly not for the most powerful of them all.

We're headed for a showdown, she thought miserably. If only he could understand her need to find her father. But then he *must* understand it. How could he not, when he knew her as well as she knew herself?

Emily put a hand to her throbbing head. Was it the result of 'porting herself out of the valley? Alec had tried to dissuade her, but for that reason alone, she had insisted. He'd finally given in, complaining (in his thoughts, anyway) about that stubborn streak of perversity in her. The truth that she'd shielded from him was that she needed to know she could do it—in case it ever became necessary.

No, she decided a moment later, it wasn't the 'porting. It was being out here. It was so noisy, and the air, even in this small Adirondack community, smelled funny. People spoke too loudly —and too much. Also, people tended to crowd each other, to invade what she had come to expect to be her personal space.

I have truly become one of them, she thought with amazement as the light changed and she crossed the street. She wrinkled her nose at the smell of exhaust fumes and had to resist the temptation to cover her ears.

She started toward the supermarket where she'd told him she would meet him. Absently, she massaged her throbbing temples, then suddenly remembered her training. She was far from being a healer and wasn't yet even as skilled as the least of the Azonyee, but surely she could do something about this headache.

She paused, pretending to gaze into a shop window as she concentrated on the headache. Within seconds it had been reduced to a barely noticeable level. With a smile, she walked on toward the supermarket.

She had made her calls: to her mother, to Peggy to check on her house and on Chaucer, to her colleague in Maine to discuss the upcoming trip to Louisiana. She'd also called home to check her machine. There'd been several calls from friends, but none from Ben. She knew she had hurt him and felt badly about that, but Ben was part of the past. So too, perhaps, were her friends.

My whole life is slipping away from me, she thought sadly. I have learned who and what I am—but I still have no place. The valley still seemed like a dream and the real world now seemed thoroughly unpleasant.

She walked into the supermarket and still more noise, and quickly found him in the frozen foods section with a well-filled cart. Alec, she'd discovered, had a real thing for supermarkets. The small markets in the valley couldn't begin to satisfy his needs. He was an excellent and inventive cook and had a barely controlled appetite for junk food as well.

He turned before she reached him, and she felt that pleasurable brushing of minds, a sort of mental caress that never failed to arouse her.

"So now you see it as we do," he said, having obviously picked up her thoughts about this world.

"How can it seem so different in such a short time?" she complained.

"The magic of the valley, I suppose," he responded as he began to select a few pints of Haagen Dasz for the cart. "I wish they had Ben and Jerry's. I like the chocolate chip cookie dough flavor."

Emily laughed, drawing a puzzled look from him until he realized that she still found the juxtaposition of two such different worlds highly amusing. Then she sent him an imaginary TV commercial touting Ben and Jerry's for the "man who's faster than a speeding bullet, the man who can conjure up anything," and they both began to laugh, drawing the attention of several other shoppers.

At least, she thought as she forced herself back to seriousness, I still have a sense of humor about all this.

But by the time they were on their way back to the valley, Emily's mood had turned somber once more. She told him how she'd become impatient waiting to cross the street and had very nearly 'ported herself across.

"I don't know how you do it, how you can move so easily from one world to the other."

"I've been doing it for a very long time," he responded. "It just takes some getting used to—and besides, your talents are new to you and it's natural that you should want to use them."

"I felt as though I were chained—trapped in my own body, for heaven's sake."

He merely smiled as his mind-voice told her that she had become an Azonyee—whether or not she was ready to admit it.

To Emily's surprise, the celebration for them was held that evening. She'd thought she would have at least a few days to consider this "marriage"— to become adjusted to the idea of it, at any rate.

She'd also expected that the affair would be attended only by family and close friends, but it seemed that the entire valley was there. It was held in the large park near the Council Building, amidst flower gardens and exotic trees and flowering shrubs, the type of place every bride would dream of.

Instead of the traditional champagne, there was a wonderfully aromatic pale gold drink whose name she couldn't pronounce. Alec told her it was made in small quantities here in the valley for just such occasions and was nonalcoholic. The Azonyee were by and large not drinkers, since they disliked anything that could affect their minds—and, by extension, their talents.

There were beautiful gifts created by various artists and craftspeople, while others had brought delicious food as their gifts. There was a dance performance especially for them, and Emily marveled anew at the beauty of the dancers. The Bolshoi would be out of business if the outer world ever saw this!

Gold was everywhere! The Azonyee tended to wear quite a lot of it even in their daily lives, but on this occasion they outdid themselves. Clothing of spun gold, soft shoes encrusted with gold threads and tiny gems—and of course, the jewelry. Even young children wore it. Leesa had given her a shimmering gown belted with braided gold studded with emeralds, pearls, and rubies. In the bright sunlight of late day, the whole assemblage was so dazzling that it actually hurt her eyes.

In the midst of this splendor, it took Emily a while to realize that while she saw almost every person wearing precious gems, no one was wearing diamonds. She asked Leesa about this.

Leesa laughed. "Yes, I guess that must seem strange to you, since the Tiyazh seem to value diamonds above all other stones. A few of us wear them, but more to balance the effect of the other gems than for themselves. Diamonds aren't really precious, in the sense of being truly rare, like emeralds, rubies, and pearls, for example. They're actually rather common. The only reason Tiyazh pay such prices for them is that the market is tightly controlled. We find that distasteful."

Emily smiled at this example of Azonyee snobbishness. They were definitely an interesting group.

At one point, Emily found Ketta, Alec's mentor, seated quietly at the edge of the group. She liked the elderly man and felt drawn to him, because of both his close relationship with Alec and his connection to her father.

He smiled as she approached. "You bring such beauty and freshness to us, Emily—a gift in itself."

"Despite my Mevoshee blood?" she asked with a smile of her own.

He hesitated for just a moment, and she thought she might have offended him. But then he nodded.

"Perhaps that is part of the gift."

"What do you mean?" Emily was surprised at his words, in view of the Council's initial deliberations about her.

He stared off into the crowd for a long time before answering, then turned to her again. "When you reach my age and are forced to live much of the time in your mind, you begin to question certain things—perhaps even to think the unthinkable. Alyeka is too young for such thoughts and couldn't really afford them, since he's still a practicing Shekaz. But there are times when I question why we live as we do."

"But Alec says that you must maintain the balance of the earth's forces, that that's your mission as a people. And the Mevoshee's as well."

"That is true, I suppose, but I think there comes a time late in life for many of us when we begin to question such a belief. And other beliefs as well—such as the rule that we must live separately.

"Have you considered, for example, that our

battles are not unlike your athletic contests? And yet such teams or individuals do not find it necessary to live separately."

"Yes, that's true—but how could you live together? They can't come here and you can't go there."

"The earth forces circle the planet, Emily. Do you not think there might be some place where *both* could live?" He stopped, then chuckled at her astonished look.

"Don't pay me any attention, Emily. These are just the ravings of an old man who is intrigued by meeting someone with both bloods in her veins. A flight of fancy and nothing more."

At that moment they became caught up in the hungry throng crowding around the tables of food and drink, and their conversation ended. But of all her memories of this occasion, it was the conversation with Ketta that would remain the strongest.

It was long after dark when the celebration ended and Emily and Alec made their way home beneath a brilliant full moon. They walked along slowly, hands clasped and minds touching gently. But without understanding quite why she was doing it, Emily shielded her conversation with Ketta from him. He knew she was withholding something, but he assumed it was her continued doubts about their marriage, and he knew that would change with time.

When they arrived home, it was to discover that the bedroom had been turned into a flower garden. The mingled scents of flowers both familiar and strange filled the room with a haunting fragrance that was at once elusive and deeply sensual. On the small table beside the bed was a gold tray with goblets and a bottle of the unpronounceable drink.

"What a wonderful thing to do," Emily exclaimed as she moved about the room, examining various bouquets and arrangements. "Who is responsible for this?"

"Among us are some who have a special gift for creating fragrances. Much time and thought goes into creating the perfect scent by mixing the flowers and then arranging them in a certain way in the room."

Emily, who'd thought that by now she could no longer be impressed by their talents, was amazed anew. Even to one as untutored as herself, there was a harmony to the arrangements. All of it blended into a silent symphony of colors, textures, and that powerfully erotic scent.

Alec watched her as she moved about the room, shimmering in the soft light as it caught her pale hair and the deeper gold of her gown. He wondered if she were truly able yet to understand the depths of his feelings for her—or even if she would *want* to know at this point.

The possessiveness of Tiyazh males was something the Azonyee disdained. Their unions were so complete, so whole, that there was no need. And yet, a part of him felt very possessive right now—no doubt because she was not yet ready to give herself up completely to what they had.

He knew he would soon have to let her go for a while. They hadn't yet discussed her trip to Louisiana and her plans to use that boy to contact her father, but they must do so soon. Soon, but not quite yet. He went over to her, wrapped his arms around her, and kissed her silken head.

"Shall we go for a swim, or just bathe here?"

"I'm not sure I could leave here," she replied huskily. "That scent is hypnotic."

When they went into the adjoining bathroom, Emily discovered to her delight that it too was bedecked with flowers. Even the water was scented. Outside the window wall, the forest was bathed in silvery moonlight.

Their love-making began as they bathed each other, and went on from there in a slow, leisurely fashion punctuated by moments when desire reached the flashpoint and brief hours when they dozed in each other's arms.

They were totally uninhibited. What, after all, could they hide from each other? How could there be any hesitation when they were so deep into each other's thoughts? Even in sleep, bodies and minds were joined, moving through a dreamscape together.

Chapter Nine

"Alec, I *must* do this." Emily knew he understood that, but she continued to find it necessary to say it aloud. "My father may well be alive, and if there is any chance I can see him, I will."

"Emily, I think you are failing to see this from his point of view. He already knows of your existence and if he'd wanted to make contact with you he would have done so. The risk for him could be very great. It isn't likely that he told anyone of your existence, and you can't know what action the Mevoshee may take if they discover the truth."

Emily conceded the point, but refused to change her mind. "It all hinges on what Toby Shaw knows—or suspects—doesn't it?"

"Whatever he might have thought, he certainly would have told his people about my showing up at that lecture—and about your interest in me. They will know that I couldn't have been that interested in Neville's book, since I'm sure they were aware of its existence at the time Neville wrote it. So they will have assumed that there was another reason for my presence.

"Furthermore, it's quite likely that they know you were brought here—or, if they don't actually know it, they might well have guessed."

"There are just too many 'ifs' and 'maybes,'" Emily grumbled. "I want the truth—and I can get that truth from Toby. Then I'll decide what to do."

"Remember, Emily, your father's life could well be in your hands."

Emily nodded solemnly. "Will you come with me to Louisiana? I know you have to stay away from Toby, but couldn't you be somewhere nearby?"

"I intend to be."

Two days later, Emily left the valley alone. Alec went with her to the boundary, but she 'ported herself through the barrier, back to that rocky ledge where she'd first seen the valley—and the shadows of the enchanted land.

She stood there for a moment as an icy wave of fear engulfed her. He was there; she knew it. She thought she could actually feel his presence. But she had a terrifying moment when she was certain she could never cross that barrier again. Before she stopped herself, she could feel her mind begin to focus on 'porting through the barrier to him.

Finally she turned away—back to the "real" world that no longer seemed quite so real. She had assumed he would at least come back to Connecticut with her, but he'd pointed out that the Mevoshee might well be watching her home now. He would follow later, keeping his distance.

She arrived at her house to the usual complaints from Chaucer and some discreet questions about her handsome friend from her neighbor Peggy. Emily shrugged off the questions, dismissing him as nothing more than a colleague, though admittedly a very attractive one.

After Peggy had left, Emily stood in her living room, reaching out with her mind to see if she could detect any Mevoshee presence. Alec had told her that she should be able to feel it if anyone were around, although he wasn't sure just how close they would have to be.

She felt nothing. Was someone there and simply keeping his distance—or would they wait until she was in Louisiana? The uncertainty annoyed her. And what if they chose to ignore her completely? Alec didn't think that likely, and neither did she, but it was still a possibility.

Toby called her the next day. She'd been half-fearing that he would tell her he couldn't go, but he sounded as eager as ever. When she asked where he was, he told her he was in London and was booked onto a flight that would put him in Baton Rouge only hours after her own scheduled arrival.

Two days later she was headed south by the kind of absurd, circuitous route the airlines used these days to torment the flying public. She was eager to see Toby and eager to return to her work, but that anticipation was very nearly buried beneath her longing for Alec.

She hadn't expected to miss him this much. It wasn't just a normal longing for an absent lover; that she could have handled. But she ached for that gentle touch of his mind against hers as much as she yearned for his physical touch. She supposed that lovers who are parted from each other often feel that they've lost a part of themselves—but none of them could have felt what she felt. A part of her was truly missing.

Surprisingly, she landed in Baton Rouge slightly ahead of schedule, and the moment she entered the terminal, she searched for any sign of a Mevoshee presence. But once again, she felt nothing. Could she and Alec both be wrong in assuming she would be able to detect them?

As she waited for her luggage, she scanned the area. No one seemed to be paying her any undue attention, except for the usual admiring glances from men. Of course, that too meant nothing. Someone could be there and avoiding her.

The steaming heat of a Southern summer struck her as she stepped out of the terminal, and she slid gratefully into a waiting cab, then hurried from the cab into the motel. How on earth could these people stand it? And how was she going to bear up once they began to work? The place felt like one giant sauna.

Hank Milton, her colleague from Bowdoin, had arrived ahead of her and had left a message at the desk for her to call him. She called him as soon as she was settled in, and they met in the quiet (and cool) cocktail lounge to discuss the project. With Hank were two students who seemed as eager as Toby was.

It felt very good to settle in to her professional role, and they had talked for several hours by the time she glanced up and saw Toby standing in the entrance to the lounge. She waved him over and introduced him to the others.

The temptation to probe his mind carefully was very strong, but Emily managed to contain herself and instead merely observed him discreetly. He seemed nervous, but that might well be because of the presence of strangers. Toby had always been shy and withdrawn.

The group had dinner together in the motel restaurant, where they passed up the Cajun items on the menu since, as Hank pointed out, they'd soon have the opportunity to eat the real thing—and probably more often than they liked.

It was late when they left the dining room. Hank and his students had rooms in another wing of the motel, while Emily had reserved a room next to hers for Toby. As they walked back after saying good night to the others, she commented that he seemed as eager as ever to go on this expedition.

He said that he was, and had even read several books about the Cajuns and the bayou country in preparation for the trip. She found his studying admirable, since most students couldn't bring themselves to touch a book over summer vacation.

"I hope your family isn't unhappy about your being away," she commented.

"No, they travel a lot, too, and they thought this would be a great opportunity for me to see if I really want to work in this field."

How very smoothly you lie, she thought. It both surprised and unnerved her, because Toby seemed incapable of subterfuge. But of course he would never work in this field—or even in this world, for that matter.

As they reached their rooms, he hesitated. "Uh, Dr. Carr, I have a really big favor to ask of you. I'll understand if you say no, but I promised him I'd ask."

"Promised whom?" Emily felt a tiny flutter of uneasiness.

"My uncle. He's really interested in what I'm going to be doing, and he's here in Baton Rouge on business. We flew over together. Anyway, he asked me to ask you if he could join us for a day or two. He'd really like to see the bayou country, and he promised he wouldn't get in the way."

Emily met his hopeful expression with outward calm. His uncle? Possibly—but she knew he wasn't interested in the bayous. She felt slightly dizzy from a wild mixture of anticipation and fear, but she managed to smile.

"I'll have to check with Professor Milton, of course, but I don't see any problem. We'll be staying at a small inn, so we'll have to be sure they have room for him."

"Oh, we can share a room if necessary," Toby assured her quickly. "I really appreciate this."

"What does he do?" Emily asked.

"He's an engineer with a Swiss electronics company, but he's actually British. My family's kind of spread all over."

"I see," she said, stifling a smile. "Is he staying here?"

"No, he's at a hotel in the city. But he'll be ready to leave with us tomorrow if Dr. Milton says it's okay."

"I'll call him now and let you know."

She did as promised, and fortunately Hank had no objections. When she called Toby, his relief was obvious even over the phone. Once again he assured her that his uncle would be "no trouble." Emily wondered if he were trying to tell her that the Mevoshee weren't her enemies—or was she reading too much into a simple statement?

She just hadn't expected it to be this easy—or this obvious. She'd been sure *she* would be the one who would have to initiate the contact. She tried to think that it was a hopeful sign. If they wanted nothing to do with her, they surely wouldn't be sending this "uncle" to make it easy.

Emily's doubts about her ability to spot a Mevoshee were laid to rest early the next morning when the stranger paused in the entrance to the dining room as their group was having breakfast. There was no doubt that this was Toby's "uncle."

He was tall, although not quite so tall as Alec, and his build was heavier. His slightly longish blond hair was a shade darker than her own, and as he walked toward them, she found herself staring into blue eyes that were a mirror image of her own. A tantalizing possibility hovered in her mind as Toby introduced him.

The name he gave was Noel Bentley, and Toby said he was his mother's brother. There was no resemblance between them, but that proved nothing. Perhaps he really *was* Toby's uncle.

He was also quite charming, although Emily noted that he paid her no more attention than he did the others. When their eyes met, Emily felt nothing more than friendliness—and that indefinable sense of his Mevoshee blood.

As he talked with Hank, Emily returned to her earlier thought. Why had it never occurred to her that she might well have a half-brother? There was at least a superficial resemblance between Noel and the image Ketta had provided of her father.

But wouldn't she know if he were her brother? She recalled how easily she'd identified her grandmother. Still, a half-brother might not be as recognizable as a full brother. How she wished she understood these things better.

Over coffee, Noel seemed to turn his full attention upon her, asking about her background and her interests. They talked easily enough, but beneath the smooth surface conversation, Emily felt the distinct murmur of things *not* being said. She had shielded her mind carefully and assumed he had done the same. She was certain that if he made any attempt, no matter how carefully, to probe her mind, she would feel it.

After breakfast, Noel said that he'd rented a Blazer and invited Emily and Toby to travel with him, leaving Hank and his two students to drive the vehicle they'd rented. Emily accepted the invitation after only a moment's hesitation. What could happen when they were traveling in convoy with Hank?

When they set out, Emily reminded herself of

Alec's warning. She could not afford to assume that any contact with the Mevoshee would be friendly, no matter how amicable it might seem. But when she stole a glance at Noel's handsome profile, she could not believe that he meant her harm. Nor could she think that of Toby.

They left Baton Rouge behind and drove out into the bayou country, where the road in many places was built up between canals and marshes. Here and there were stands of dead cypress and big, ugly oil-drilling rigs.

Emily had read that the bayou country and its way of life were disappearing rapidly, thanks largely to the lure of profit dangled before the eyes of residents by the big oil companies. The incursion of salt water into this fragile ecosystem had already affected the fishing and shrimping that had for generations been the dominant industry. And now, according to Hank, even the oil industry jobs were disappearing because it was too costly to bring up the oil that remained.

"This is a tragic, dying place," Noel remarked as they passed through a small settlement where ramshackle houses stood on pilings and small, battered boats squatted next to tumbledown docks.

Emily agreed, wondering aloud how people could sell their heritage and destroy their future here for what had obviously been no more than temporary gain.

"Just about anyone can be tempted by enough money," Toby said. "The world is full of examples of that."

This world, Emily thought—but not the worlds we know. And for a moment, she felt a true bond with them: outsiders staring in dismay at an alien world.

For the first time since he'd become a fully trained Shekaz, Alec knew a feeling familiar to all lesser beings: a sense that things were beyond his control. The only time a Shekaz could experience such a feeling was during a battle about to be lost, and since he'd never suffered that, all of this was painfully new to him.

He had followed Emily to Baton Rouge, keeping his distance from her even as he longed to be with her, or at least to reach out and touch her mind. She'd given him her itinerary, so he knew she was staying at a motel near the airport. Therefore he opted for one of the large hotels downtown.

But no sooner had he checked in than he'd felt it. He was more talented than most at detecting the presence of their adversaries and lightning-fast at erecting his shields. It wasn't likely that he'd been spotted, but he knew that a Mevoshee was somewhere nearby.

He stretched out on the bed and considered the situation. What were the odds against one of them being here at this time for any other reason? Very long indeed. Whoever it was, he or she was here because Emily was here. And he had no safe way of finding out if it was a Shekaz, although he suspected that would be the case. Knowing of his connection to Emily, it was unlikely they'd send anyone but another Shekaz.

He thought about finding another hotel. His shields were only so good. If the two of them chanced to meet face to face, there would be no hiding. On the other hand, he would be safe enough if he stayed in his room.

The next morning, after ordering his breakfast, Alec called the motel where Emily was staying and ascertained that the group had already checked out. Then he cautiously reached out to seek the unknown Mevoshee. Nothing. Just as he'd expected. He ate his breakfast and checked out, then drove to the motel where Emily had been staying.

He approached the desk clerk, and two discussions began simultaneously. Aloud, he inquired about Emily's group, certain that even in a busy motel she would be remembered. He said he thought an old friend of his might have joined them this morning when they left. And even as he spoke, he was pulling the desired information from the young man's mind.

Noelo! Alec recognized the mental image immediately, although the clerk hadn't known his name. Alec knew Noelo well indeed; the two of them had been joined in battle twice. And that made him a logical choice for this mission, since Noelo would be particularly sensitive to his presence.

He thanked the clerk and left deep in thought. When Noelo's image had come to him, he had made the same connection Emily had earlier. Was it possible that he could be her half-brother?

Or might they simply want her to believe that, so she wouldn't feel threatened?

He followed the route he knew they would have taken, still thinking about Noelo. He knew Noelo couldn't be much older than Emily herself, and that argued very strongly against the possibility of his being a half-brother. Adultery simply didn't exist among them, and it seemed very unlikely that Turan would have married and produced a child so quickly after his affair with Susurra.

The more he thought about Noelo, the more troubled he became. His two battles with Noelo had left him with a certainty that there was a darkness within the Mevoshee. Alec hadn't been able to penetrate it, but he knew it was there. Noelo was powerful, but his powers were limited by that darkness.

What he wanted in that moment was to find Emily and take her away—back to the valley. But Emily had made her decision, and all he could do was stay as near as he dared and protect her to the extent he could.

Toby was the one who gave voice to their collective relief when the group at last pulled into the parking lot of the small inn.

"At least it doesn't look as though it's ready to sink into the bayou like everything else we've seen for the past hour."

Emily laughed. "Toby, when you've done field research as long as I have, you'll see worse, believe me. Often it seems that only in places like this can we find folk mythology still existing."

"It's true that this is not a lovely place," Noel said. "But I can see what you mean, Emily. Folklore survives now only in such places. In the rest of the world, change has destroyed all that."

Their eyes met briefly, and Emily was left with the distinct impression that Noel's observation, while certainly true, had been made solely to please her.

The man was almost impossibly charming. His wide-ranging knowledge and his very British wit made it impossible for her not to like him. But she still would not allow herself to trust him completely.

The inn, which had been recommended to Hank by someone familiar with the bayou country, proved to have some charm of its own, albeit a seedy sort of charm. The group gathered in the small lobby and Emily looked around, her mind fixing on the phrase "shabby dignity" to describe the place.

What happened next occupied only the briefest possible span of time—so brief that Emily didn't truly begin to realize its ramifications until she was in her room.

As the group was milling about the front desk, a man appeared at the top of the staircase that led to the second floor. In scarcely more than a blink, Emily realized that his resemblance to Alec was superficial at best—but for one heart-stopping moment, she saw only that tall, lean build and that thick black hair. And Alec leapt into her mind atop a tidal wave of longing.

She turned back to the group just in time to see Noel swivel his head sharply in her direction, almost as though she'd spoken. His gaze passed slowly over the dark-haired stranger as he left the inn, then returned to Emily silently.

Shaken, Emily hurried to her room as quickly as possible, sank down onto an overstuffed chair, and tried to assess the damage. There was no doubt in her mind that *something* had been communicated to Noel; the only question was *what*.

Could Noel have made the connection between the stranger and Alec—or might she have unwittingly made that connection for him? Of course, the connection between Alec and her would already be well known to Noel, thanks to Toby—but now, thanks to her foolish longing for him, Noel might know even more.

Did that really matter? Would Noel be unwilling to help her reach her father if he knew the true relationship between Alec and her?

She leaned her head back against the chair. Questions. That was all she had. Too many questions and no answers. And she felt so alone—and so unable to cope. She, who had lived a life of total independence.

Her thoughts were interrupted by a light tap on her door, followed by the door swinging open. Noel stood there, looking rather surprised.

"I'm sorry, Emily. I didn't mean to barge in, but your door must not have been latched." He cocked his handsome head and peered closely at her. "Are you all right? You're looking a bit peaky."

She stood up and waved a hand in dismissal. "I'm fine, Noel. It's just a slight headache. Travel does that to me sometimes."

"Well then, perhaps you'd rather rest for a while. Hank and the students are going to find his contact and make some arrangements, and I thought we might stroll about the village a bit."

"That sounds like an excellent idea. Fresh air and exercise will probably do more for me than an aspirin. I'll be with you as soon as I change."

He left and Emily unpacked quickly and changed into jeans and a T-shirt before she could change her mind. She had no option now but to proceed as though nothing had happened—and wait for him to make a move. Besides, they would certainly be safe in the village.

The village was only a collection of two dozen homes, a small grocery store, a church, and a disreputable-looking bar from which a great deal of noise erupted, even in the middle of the afternoon. A few old people were about and several large, noisy groups of children scampered by, pausing briefly to stare at them before continuing on their way.

Noel began to question Emily about her family, a subject he'd raised during their journey here. She explained that she'd been adopted.

"Have you ever tried to find your real parents?" he asked.

Knowing she could be treading on dangerous ground, Emily explained the circumstances of her birth.

"That's quite a story," he said when she had finished. "Enough to make one believe in the old tales of fairies leaving babies, or whatever it was."

Emily laughed, and hoped it sounded natural. "Actually, my mother used to call me her 'fairy child.' And I've always thought that my origins might have had something to do with my choice of a career."

"Indeed. I was just thinking that as well. Folklore is really a sort of collective search for a heritage, isn't it?"

"Yes, I think that's a good description—one I've used myself."

"If you had the opportunity, would you want to meet your real parents?" he asked suddenly.

Emily was too startled to reply quickly. A shiver of anticipation ran through her. Then she nodded. "Of course—that is, as long as it wouldn't cause harm."

"But what if they turned out to be . . . different from your expectations? Surely you must have fantasized about them."

Feeling as though she were negotiating a verbal minefield, she chose her words with great care, while trying to maintain a facade of casualness.

"Oh, I fantasized about them when I was young, but I don't think I really have any expectations now. Just curiosity—and a need to know."

They had reached the end of the village and paused to stare off into the distance where two oil rigs perched in the marshy land like ungainly metallic birds. He was silent for a moment, then surprised her again with his next question.

"Would you hate them for having abandoned you? I should think it would be natural."

"No, I don't think so. There are many reasons why parents might have to give up a child, and I'm sure they would have suffered more than I did, since my adoptive parents were wonderful."

Then he smiled at her—a genuine smile, she thought. "Forgive me, Emily, for intruding upon your privacy. That was very un-English of me."

Emily laughed and stifled her disappointment. The subtle change in his tone indicated that he had no intention of pursuing the matter any further.

Feeling frustrated, Emily sought and found an opportunity to approach the matter in a different manner. They had begun to talk about her work once more, and she mentioned several recent projects, then casually mentioned Neville's book.

"It's quite interesting," she said after giving him a brief description of both author and book.

"But surely there have been many such tales?" Noel asked. "I'm not that well read in that area, but practitioners of magic are rather common in folklore, aren't they?"

"Yes, but not quite like these: two tribes, existing through the ages in their enchanted lands, and moving with ease between their worlds and ours."

"And were you able to discover the location of these people?"

"No, not really—just that it's upstate New York, in the Adirondack region. I might try to pursue it at some point. It would be interesting to see if there are any local legends up there that would tie in with it."

"Do you believe in magic?"

She laughed. "Don't we all? Anything we don't understand—or don't *want* to understand—can be called magic." Then she added more seriously:

"I do think there are forces in this world that are presently beyond our understanding— psychic talents, for example. There is certainly ample evidence that some people are quite gifted, although not as gifted as Neville's 'magic races,' of course."

He chuckled. "Yes, I would imagine they could create quite a stir, couldn't they—if they made themselves known, that is?"

"Actually, Neville's old woman said that if he were to encounter one of the Shekaz, he would know it."

"But perhaps only if the Shekaz wanted to be known," Noel said.

Early the next morning, the group set out for their first full day's field work. Emily was eager to begin, if only because it would take her mind off the tantalizing but ultimately unsatisfying conversation with Noel. She felt she had gone about as far as she dared at this point, so the next move was up to him.

Hank's contact was a recently retired schoolteacher, herself a Cajun and a native of the parish. The woman lived in a remote village and had agreed to gather some of the most knowledgeable local residents for a day-long discussion. They had both agreed that this would provide an excellent opportunity for the students, since all of them would be taking notes separately, then comparing them later.

Hank had already visited southern France, the place from which the people known as Cajuns had originally come, and they were both eager to see if the lore of that region had been carried along to Louisiana.

More than two hundred years had passed since the ancestors of these people had left France for Nova Scotia, where they had established a colony known as Acadia. Then, in the 1800s, they'd been driven out of Nova Scotia by the British and had migrated to Louisiana, where they were well received by the French already living here. They'd quickly returned to the fishing and trapping that had been their livelihoods in Nova Scotia.

The term "Cajun" was a corrupted form of

"Acadian," and the tale of these people had been immortalized in Longfellow's poem *Evangeline*.

Like so many once tightly knit groups, the Cajuns were now scattered, and since their once-thriving fishing business had been reduced by the environmental damage wrought on the bayous by the oil companies, it seemed unlikely that small communities like the one they were visiting would survive for much longer. Emily and her colleagues often felt as though they were only one step ahead of such dispersions, and that frequently lent an urgency to their work.

After several wrong turns, they finally found the village and the small, neat clapboard home of Helene Duchault. To their delight, the retired teacher had gathered a dozen people, most of them elderly, and all of them eager to talk.

Because the house was small and the weather pleasant, their hostess and her neighbors had set up tables and chairs in the yard. It was apparent that they'd decided to make a party of this, and true to Cajun custom, the tables were laden with more food than could be eaten by a group twice the size of this assemblage.

Emily, who had eaten far too much of the inn's excellent food the evening before, nevertheless found herself becoming hungry again as she looked at the wonderful array of food. The students, being students, needed no urging to dig in. Emily had observed long ago that the thirst for knowledge seemed to be accompanied by a hunger for food of all kinds at any time.

In addition to the food, it seemed that they were to be treated to entertainment as well. Two elderly men were busy tuning up their fiddles, while another appeared just after they arrived, carrying a well-used accordion.

The day passed quickly. No one observing the group would have guessed there was any purpose to it other than to have fun, even though the guests carried recorders or scribbled regularly on yellow notepads.

Noel, who spoke French fluently, was forced to give up in his attempts to converse with them in that language. "It isn't French," he complained to Emily and Hank at one point. "Just when I think I understand what they're saying, they toss in something totally incomprehensible."

Hank explained that the Cajun tongue was actually a mixture of French, Indian, Spanish, Italian, and English—"a true gumbo," he said with a grin and gesturing to the dish he was devouring.

Their hostess introduced Emily to a latecomer to the party whom she described as a "treater." The woman was a trained nurse who worked at a local clinic, but who also practiced her own ancient healing rituals. When Emily asked if the clinic doctor knew this, the woman nodded.

"He sends patients to me sometimes," she said with a decidedly Gallic shrug. "He is Cajun, too."

As the day drew to a close, the musicians were joined by a younger guitarist, and another of the group produced a triangle. The music was alternately sad and happy—and utterly captivating.

Drowsy from all the food and the heavy heat, Emily found a shady spot on the fringes of the crowd. A moment later Noel joined her, and she began to talk about her discussion with the treater.

"Do you believe that the body has the power to heal itself?" he inquired when she had finished describing the woman's methods.

"Of course. I've never doubted it."

"Oh? Have you perhaps discovered some of those talents in yourself?" he asked in a light, teasing tone.

Emily hesitated briefly, then nodded. "Perhaps."

"Tell me about them," he urged.

Oh, I can levitate and 'port myself and move small objects and cure headaches, she said to herself. Aloud, she said only, "Nothing, really—just certain feelings about people or events that I can't really explain."

"I see. And do those feelings tell you anything about me?"

She turned to stare at him—and took the plunge. "They tell me that you aren't what you seem to be, Noel."

She was disappointed when he feigned shock at her words. "Then what do you think I am?"

"I'm waiting for you to tell me."

His gaze slid away from her. "Honesty can sometimes be dangerous, Emily."

Then, abruptly, he turned those piercing blue eyes on her again. "You have not been entirely honest with me, either."

"Oh?"

"You said you intended to pursue the clues that you found in Neville's book at some time in the future. But in fact, you have already done so."

So there it was. Should she deny it? She decided to counter with a question of her own.

"How could you know that?"

He smiled. "Because I have 'feelings,' too."

Suddenly, unaccountably, Emily panicked. She struggled to find some safe reply, but before she could, Hank had come up to join them.

After that, she managed to prevent any more discussion by remaining with the others. She didn't understand her sudden withdrawal, but decided to trust her instincts. She even maneuvered it so that she would travel back to the inn with Hank, rather than risk being alone with Noel and Toby—and once back there, the group remained together far into the night, discussing the day's work.

Hank announced that he'd secured the services of a young man in the village to take them deep into the bayous, to a small settlement that could only be reached by a pirogue, the flat-bottomed boats the Cajuns used to travel through the shallow bayous.

"It'll be a great trip, Emily." Hank grinned. "Alligators, mosquitoes, all sorts of interesting flora and fauna."

"Actually, I was planning to follow up on some leads the treater gave me. She gave me the names of several other treaters, and also told me about a local historian who sounds interesting."

"Well, perhaps we should split up then," Hank said. "But our guide is going to be disappointed. I think he only agreed to take us because of you."

"Please give him my regrets," Emily replied sweetly. "But this sounds like a trip I could live without. Mosquitoes are entirely too fond of me, and the only place I want to see an alligator is on the other side of a chain-link fence."

Then Hank asked Noel if he wanted to join them, but Noel said he thought he'd look around a bit on his own and then return to Baton Rouge. He didn't look her way at all.

Despite her tiredness, Emily had difficulty falling asleep. She now feared that she might have lost her only chance to make contact with her father. What if Noel just left? She still couldn't understand that panic that had come over her.

Oh, Alec, she thought. How I need you now. Damn you anyway, for becoming a part of me and then leaving me like this.

It helped not at all to know that *she* was the one who had separated them. Logic played no part in it.

Alec stretched out on the lumpy mattress and stared at the sleazy motel room with its cracked vinyl chair and battered dresser and plastic vase filled with garish plastic flowers that could not possibly have been intended to imitate anything in nature.

He was a snob, pure and simple, and had he been accused, he wouldn't have bothered to deny it. With unlimited funds at his disposal, he always stayed in the best hotels and ate in the finest restaurants.

The spicy, unrecognizable food he'd eaten earlier sat uneasily in his stomach—perhaps the worst insult of all, since he'd foolishly believed that the little restaurant next door would be one of those glorious discoveries and he'd be sampling the best of Cajun cuisine.

Alec was frustrated, a feeling virtually unknown to a man who always ordered the world around him to suit his needs. But here he was, relegated to a passive role, waiting in a dump of a motel.

Furthermore, he didn't understand the nearly overwhelming need for Emily that left him unable to achieve the inner serenity he'd always been able to find. When he and Janna had been separated from time to time, his need for her had been nothing more than a small but manageable emptiness. But what he felt now was a huge hole—so large that it seemed to him he was only an empty shell.

He lay there listening to the rhythmic rattle of the old air conditioner, hoping it would lull him to sleep, and wondering how many more days of this he would be forced to endure. But despite his best efforts, sleep wouldn't come.

Finally the thought that had been hiding there all the while crept stealthily into his consciousness. Did he dare to go to her now, in the middle of the night when Noelo would be asleep?

He drew his dark brows together as he tried simultaneously to ward off the temptation and examine its possibilities. He knew he didn't dare risk going over there. Even in sleep, Noelo could easily become aware of his presence. But what if he left his body behind?

Not all Azonyee possessed the talent known as astral projection or out-of-body experience in the Tiyazh world—but Alec *did* have that ability. How much of the powerful aura of a Shekaz would cling to his spirit? Surely not enough to draw the

259

sleeping Shekaz's attention.

A shiver of anticipated pleasure shot through him as he contemplated the notion. He *did* pause long enough to berate himself for behaving like a lovesick Tiyazh—but by now the need had become too great.

Emily drifted up from deep sleep, but not quite into wakefulness. In this trancelike state, she was aware of something that her brain registered as being Alec. But she did nothing more than murmur his name, then roll over slowly onto her back.

Ghostly lips touched her cheek, brushed against an ear, moved slowly along a bare shoulder. She made a soft, throaty sound of pleasure, but remained suspended in that strange place.

The feather-light touches continued, a mouth moving softly against her throat, a tongue toying with her nipples, making them hard and sensitive.

She began to struggle toward wakefulness as that ghostly touch continued, moving downward now—across her stomach to the place where a throbbing need was building.

But the struggle was too much and she gave it up, giving herself over instead to sensation piling upon sensation. Her body was being driven into a hot, damp frenzy as she drifted in a dark, voluptuous haze.

She moaned again as she felt him enter her— big and hard and wanting as he thrust deeply into her, then retreated and thrust again, filling her, making her whole.

It went on and on—or so it seemed. Time was as insubstantial as everything else as she moved along the edges of darkness, then suddenly arched into a blinding explosion of ecstasy. Sated and quivering, she slipped down once again into sleep.

Chapter Ten

When she awoke in the morning, Emily could still feel that final, lingering brush of lips against her eyelids, of a mouth lightly touching hers. She tried to cling to the memory, but it had begun to fade the moment she opened her eyes.

At first she thought it had been nothing more than a particularly vivid dream. But her body ached pleasurably with the unmistakable aftermath of love-making.

He must have come to her in the night, after all, 'porting himself into her room, then stealing away again. But he'd told her he didn't dare do such a thing, that if there was a Mevoshee nearby —particularly the Shekaz he expected them to send—he or she would be able to detect his presence even in sleep.

And yet she knew he *had* been there. There was

even a lingering presence in the room, something she couldn't define but definitely recognized: the residue of a powerful sorcerer.

Emily went downstairs to join the others for breakfast with considerable trepidation. What would happen if Noel knew he'd been here? This morning might well be her last chance to convince him to help her reach her father, and both she and Alec believed that if the Mevoshee knew of her true relationship with Alec, they would turn their backs on her.

But if Noel knew anything, he hid it well. He greeted her pleasantly, then resumed his conversation with Hank. When their eyes met, Emily came dangerously close to probing his mind, drawing back only at the last possible moment. There was a very fine line between the ordinary probing for subtle signals and true mind-reading, and she knew she'd pushed against that line. But Noel registered nothing.

The others left immediately after breakfast, eager to be off on their adventure through the bayous. Emily and Noel walked out with them, then stood watching as they left with their guide.

"Are you leaving now as well, Noel?" she asked as casually as she could.

"I thought I might drive around the area a bit," he replied. "Then I must return to Baton Rouge early tomorrow morning. Could we have dinner together tonight?"

She agreed quickly, glad for the temporary reprieve. She still didn't feel ready to confront him, and that rapidly approaching deadline weighed heavily on her all day long. Normally the most meticulous of researchers, Emily realized as she returned to the inn late in the afternoon that she had performed more poorly than any undergraduate this day.

Some twenty miles from the inn, she passed a shabby motel. Since she was preoccupied with thoughts of the evening ahead, an awareness of the man getting out of an old pickup truck was very slow in coming. And by the time she realized it was Alec, she could already feel that welcome brushing against her mind.

Emily literally stopped in the middle of the road, causing an old station wagon behind her to swerve off the road with a loud screeching of brakes. She quickly pulled off the road herself and smiled apologetically at the occupants of the wagon as they drove past glaring at her. Then she turned around and drove back to the motel, her hands shaking so badly she could barely hold the wheel.

Alec stood there waiting for her, plainly worried at her near-accident. She decided to forgive herself for not having recognized him immediately. He was just barely recognizable now in old jeans, a faded knit shirt, and a baseball cap imprinted with the name of a hardware store.

He came up to her the moment she pulled in, and there was a frustrating moment when they both tried to open the door. She would have rushed into his arms immediately, but he gave her no opportunity as he half-dragged her into one of the units.

"Inside—quickly. We're too visible out here."

After pushing her inside, he demanded the keys to her car and said he wanted to move it around back. While he was gone, Emily looked around with amazement that turned quickly to amusement. This was definitely not his style. And that baseball cap. She began to laugh.

"I'm glad *you* find it so amusing," said a dry voice in her mind. Then the door opened and he was there again.

He lifted the cap from his head and sent it flying across the room—without touching it, of course. Emily laughed in sheer pleasure: the pleasure of seeing him and the pleasure of having that quiet voice in her mind again. But above all, it was the pure joy of feeling whole again.

He nodded gravely, his eyes devouring her. Being apart from you has been a very humbling experience, his mind told hers, and she knew that he had shared her pain and longing.

They moved into each other's arms, already fumbling with their clothes. But as her body felt that welcome heat of desire, she remembered the night before. How could she have forgotten?

How indeed? his mind-voice asked humorously. But Emily could detect a certain embarrassment. She drew back and frowned up at him as he slid her shirt off her shoulders.

So he hadn't really been there—at least not in the flesh. And his lack of control troubled him. She let him know that Noel seemed not to have known, and then they shared the information and she understood who Noel really was.

All of this was conveyed without a word. The only sounds in the room were the whispers of clothing being shed and the soft sounds of two people rediscovering each other's bodies.

They fell back onto the lumpy bed in a frenzy of need and joined with a rough urgency that would not have happened had they not both known that the other wanted it so. Mere moments passed before they were both driven over the edge, fused together by the heat of their combined passion.

Afterward, they lay as they always did, bodies still joined and minds roaming together over the past few days and the evening yet to come.

Alec voiced the silent opinion that Noel would not have betrayed himself to the extent he had if he didn't intend to carry it further.

"Yes," Emily said aloud. "But that doesn't necessarily mean that he intends to help me reach my father—or that he even knows Turan is my father, for that matter."

"I think he knows," Alec replied. "It's not likely that you're good enough yet to shield your thoughts completely from a Shekaz. And I doubt very much that you could hide your Mevoshee heritage from him. My guess is that he already knows the truth—or some of it, at least. He may not know yet that Turan is your father—or he might have known before he came here. But Noelo cannot be your brother, Emily."

He then explained why, and Emily nodded. "I think I already knew that, although for a different reason. I'm sure that if he were my brother, I would have felt it—just as I felt it with my grandmother."

She could sense an uneasiness in him, and probed at that until he sighed and explained.

"There is something in Noelo that troubles me—something dark. But it may not be anything that would cause problems for you."

"I must see this through, Alec. I can't come this

close and not make this one last effort to know my father.''

She felt his understanding and kissed him softly—but she also continued to feel his uneasiness. Then she got up reluctantly.

"I must go now. He'll be expecting me."

He lay on the bed watching as she dressed, and she knew he was shielding his concern from her because he knew this was something she had to do.

"Will you come to me again tonight?" she asked hopefully, although she thought she already knew the answer.

"We cannot risk that again. Noelo may be even more on guard after you talk tonight." But privately he suspected that Emily would be unable to keep the secret if Noelo chose to probe. He might already know—and that was what troubled Alec most right now.

She bent to kiss him, started toward the door, and then paused. "If he is willing to take me to my father, will you follow us?"

"Yes—at a distance. But I cannot get too close to their land, and I cannot reach out to you while you are there."

Still she hesitated, and he felt her thoughts being torn between the desire to know her father and her fear of being cut off from him. Finally, with a choked, whispery "I love you," she was gone.

"You look . . . a bit tattered," Noel said as she hurried into the inn. He'd obviously been waiting in the lobby for her.

Tattered? An interesting choice of words, she thought: tattered and torn. It was exactly how she felt at the moment.

"It was just a very hectic day. I seemed to spend most of it being lost."

"Well then, perhaps an early dinner is in order. I spent much of my day being lost as well, though I prefer to think of it as being an adventure."

"Yes, an early dinner would be fine—just as soon as I shower and change."

Emily hurried to her room, wondering if she'd effectively shielded her thoughts of Alec from Noel. She hadn't expected to have to face him until later.

Until now Emily had reveled in her newfound powers without giving very much thought to their limitations. But at the moment she was far more aware of her lack of power as she felt caught between two Shekaz: a novice playing with experts.

She showered and changed into a pair of pale, loose-fitting linen slacks and a bright blue silk shirt, then braided her hair into a single long plait and tied it with a matching ribbon. All the while, she thought about the evening ahead. Even in the privacy of her room, she would not allow herself to think about Alec.

She found Noel awaiting her at the bar that ran along one wall of the dining room. He picked up his drink and ushered her to a table, and she noted the glances they received from the other customers. It was easy to see why they attracted such attention; they were a striking pair with their matching blond hair and blue eyes.

"You look refreshed—and very lovely," Noel

said as he seated her.

Emily smiled her thanks and thought for the first time about the possibility of a competition between the two men over her. Surely not. If Noel knew about Alec and her, wouldn't such a thing be unthinkable? But the nagging thought lingered all through dinner.

They talked easily enough. Noel, as she'd observed before, had a great deal of charm and was an excellent listener. She could only hope that he wasn't "listening" to more than her spoken words. And now that she knew he was a Shekaz, she wondered too if a large part of that charm might not be the powerful aura they seemed to possess.

Emily had met some of the other Shekaz during her stay in the valley, and while she found all of the Azonyee (with the exception of Menda, the Council Leader) to be thoroughly likable people, there was no doubt that the Shekaz stood out even among them. Virtually unlimited power conveys an aura all its own.

After dinner, Noel asked her if she thought she could endure a short trip. "There's a place I'd like you to see. It's not far."

Emily hesitated. She had wanted to remain in public places with him; that seemed to her to be the prudent course, especially given Alec's uneasiness about him. But she found herself agreeing. This man represented what could well be her only chance to reach her father.

He drove out of town, then turned onto a narrow dirt road built up through bordering marshlands. They passed one small house—and then nothing more.

"Where are we going?" she asked as they continued deeper into the wilderness.

Perhaps Noel caught the slight uneasiness in her voice, because he turned to her with a disarming smile. "I thought you shouldn't leave here without at least a brief trip into the bayous."

He turned onto yet another, even narrower dirt road that ended a few hundred yards later at a small, ramshackle house. She turned to him questioningly, but he was already getting out to greet an elderly man who had come out of the house. It was obvious that he knew the man, and the two began to converse rapidly in French. Emily was surprised to hear Noel talk in what sounded very much like the Cajun dialect of their host.

Then he switched to English as the man led them around to the back. After performing the introductions, he explained that he'd been here earlier and had arranged to borrow the man's pirogue to take her for a short trip into the bayou.

Emily stared doubtfully at the little boat tied up to an old dock, then peered out at the forbidding swamplands beyond, where webs of Spanish moss dripped from trees and clumps of long grass protruded through the dark waters. The whole scene looked like something from an old horror film. *The Creature from the Black Lagoon* came unpleasantly to mind.

Noel laughed. "Come along, Emily. I was out here earlier and René can testify to the fact that I can handle the boat. We won't go far."

"What lives in there?" she asked suspiciously, envisioning the hideous, lizardlike creature from the film.

"Nothing you need worry about." He grinned. "And there's a rifle in the boat just in case."

"If that's meant to reassure me, it doesn't," she said, nevertheless allowing him to hand her into the flat boat.

Noel started the small outboard motor, which effectively cut off further conversation as they skimmed over the water. Within moments, their host and his dock were gone from view.

In spite of her misgivings, Emily was fascinated. This was an utterly alien landscape, a watery wilderness that seemed simultaneously to be both dying and timeless. She could not shake the sense of being in a film, and still expected the creature to rear its ugly head at any moment.

Noel piloted the boat slowly and smoothly past clumps of cypress and half-submerged logs. The strange Spanish moss brushed against her head and shoulders, feeling like giant cobwebs. The sun was low in the west behind them, casting the swamp ahead into deep shadow, while the tops of the tallest trees still touched the sunlight.

Then Noel suddenly cut the engine. In the silence, Emily heard several small splashes and whirled about to see some small, dark shapes slithering into the water about fifty feet away.

"Those are nutrias," Noel explained.

"What was that orange I saw?"

"Believe it or not, their teeth. I got a close look at one earlier when I was out with René. They're amazingly tame, despite those teeth."

One of the creatures swam closer to the boat and Emily frowned at it. The bright orange teeth seemed more like curved tusks. "They look like overgrown mutant rats."

"Apparently that's what the fur-buying public thought, too, so they aren't trapped much anymore." He waved an arm about them.

"Isn't this incredible? I've never seen anything like it and I wanted to show it to you."

His enthusiasm was infectious, and Emily laughed. "I'm glad you brought me here. Thank you—even if this place is going to give me nightmares. I spent too much of my childhood watching horror films." She told him about the *Creature from the Black Lagoon* and he nodded.

"I thought of it too. It's a classic. But René assured me that he hasn't even seen an alligator out here in a long while."

His expression grew solemn. Emily felt a tiny shiver begin to grow in her, and it escalated rapidly with his next words.

"Actually, I had *two* purposes in mind when I brought you here. I also wanted a quiet place for us to talk—and we *must* talk, Emily."

She nodded, struggling against both excitement and fear.

"You have met the Azonyee—your mother's people," he said quietly.

"Yes."

"And you know who . . . what I am."

"Yes." She took a deep breath. "And I know that my father is Mevoshee."

"Then you know too that you are unique—that such a thing has never happened before?"

She nodded, then asked a question of her own. "Are we related, Noel?"

"Not closely—distant cousins. There aren't many of us, you know, so we're all related to some extent."

"My father—is he still alive?"

Emily couldn't hide the relief and pleasure that washed over her when Noel nodded. But she hurried on. "Does he want . . . is he willing to see me? I very much want to meet him."

"Yes, he wants to see you. That is why I was sent here—to bring you back to him."

"But why didn't he come himself?" she asked.

"Because it could have been dangerous. We couldn't know if you would be alone, or accompanied by one of the Azonyee. Your father was once a very powerful Shekaz, but his powers have waned with age. He's sixty-seven."

"Has he suffered because of . . . what he did?"

"No, it is all too far in the past now, although he might have if it had been known at the time. He told us only when Toby informed us about you. But what of your mother? She could not have hidden it as easily as Turan did."

"My mother is dead," Emily replied softly. It hadn't occurred to her that her father wouldn't know that. "She killed herself just after she returned to the valley."

Noel stared at her in shock, then turned to stare off into the gathering gloom. "That will be very hard on Turan. He never married, so I know he never forgot about her."

Emily was touched by his obvious concern for her father. "I won't tell him if you think I shouldn't—but I'm not sure I can keep it from him."

"You can't," Noel replied. "Have you been trained by the Azonyee?"

She nodded.

"I thought as much. When you returned to the

inn this afternoon, I thought you were shielding your thoughts from me."

They stared at each other, and Emily felt a tentative touch against her mind. She strengthened her shields and gave him an imploring look.

"Noel, please don't pursue this. I am in a difficult position—caught between the Azonyee and the Mevoshee. I must remain neutral."

"But *are* you neutral, Emily? I know that Alyeka is the one they sent after you, and several times since we've been here, I've thought I sensed his presence. We have fought twice, and that means there is a bond of sorts between us. When you returned to the inn earlier, I was certain I felt something of him. I know they would have sent someone to watch over you, and he would be the logical choice."

"Why?"

"Because he is their most powerful Shekaz— perhaps the most powerful ever. I should know." There was a brief trace of bitterness in his voice, but it was gone quickly. "This is a unique situation, and they would naturally choose their best —especially if they believed we might try to harm you."

"And will you try to harm me?"

"No. Your father gained a guarantee of your safety before I was sent here. You will come to no more harm among us than you did among the Azonyee."

"The Azonyee came close to deciding to kill me," she stated flatly, then immediately regretted her words. She had not shielded her memories quickly enough and could feel his surprise as she saw his eyes widen.

"Alyeka was willing to risk himself for you?"

"Noel, please. Keep Alec out of this." But she knew it was too late. She wanted desperately to probe his thoughts, but she didn't dare risk his anger, and besides, she knew he could hide them from her. Even in the midst of her pleasure over the prospect of seeing her father, Emily could not quell a certainty that something dark was hanging over her.

Less than twenty-four hours later, Noel and Emily were driving through the Scottish Highlands, en route to his home. Emily had left a note for Hank explaining that a "family emergency" had arisen and promising to get in touch with him as soon as possible. She made no attempt to contact Alec, but assumed he would know where she was going, and would follow as far as he dared.

Noel did not mention Alec again, but his earlier charm had disappeared. He was polite but distracted, and she was sure that he'd guessed the true nature of her relationship with Alec, thanks to her failure to hide her memories.

Still, she didn't feel threatened by him. These were not violent people, and whatever unpleasant thoughts he might be harboring, he wouldn't act upon them. Neither was she concerned about Alec's safety. Even Noel acknowledged that he was too powerful.

Her thoughts turned to her father, and she was surprised to discover within herself a residue of anger and bitterness. She so very much wanted to be happy; after all, she was about to reach the goal of a lifetime, and her father wanted to see her as well.

But she couldn't drive away that anger. He had a lot of explaining to do, despite Noel's words about his never having married because of her mother. The fact remained that he had abandoned her mother—and when she was pregnant, at that.

Noel turned off the main road onto a narrow gravel road that ran between steep, craggy hills. He broke his long silence and turned to her.

"This will be a difficult meeting for your father, Emily. He has held his feelings very closely over the years, and it will be difficult for him to set them loose now."

Emily said nothing, but she thought about her grandmother and knew it wasn't enough just to *meet* her father; she wanted that unquestioning love from her own flesh and blood.

"If none of this had happened, he would never have attempted to contact me, would he?" she asked.

"No, he probably wouldn't have, because he would have been afraid to draw attention to you. Had she lived, I think your mother would have done the same. Perhaps you do not yet fully understand us, Emily—how bound by our rules and our traditions we are."

He turned from the gravel road onto a dirt road barely wide enough for the Rolls Corniche. It appeared that the Mevoshee were as addicted to luxury as the Azonyee. They'd flown over on the Concorde, after a private jet from Baton Rouge, then followed that with another private flight to Scotland.

The dirt road ended at an abandoned farm, and Noel pulled the Rolls up to the barn, a stone and timber affair that was clearly old, but in good repair. As Emily watched, the huge barn door began to swing open. She'd assumed someone was inside until it had opened completely and Noel was driving inside, where he parked the Rolls alongside two others and several Land Rovers.

It wasn't until they had walked out of the barn that Emily realized it was Noel who was using his magic to open and now close the barn door.

"Does anyone live here?" she asked, looking toward the farmhouse.

"No, we own the farm. We bought it some years ago because of its convenience as a storage place for vehicles."

Carrying their luggage, they walked around behind the barn, where a sloping, rocky field ended in a narrow, tree-enclosed valley. Noel gestured. "This is our home. Give me your hands."

Emily did as told. It was difficult, with them both carrying their bags as well. But the blackness came—and went quickly, before she even had time to decide if she felt anything.

She assumed she was in Noel's home. The large living room was starkly modern, all brass and glass and soft leathers and suedes. At one end of the L-shaped space was a handsome grand piano. He saw her interest in it.

"My chief hobby," he said. "Do you play?"

"I did, but not in years." She went over to examine it and touched a few keys. She'd never heard better sound quality, although there was no brand name visible.

"It was built by a craftsman here—a cousin of yours, actually. His whole family makes instruments."

His mention of her family drew her away from the piano. How wonderful to think that she had an entire family here. She'd been afraid to hope for such a thing.

"Can I see my father now?" she asked eagerly.

"Yes. His house is close by, and he will know of your arrival."

Noel led her out of the house and along a footpath that bordered a small, swift stream, then turned away from the stream and went uphill through a short stretch of woods. They came out of the woods and began to descend into a narrow valley. Ahead of her, Emily saw a garden very much like Alec's, with waterfalls and exotic plants. But here there were sculptures as well— marble, from the look of them. They gleamed in the bright sunlight.

Emily was about to ask if the home that lay at the far end of the garden was Turan's, but her question was answered before it could be asked. A man came out of the house and walked toward them.

She was vaguely aware of Noel's turning away, but her gaze remained locked on the figure that approached her. He stopped about twenty feet away: a tall, still powerful looking man who wore his years amazingly well. His once golden hair had gone pure white, as white as the sculpture

278

beside which he'd paused.

Emily had stopped too, her heart pounding, but her body suddenly unwilling to take those final steps. Then he raised his arms in a clearly welcoming gesture and she moved toward him, her own hands outstretched to meet his.

They stood there silently for a long, long while, hands clasped as they stared at each other. Although she made no attempt to touch his mind, it happened. It was impossible to tell which feelings were his and which were hers. Pain and longing and joy and love.

"Father," she said aloud, her voice choked.

"My daughter," he replied in a deep, husky tone. "You are even lovelier than young Toby's memory of you."

Do you see my mother in me? she asked silently, then quickly drew in her thoughts—but not before she saw the pain in his eyes and felt it in her mind.

"I . . . I'm sorry. I didn't mean to . . ." she stammered, then stopped in embarrassment.

He squeezed her hands gently. "You cannot entirely shield your thoughts from me, Emily. Come. We will sit in the garden and eat while we talk."

He led her toward the house, through a garden she now saw was even more elaborate than Alec's and as big as Ketta's. She paused before a particularly beautiful free-form sculpture and reached out to touch it. It felt cool, like marble, but the texture was different in some places.

"It is marble—a type that exists only here. The texture is the result of careful rubbing."

"*You* created this?" she asked, knowing it to be

279

so even as she spoke.

"Yes. It is a good hobby."

"Azonyee Shekaz have such gardens as well," she said. "I have seen several of them, but this is more beautiful because of the sculptures."

Subconsciously she had been comparing it to Ketta's, and when she turned back to Turan, she saw his smile.

"Ahh, Ketta, my old opponent. So he still lives. We fought twice to a draw, you know."

She nodded. "He told me and showed me what you look like. He has great respect for you."

"And I for him." He gestured her to a table and chairs in a corner of the garden, where a large tray of fruits and cheeses and a loaf of bread awaited them.

They sat down and began to eat. He asked how she had known he was her father. Emily told him how her mother had remembered him, then found herself forced to explain still more. But by the time she had finished, she realized that he had asked as a way of asking about her mother. And no sooner had this realization struck her than she knew that he now understood the truth.

He sat quietly, his blue eyes fixed on some spot behind her. Then he shifted them back to her again. "I too considered taking my life. Perhaps I should have done so. At least she has been spared the pain I have known all these years. I will try to remember that."

In that moment, Emily knew she could never feel any bitterness toward this man—but she still needed to know what had happened.

Turan nodded slowly. "Yes, of course you must know. And it would be understandable that you should hate me for abandoning you. But hear me out first."

So, as the sun drenched his garden and its warmth brought the mingled scents of thousands of flowers, Turan told her the story.

They had met by accident. Both were in love with the paintings of Rembrandt, and the Metropolitan Museum of Art in New York was holding a major exhibition of the works of the Dutch master. Fate placed them both there at the same time.

"There are protocols for such chance meetings, as you may know," Turan said. "Both parties are to leave immediately, with no hesitation that could in any way be construed as a challenge.

"We should have known of each other's presence more quickly than we did, but I think we were both too involved with the paintings. Besides, the exhibit was very crowded and for us, the thoughts of the Tiyazh can seem like static—interfering with the normal awareness we have of each other."

In any event, they found themselves in the same room before each recognized the other's presence. And both hesitated instead of leaving as dictated by their protocol.

"I think I intended to leave, and I'm sure she did, too—but then it seemed that neither of us *could* leave. But we didn't speak at all. We just moved along with the crowd, keeping slightly apart but always aware of each other. And then we left together."

He closed his eyes and Emily saw the scene: the two of them, standing on the wide steps of the museum on a bright winter's day, perhaps ten or twelve feet apart, with other museumgoers passing between them, totally unaware of the drama taking place. It was an image Emily would always treasure.

"I think we both reached out at the same moment—with our minds, I mean. But we were horrified at what we were doing and quickly withdrew. Still, an agreement had been reached: we would meet again."

Their next meeting was three months later, at the Rijksmuseum in Amsterdam, home of Rembrandt's great masterpiece *Night Watch*. Both were still wary, but they began to talk.

"Anyone listening would have found us to be very correct, very formal—especially given the fact that this was the decade of the sixties. I suspect we sounded rather Victorian." He smiled.

And so it had begun. Emily had imagined a brief, passionate affair, but she was wrong. Over the next two years, they met often, but only to talk—at first aloud and then through their minds.

"Each time we met, I expected she would show the courage I lacked—the courage to end it."

He paused briefly and Emily felt the turbulence of his thoughts and even saw some of the images: the two of them on the terrace of a ski lodge with Alpine slopes in the background, a sailing expedition somewhere in tropical waters, what she thought was Central Park on a bright spring day.

"Electrical storms have a powerful effect upon us," he went on. "We were walking along the banks of the Seine when the storm came. Her hotel was closer, so we went there."

He paused once more and smiled at her. "And

that, my daughter, is the day you were conceived."

"But you both must have *wanted* that to happen," Emily said, frowning. "I know you can control . . ."

He interrupted her with a heavy sigh. "Yes, we did want it. It's difficult for me to explain that now. I think we both understood that it had to end for us, and we wanted desperately for something of us to continue to exist.

"We parted the next day—and I never saw her again. She had been planning to study art in New York, so she was sure she could conceal the pregnancy."

"That's what she did," Emily told him. "My grandmother told me that. No one suspected a thing, although Grandmother began to suspect it after her death."

"She intended to give you up for adoption, of course—to find a suitable Tiyazh family. But something went wrong. I can only guess that she found herself unable to take that step, then panicked and left you on the hospital doorstep to avoid being questioned by an adoption agency. I think she may have been irrational by then."

"But how did you find me?" Emily asked.

"Sheer luck. If she'd gone through with her plan to work with an adoption agency, I probably wouldn't have found you.

"Susurra wasn't the only one who was irrational at that time, Emily. I spent the months of her pregnancy in agony. Twice, I left the valley intending to go to her—and the third time, I did.

"At the time, I had decided that we would both

forsake our people, our heritage, and live in the Tiyazh world. I was determined to convince her we could do it, even though I knew it would never be permitted. But when I sought her out at the art school, I learned that she was gone. I found someone who told me that she'd had her baby, and then disappeared."

He stopped briefly and Emily felt his pain course through her as well.

"I knew she must have gone home, and of course I couldn't follow her there. I remember thinking then that she might have gone home to die, and I even considered going up there and flinging myself at that barrier to kill myself. As I said, I wasn't rational.

"But then I saw the article about you in the newspaper, together with a picture—and I knew. The article gave the names of the couple who had temporary custody of you and said that they intended to adopt you if the real mother didn't show up.

"So I simply bided my time, returning home for a while to try to regain my sanity, and then going back to New York to find a way to see you. I wanted to be sure that you had a good home. And you had. I never met your stepfather, but through your stepmother, I knew he was a good man."

"And you never tried to see me again?"

"No." He reached out to take her hand. "I wanted to, Emily, but it would have been a selfish thing to do."

"Noel said that no one here knew until Toby told them about me."

"That's true. I never told anyone—not even my

284

family, from whom it was difficult to keep such a secret."

"Has telling them now caused any problems?" she asked fearfully.

"If you mean trouble for me, no. It is too far in the past now. And it has allowed me to become closer to my family again. I've discovered that they all suspected something had happened to me—but none of them had ever guessed what it was.

"But as to you—you are a problem, Emily." When he saw her expression and felt her fear, he quickly shook his head and sent a soothing thought.

"No, no one will harm you here any more than the Azonyee did. But you present all of us with a problem. We live in our traditions, and your very existence changes all that."

Chapter Eleven

Emily spent the night in her father's house, sleeping in a bed set up for her on a small, screened sunporch that jutted out into his garden. She awoke in the morning to a soft breeze filled with lovely fragrances and an eagerness to face the day. Today she would meet the rest of her family.

She sat up in bed and saw her father's white head as he moved about his garden. They'd stayed up late, talking, mostly about her life. But she'd withheld from him the most important part of that life now: the man she yearned for even in the midst of all this happiness. She wondered if he might know. Probably not, or surely he would have questioned her.

She got out of bed and went to stand at the screen, still watching him. Had she brought happiness into his life? She wanted to think so; certainly he seemed as pleased about their meeting as she was. But hadn't she also brought back all the pain of that long-ago love?

He started back toward the house, then stopped when he saw her there. His smile gave her her answer even before she felt that warm, gentle touch against her mind—so different from Alec's and yet so like it, too.

Emily had expected a small family celebration and so was totally unprepared for the crowd that awaited them in the village park. Seeing her surprise, Turan explained that a "few friends" were present as well.

The similarities between the two enchanted valleys were so great that when Emily saw the crowd in the park, she half-expected to see familiar Azonyee faces. The architecture was the same, the land was quite similar, and the voices that carried to her as they approached spoke the same language. But it wasn't long before Emily felt the difference.

Through Alec, she had gained some understanding of the powerful psychic bonds within families—but here she felt it herself. She was welcomed not as a stranger who happened to be related, but as one of them. Their warmth and love and acceptance flowed through her. No Tiyazh family, however close, could duplicate this unique bond.

After a time, she began to feel quite overwhelmed by it all. Neither of her stepparents had come from a large family, and neither of them was particularly close to the relatives they had, so Emily had never known even an ordinary extended family, let alone the all-encompassing tie she found here.

She slipped off to the sidelines of the celebration and noted with gratitude that no one made a move to stop her. They understood, and that understanding in itself was overwhelming.

A short time later, as she sat beneath a tree watching some children playing the ball game she'd seen in the Azonyee valley, Turan came to join her.

"I . . . this is almost too much for me," she said with an apologetic smile. "I didn't understand what it would be like to have a real family."

"You will always have a family here, Emily—but I know that you cannot stay."

She gave him a surprised look and received in return a gentle smile.

"I think it is time we talk of Alyeka."

"So you knew all along—or did Noel tell you?" Noel was at the celebration, and Emily had just learned that her father had been Noel's mentor.

"He did not know, although he suspected. No, you could not keep such a thing from me, just as you cannot keep Alyeka from your thoughts. I am sorry that I can never know him, but I am happy for you both. I know he is a good man."

"But you haven't met him?"

"No, but I think he may well be the most powerful Shekaz either of our people has yet produced. Certainly he is the most powerful now alive. And that means he must be a very good man. Do you understand what it takes to make a Shekaz?"

"Yes, I think so. Or some of it at least."

"It has always been our belief that the earth

forces can be harnessed only by true goodness, by a mind free of the usual human faults. I'm not so sure that's always true, but when a Shekaz wields the power Alyeka has, I think it *is* true."

"He *is* good—kind and gentle and patient. He understood why I needed to try to contact you and made no attempt to stop me, even though I know he worried. And he accepts that I will never truly be one of you, that a part of me will always be Tiyazh."

Turan was silent for a while, then spoke in a musing tone. "I find myself wondering, Emily. Is there some hidden meaning to this union between a truly unique woman and a man who may be the most favored among us?"

"What do you mean?"

He shrugged. "I don't know what I mean. Perhaps I am merely a rambling old man."

His words brought back a similar remark from Ketta. She told him about Ketta's statements, about his questioning of the belief that they must live separately. Turan stared at her for a moment, then nodded solemnly.

"Yes, I too have thought about that—and for much longer than Ketta has. I began to question that when I left your mother and came back here. Like Ketta, I wondered if there might not be a place in this world where the forces would permit us both to live. If things had been different, we might have found such a place together."

"But you thought you could simply live in the Tiyazh world."

"I thought that only when I was irrational. None of us can be gone too long from our valleys. We draw our very lives from the forces here. It's always been our belief that we could not survive for long in the outer world."

"You mean that you would lose your powers?" Emily asked uneasily.

"Yes, but more than that. What you think of as being 'powers' or 'talents' are so much a part of our lives that we could not survive without them. It is difficult to explain, Emily. Think of yourself suddenly being thrust into a world where you could not speak or hear or move about. That is what it would be like for us without our powers. A living death."

He looked at her sadly. "I must tell you this, although I wish it could be otherwise. I think that at some point you will be unable to come here. The longer you live among the Azonyee, the greater will be their influence over you. And the day may well come when that influence will be too great for you to be able to enter this valley."

"So I will lose my family again," she said in a choked voice.

"Perhaps I am wrong. There is no way to know."

Emily lingered in the valley for another week, missing Alec and yet filled with the pure joy of having discovered a family. Cousins, she decided, were the greatest pleasure of all. As the only child of two adoptive parents who themselves had been only children, Emily had never known what it could be like to have others of one's own age who were bound by blood.

Her favorites were a brother and sister, Mesav and Kalera. Mesav was two years younger than Emily, but was already regarded as a master craftsman. It was he who had built the piano she'd admired in Noel's home. Although he was capable of great intensity where his work was concerned, he was otherwise an easygoing and very funny man who traveled as often as possible to the outer world and had a special fondness for America—and American slang in particular.

Kalera, his sister, was Emily's age and a Shekaz. Anyone seeing the two together could have been forgiven for thinking them sisters. Kalera was an inch or so taller than Emily, but possessed her slim, graceful figure. Her hair was a brighter shade of gold and her eyes were a striking blue-gray. She had that aura of inner strength and calm that all Shekaz had, but she was also bright and lively and interested in everything.

She was particularly fascinated by Emily's relationship with Alec, of whom she'd heard, of course. And so it was to her that Emily confessed all her doubts and fears, not because she believed her cousin could resolve them, but simply because she needed to talk about them.

Kalera had a secret passion for romance novels and found this improbable union to be the best story she'd yet heard. "It's so incredibly romantic, Emily," she enthused. "Not like it is for us, you know. We don't have romance. We have friendships that eventually become physical unions." She sighed. "It's rather boring, in a way."

One evening Kalera made a confession of her own. They were seated in Turan's screened porch, enjoying the cool evening breeze.

"I met an Azonyee once—actually talked with him," she said, pausing as Emily stared at her.

"Oh, it was only once—but something was there, something between us. He was a Shekaz, too. I won't tell you his name because Alyeka might find out."

She leaned forward in her chair and stared hard at Emily. "And I can't believe that I'm the only one who has done that, either. No one will talk about it, of course, because if it became known, the Council would ban all travel."

"Do you think, then, that this might have always happened?" Emily asked, fascinated by this revelation.

"I doubt it. And when it has, it's probably been only among Shekaz. We spend more time outside and we're better able to shield our thoughts— even from our families. It's quite amazing, really, that your mother was able to hide her knowledge of Turan from her family. Few other than Shekaz could do that.

"I think we're changing. We younger ones do talk about that sometimes. We understand and honor our traditions and our heritage—but only up to a point. The older ones, and particularly the nastranos, would have us believe that mere questioning of our lives could result in the earth forces abandoning us—but that simply isn't true. If it were, I couldn't be a Shekaz.

"And look at Turan. No one ever broke the rules as he did, and yet he continued to be our most powerful Shekaz. You should have seen the look on Teera's face when he told us what he'd done." Teera was an aunt who was a nastrano. "She had the look of a woman who has just seen all her beliefs shattered."

"Well, that certainly explains why Teera has

been less friendly toward me than all my other relatives here," Emily said.

After Kalera had gone and Turan returned, Emily told him what Kalera had said about his being living proof that their beliefs were wrong. She expected him to agree, but he merely shrugged.

"There is no way to know, Emily. When you get older, you learn to live with unanswered questions. No one really understands the earth forces —not even Shekaz and nastranos. We use them, or are used by them, but we don't understand them."

But Emily could not live with unanswered questions. She recalled that Mabel Smithers, the retired schoolteacher in New York, had said much the same thing: that one got used to living with unanswered questions. Perhaps so, but it would take many more years than she had now to convince her of that.

She was eager to discuss all this with Alec, and that eagerness only stirred an already smoldering desire to be with him again. Still, she hated to leave this place—and especially her father. She knew that she was bringing as much joy into his life as he was to hers.

Perhaps he was right when he said that the day would come when she could not enter the valley of the Mevoshee—but with the optimism typical of youth, Emily was sure that day must be far away. After all, she felt as comfortable here as she did with the Azonyee. And her father had admitted that none of them truly understood the forces that shaped their lives.

* * *

If Emily's need for Alec was rapidly reaching the point where she could no longer be apart from him, Alec's need for her had long since passed that point. And added to that was the pain of separation from his home.

Alec had now been away from the valley for nearly two weeks—perhaps a record for Shekaz, who, more than any others, had to remain close to the forces that granted them their extraordinary powers. It was true that he'd spent much longer periods away from the valley during college, but he hadn't then been a fully trained Shekaz. The training began at age twelve, but was interrupted when they went outside to be educated. By the age of twenty-five, their training was complete and they went forth into their first battles. After that, the need to be nourished by the forces within the valley kept them close—even those like Alec who enjoyed travel in the outer world.

During the time when Emily was delighting in her newfound family, Alec was traveling about the Highlands, staying just barely outside the perimeter of the Mevoshee home.

Although events were about to occur that would make him forget about it for a long time, Alec too was wondering about the forces that determined their lives: the forces that were now keeping him away from Emily.

Perhaps Emily had set such thoughts in motion even before this, as she plied him with questions that no Azonyee would ever ask. What were these forces? Did he think of them as gods? Were they capable of free will—or were they simply *there*? What did he think would happen if the Shekaz no longer fought each other?

These thoughts circled in his mind even as he himself circled ever closer to the Mevoshee land —close enough at times to feel that unmistakable repulsion, like a magnet with the wrong poles butting against each other.

Then a morning came when he awoke to a certainty that he would see her that day. He was desperate enough to believe it, although he knew that precognition was not among the gifts his people possessed.

He showered and dressed in rugged hiking clothes, then left the small inn and drove to the edge of the Mevoshee land nearest a main road. He left his rented Bentley in the car park of a town and began to hike through the hills, struggling against the force that tried to repel him, ignoring the certainty of his waning powers and concentrating only on his need for Emily—as though that need alone could bring her back to him this day.

Alec was not totally unaware of the danger of his actions, but for the first time in his life, he chose to ignore those warnings.

Turan nodded as Emily turned to him. They were seated in his garden in the gentleness of a gathering twilight.

"Yes, child, I know it is time for you to go. I have felt that need building in you."

"I'm afraid of that need," she confessed.

"Perhaps you will always be a bit afraid of it, Emily, since you were not raised among us. But it's natural and you shouldn't fight it."

So the next morning Emily, Turan, and Noel

walked along the path that led to the boundary. They could easily have 'ported themselves, but Emily thought that 'porting made too abrupt a departure. She wanted to savor these last moments here.

They walked along mostly in silence as Emily and her father felt each other's thoughts, while Noel remained discreetly apart from them in his own thoughts. Emily was glad that Turan could understand her ambivalence at this moment. Any attempt to put it into words would surely have failed. She wanted to stay close to him, yet wanted desperately to return to Alec.

When they reached the boundary, Turan gathered her into his arms, and father and daughter shared some last loving thoughts. Then she reluctantly walked over to Noel, who would 'port her through the barrier and see her on her way.

Noel's arms were already encircling her lightly when she turned for one last look at her father. A sudden frown creased his face, but Emily's question was swallowed up in the blackness as they left the valley.

Alec felt her presence as a rush of warmth through his body and mind. He walked faster, eager to feel her conscious presence in his mind and not just an awareness of her nearness. He was very close to the perimeter now, but his only thought was of Emily.

Emily was disoriented this time, and so clung to Noel for a moment. Had she imagined that frown on her father's face? Surely she had. Perhaps he'd just been squinting into the sunlight. The dizziness subsided quickly and she backed out of Noel's arms. They walked toward the barn where the cars were kept.

"I'll drive you into the village," he said. "You'll be able to get a train there."

"Thank you," she murmured distractedly, still worried about that look on her father's face.

Noel was silent as he backed the car out of the barn and started out. Emily had seen little of him since he'd brought her to the valley, and now felt rather guilty about that. He had been very kind to her. She made several attempts at conversation, but he seemed preoccupied, so she gave up and lapsed into her own thoughts.

Then, as they were driving along the gravel road that led to the highway, Noel suddenly made a sound and quickly pulled off the road. Emily thought he sounded pleased about something and looked at him questioningly.

"It won't be necessary for me to drive you to the village. Alyeka is here."

"He is?" Emily asked excitedly—and immediately reached out to find him.

Alec stopped when he felt that gentle touch of her mind against his. But in the next instant he felt a powerful jolt: Noelo! And even as he shielded his mind, Alec knew what was to happen.

Noel got out of the car and started up a hillside. Emily hurried to follow him. "Noel, what are you doing? If Alec is here . . ."

The rest of it never came out as Noel paused briefly to look back at her. The force of his anger made her stagger backwards until she lost her footing and fell onto the road.

He intended to fight Alec—not just fight him, but *kill* him—here where he had the advantage!

"No!" she screamed, even as she tried to make contact with Alec. She knew he was here; she'd felt him for just a moment. But there was nothing now.

She picked herself up and started up the hillside after Noel. Above her, the heavens were growing very dark, and even as she struggled up the steep bank the first crash of thunder sounded.

It seemed forever before she had gained the summit. But then she saw Alec, on the far side of the broad hilltop. "Alec," she screamed into the howling wind, "Noel . . ."

But before she could warn him, something unseen pushed at her, sending her tumbling partway down the hillside again. She lay there stunned and bruised, then gathered her strength and started back up again. But the moment she tried to move forward, she came up against an invisible wall—just like that day when he'd prevented her from running away from him at the edge of the valley.

The moment Alec saw Emily appear over the edge of the hillside, he pushed her away, then erected a barrier to keep her away—and keep her safe. Then he turned to face his enemy—for that was what Noelo had become. No longer was he simply an opponent.

Alec reached deep into the earth to find his power. It came to him at last, but he could feel its weakness here on the edge of the Mevoshee land.

He was still gathering it carefully when Noelo struck his first mind-blow.

Emily limped back and forth along the hillside, seeking the end of the invisible wall. Suddenly it seemed to collapse and she fell forward, then began to scramble up the hillside again.

She reached the top and peered through the gathering darkness and the sheets of wind-driven rain that were sweeping across the plateau. She could see both men now. They stood about fifty feet apart, bracing themselves in wide-legged stances with their fists clenched at their sides. Overhead, lightning flashed and thunder rumbled.

It seemed to Emily that the very air between them shuddered. How could they fight in the midst of a storm? And yet they obviously were fighting. She saw Noel take a few unsteady steps backward, and in the flash of lightning that followed, she could see the surprise on his face. Did that mean that even here Alec could beat him?

But then Alec staggered and raised an arm to ward off an invisible blow. Even as he struggled to regain his feet, she could tell that Noel had struck again.

I must stop this, she thought. Alec cannot win. But what could she do in this battle of titans?

She started toward the middle of the hilltop, intending to put herself between the combatants. But Alec turned toward her, and she was flung back again. In that moment when he was distracted, Noel struck out at him and he staggered to his knees.

"No!" she shouted, now concentrating on Noel. A rage built within her, surging like a wildfire. "No!" she screamed again.

Suddenly she saw her father appear at the edge of the hillside beyond Noel. It was the last thing she saw before she crumpled to the wet ground.

Emily awoke shivering. Rain stung her face as she lay there fighting her way back to consciousness. The darkness began to drain away from her mind, leaving in its wake bits and pieces of memory that finally coalesced into sudden, terrifying awareness.

She pulled herself into a sitting position, gritting her teeth against the pains that wracked her entire body. The rain was heavy, obscuring her vision, but the thunder and lightning had moved on. All she could hear was a low, distant rumble.

She saw three bodies scattered along the hilltop in a rough triangle. Noel was closest and she moved stiffly toward him, recalling that blinding rage she'd projected at him. He lay still and she stood there over him, horrified at the thought that she might have killed him—until her still dazed brain reminded her of *his* intentions.

Then she ran to her father, who was next closest. It took only a few fumbling moments for her to see that he was alive, and then she was off again, lurching in an ungainly fashion across to the final body, willing it to rise.

He was so still. She stopped several feet away, reaching out with her mind when she was afraid to move closer. Nothing. She was reaching into emptiness. With a cry of protest, she sank to her knees and stared at him. Then she rubbed her eyes and stared again. Yes! She could see it now—that slow rise and fall of his chest beneath the shirt that was plastered to his body.

She crawled the remaining distance to him on her hands and knees, all the while making strange mewling sounds in her throat. He wasn't dead; he was just unconscious. That's why she couldn't reach out to him.

Still, she reached for his hand fearfully, gripping it tightly only when she felt the warmth of living flesh. She brought it to her mouth, then bent over him and brushed his lips with hers. His breath fanned softly against her face as she lingered there, staring at him as though she could will him back to consciousness.

Finally she sat up again and looked back over at her father. She had to get him home, and she had to get help for Alec. But how could she do either when she wasn't sure that she could even pull herself to her feet? She ached all over and when she tried to get up, her vision blurred at the edges.

She was trying to summon up the energy to go to her father again—and to check on Noel—when she blinked in disbelief. Figures suddenly materialized between them: four, no, six of them. She rubbed her eyes, certain it must be a hallucination. But then one of them was running toward her, calling her name, while the others separated to go to Noel and her father.

"Mesav!" she breathed in relief. "Oh, thank God you're here! They . . . Noel tried to kill Alec. Father . . ."

Mesav knelt down beside her. "Just let me see it, Emily. It will be faster that way."

She nodded and opened her mind to him. After a moment, his gaze moved from her face to Alec. "Alyeka lives." He paused, then nodded. "Turan also lives. But Noelo is dead." He had gotten the information from those who surrounded the other two men.

Emily saw then, as the day began to brighten, that one of the figures beside her father was a nastrano whom she'd met. Mesav apparently heard her desperate hope because he shook his head even before she could ask the question.

"Our nastranos cannot help Alyeka. We must get him away from here. He is too close to our land. I do not understand why he would have ventured so near."

But Emily did. She sat there holding his lifeless hand as the tears ran down her already wet face. He had come here for her.

Mesav left her there and went to confer with the others. She looked up and saw him walking back with another man. The rest of the group had gathered around her father or around Noel's body. Both men were lifted from the ground—and they all vanished.

"We will carry Alyeka to the car," Mesav said. "We cannot 'port him there because it would be dangerous to use our powers near him. Or so we think." He sounded very confused.

He helped Emily to her feet, and when he had assured himself that she could walk, he motioned to the other man and they lifted Alec between them. The group then struggled down the mud-slicked hillside to Noel's car and deposited Alec in the rear seat.

Mesav turned to Emily and started to ask if she

could drive, but when he saw her sway against the side of the car, he picked her up and carried her around to the passenger seat, then got into the driver's seat himself. There was a brief conversation between Mesav and the other man, who then turned away—and vanished. Emily reached around into the back to take Alec's hand once more and fell away into darkness.

She awoke to Mesav's soft voice calling her name. But before she responded, she reached again for Alec's hand. It felt warm, but still lifeless.

"Where are we?" she asked, peering out at the unfamiliar countryside.

"Not far from Aberdeen," Mesav replied. "Emily, you must summon help for Alec. Even though I'm not a Shekaz, I think it is bad for me to be near him, and you cannot get him home on your own."

"I . . . I've never done that," she said, knowing that he meant she must try to contact one of the powerful telepaths. "But I do know a phone number."

"The telepath would be better. Try to make contact. Keep it simple. Your name. Alyeka. Aberdeen. That will tell them all they need to know."

She closed her eyes and concentrated, repeating the words over and over with increasing desperation. Then, just as she was about to give up and ask Mesav to stop so she could call, there came a very faint, soothing touch against her mind.

What neither Emily nor Mesav could have known was that her "call" was unnecessary, except perhaps to pinpoint the location. All over the world—from a vacationing Azonyee couple in Nepal to a Mevoshee on a photographic safari in the Serengeti to two Shekaz about to battle in Canada's North Woods—members of the magic tribes knew that some cataclysmic event had occurred near the Mevoshee lands. And in the two valleys it felt like a silent earthquake that left objects untouched but tilted minds in a crazy fashion for several minutes. Nastranos in particular became dizzy and incoherent, an effect that lasted for some time after the others had regained their mental equilibrium.

Nothing remotely like it had ever happened before. But even as Emily reached out to a telepath in London, a young Shekaz who happened to be visiting Edinburgh was already aboard a hastily chartered flight to Aberdeen.

Mesav drove to the airport, saying that this would be the logical meeting place. By now uncertain that her message had in fact been received, Emily wanted to go call the answering service. But Mesav stopped her, saying that they couldn't just leave an unconscious man unattended in a car, and he thought it would be even worse for Alec if he was left alone with him. Her presence might be mitigating the effects of a Mevoshee presence.

Then, seeing that she was clearly worried that her message might not have been received, he offered to make the call for her. She gave him the number and he left the car.

Emily sat there holding Alec's hand and praying that no one would get too nosy. Mesav had parked the car in a secluded spot, but she still imagined a crowd gathering, the police arriving . . .

She kept shifting her gaze from Alec to the terminal where Mesav had disappeared, waiting anxiously. How long would they have to wait? Would Mesav be able to tell her? If only Alec would stir, show some sign of life. And what about her father? How could she have forgotten about him? He was an old man, no matter how healthy he'd seemed.

With all this running through her brain, it was no wonder that she failed to see the young woman approaching until she was nearly beside the car.

Emily stared at her as she lowered her head and peered into the back seat briefly, then opened the door.

"He's fine—just resting," Emily said with false brightness. Her eyes met those of the young woman, and she felt that flicker of recognition. But she didn't quite trust it; she'd never seen this woman before.

"How could you have . . . ?"

Her question trailed off as the woman suddenly straightened up and turned to look behind her. Mesav was returning, his normally pleasant features gathered into a frown. The woman turned back to Emily.

"My name is Lilleet. We felt something. I was closest so I was sent here."

Mesav had stopped a few feet away and was watching her warily.

"Mesav drove us here," Emily said to defuse the tension. "He is my cousin. We had to get Alec away from the Mevoshee land."

"Do you have a plane?" Mesav asked, addressing the woman for the first time.

She nodded and pointed to a small hangar some distance away.

"Then I will drive over there and help you get him aboard."

Even in the midst of her concern for Alec, Emily could not help noticing the tense awkwardness between the two as they got Alec onto the waiting plane. The pilot looked dubious at his lifeless body, but at a glance from Lilleet, he climbed into the cockpit and waited silently.

Emily stretched up to kiss Mesav on the cheek before climbing into the plane herself. "Thank you, Mesav. And I know Alec would thank you, too. But I must know about my father."

"I am sure he will be fine, Emily. But I will give you the number and you can leave a message for me, telling me where and when you can meet me."

Then he exchanged one last glance with Lilleet and walked back to the car.

The next hours were a jumble of private flights. At some point—Heathrow, she thought—they were joined by two other Azonyees, young men who took charge of moving Alec from one plane to another. Lilleet had demanded to know all the details the moment they took off, and Emily assumed that she had passed these on to the two men at Heathrow as they stood in a silent group. She could have eavesdropped, but she was too tired.

There was a short delay while one of the men went to another man who'd remained outside the plane. Beside him stood what Emily assumed was a British customs agent. The man simply stood there unmoving, a clipboard held in one hand. Then the man outside the plane led him off. Clearly, Azonyee magic had circumvented official curiosity.

The other two joined them in the sleek little jet, and Emily drifted off into exhausted sleep listening to their quiet murmurings in the Azonyee tongue. Alec was strapped into the seat beside her, and she still clung to his hand as the jet circled in a wide arc, then flew westward into the late afternoon sun.

Chapter Twelve

Emily walked into the small restaurant at the Plattsburgh Airport, glad to find it as empty as she'd expected. She saw Mesav at a small table in a corner. Rather to her surprise, he got up and kissed her lightly on the cheek. Such displays weren't common among his people, who showed affection in more unobtrusive ways.

As soon as they had seated themselves, he studied her carefully. "You do not look well, Emily. Is it Alyeka?"

Emily nodded. "Yes, I . . ." She stopped, then tried on a smile. "I don't want to talk about him just yet. Tell me about my father."

"Turan is well. He has recovered completely— enough so that he wanted to come here himself. But the nastranos convinced him he should not leave the valley for some time yet. He hopes you will come to see him soon, although he understands that you cannot come now."

This time, Emily's smile was genuine. "I'm so happy to hear that. I've been so worried, especially after seeing . . ."

She broke off abruptly as the waitress came to take their orders. Then, before Mesav could ask any questions, she asked what Turan remembered of that day on the hilltop.

"He recalls no more than you did," Mesav replied. "He saw immediately that Noelo intended to kill Alyeka and tried to stop him. No one really knows who was responsible for Noelo's death. It could have been Turan or you or even Alyeka himself. But there is no doubt that Noelo intended Alyeka's death."

Mesav sighed heavily. "The subject of Noelo has been debated so many times among us, Emily. How could a Shekaz do such a thing? Turan blames himself, although no one else does. He was Noelo's mentor, you know, and he thinks he should have seen that darkness in him.

"But there were always doubts about Noelo, according to what I've heard—and some of them were raised by Turan during his training.

"The general consensus is that he suffered from what the Greeks called hubris: excessive pride. No one had ever beaten him except for Alyeka, and when he saw the opportunity to get rid of Alyeka, he seized it, believing, no doubt, that if Alyeka were gone, *he* would be the greatest."

"But how could he have hoped to get away with such a thing?"

"We can never know what was in his mind, but

we think he intended to cast the blame onto you—to say that Alyeka's union with you had made him insane with jealousy in the manner of a Tiyazh. He could have said that Alyeka initiated the attack because he found the two of you together."

"But that would never have worked. I would have told the truth."

"I think it was his intention to kill you as well, Emily," Mesav said sadly. "But it is all theory, of course. That is all we have."

They paused as the waitress brought their lunches, and as soon as she had gone, Mesav fixed her with a determined look.

"Now we must talk of Alyeka. We wish to know how he is, Emily. We all feel that we bear a great responsibility for him."

"It's . . . difficult to speak of him, Mesav," she said slowly. "He is well physically, but his mind . . ." She paused again, then went on in a choked voice.

"He exists; he does not truly live. I can think of no other way to put it. Sometimes he knows who I am; other times he doesn't. He's always kind to me. There's no violence in him. But there is no life, either.

"What I think I miss most is feeling that wonderful sense of inner peace in him. I could always feel that, even when our minds weren't touching. I felt it the first time I saw him, although I thought it was arrogance then."

Mesav nodded. "All Shekaz project that, but given Alyeka's greatness, you would have felt it even more in him."

"At first they wouldn't let me near him. They

said that my Mevoshee blood could harm him more. But then Ledee, the chief nastrano, said there was nothing more they could do for him and it would do no harm for me to be near him.

"I foolishly believed that *I* could heal him when they'd failed. I thought our love would be enough. But I was wrong." She spoke the final words very softly, as though loath to say them at all.

"Nearly a month has passed and there is no change. Every time he recognizes me and seems pleased to see me, my hopes soar. But it never lasts. This is the first time I've been away from him."

"And what are the nastranos saying now?"

"Very little. No one ever says anything definite. Perhaps they don't know—but I think they do. I think they know he will never change. I can see it in their eyes even though they shield their thoughts from me."

Mesav nodded sadly. "Such things have happened from time to time after battles. I have heard about it."

Emily felt compelled to go on. She hadn't really spoken of him to anyone other than the nastranos and his family and Ketta. It felt good to talk to an outsider—and a cousin.

"Most of the time, he speaks in his own language. I have had to learn it as best I can, but I've never really been good with languages. And he talks often of Janna, his dead mate.

"I try not to feel hurt when he talks about her—but I am. The nastranos tell me that it's normal for him to regress, to go back to a happier past. They say that by doing so, he is clinging to . . . to what sanity is left to him."

Mesav reached out to cover her hand. "Emily, acceptance of such a thing would be hard even for us—and acceptance is one of the foundations of our beliefs. Let yourself be angry. That anger needs to come out. Then, perhaps, you will come to accept."

"There are times when I wish that I'd left the valley as soon as we got him back here," she said. "At least then I could have remembered him as the man he was."

"That is Tiyazh self-deception—and it would not have worked for you," Mesav stated.

"Do *you* think he could come out of this, Mesav?" she asked suddenly.

"I do not know. No one does. From what I have heard of such cases, I would have to say no. But this was different—in many ways.

"First of all, this was not an ordained battle, and that has never happened before. Secondly, *you* were involved—not only his mate, but also of unique blood. And thirdly, Turan was there as well, and used his powers to stop Noelo. That too could have affected Alyeka, for better or for worse.

"Three unique circumstances, Emily. And only one of them would make it impossible to predict the outcome for Alyeka."

"There was something else," Emily said, "and no one understands that, either."

"Ah yes, the thunderstorm. I'd forgotten about that. We do not understand that, either. No one should have been able to call on the earth forces at that moment."

"Much of that day is hazy for me, Mesav, but I do remember that it was a beautiful day, and I *don't* remember any storm clouds gathering when Noel and I 'ported through the barrier.''

Mesav looked surprised. "Then it is possible that the storm was not an ordinary one—that it was part of the forces present there. You know that the battle was felt by us all over the world. A friend of mine was in Africa, and he even felt it there. That's another thing that has never happened before.''

"Yes, they told me that. Ledee said she had never felt such a sudden draining away, then a surge, within the forces.''

"That's what our nastranos felt, too. Emily, perhaps it would be good for you to leave the valley for a while, for your own sake. Come to visit us. Your father would be happy to see you and so would the others, since it would show them that you bear us no ill will.''

"I've been thinking about that," she said slowly. "I just don't know how much more I can withstand. It hurts so much to see him this way.''

"It would not be disloyal of you to leave him for a time.''

"Leesa, Alec's sister, and Ketta, his mentor, have said the same thing. And the nastranos see no harm in my leaving for a while.''

"Then I will tell Turan to expect you.''

By the time they left the restaurant, Emily had agreed to visit the Mevoshee in a week's time. After Mesav boarded his flight, she went to call her mother. It took every ounce of will to sound happy and carefree, and by the time she hung up, she felt so drained that she could barely make it to the car.

When she walked into the garden a few hours

later, she found Alec propped up against cushions. He spent much of his time here, although she didn't think he really saw the beauty he had created.

She walked slowly through the new part of the garden that she had made. Everyone had encouraged her in this, and Ketta had come often to make suggestions and to help her. Alec sometimes came to watch, and a few times she thought he'd seemed interested. But then his gaze would turn inward again, and she would know he was gone.

"Alyeka," she said softly as she approached him. She used his Azonyee name now, since he himself spoke only in that language. He looked up immediately, and she felt yet another foolish surge of hope.

"Emily," he said, and for a moment the ghost of a smile seemed to move across his mouth. She sank down beside him.

"Did you miss me?" she asked with foolish eagerness. "I was only gone for a few hours."

"Emily," he said again, his voice low. It almost sounded as though he were trying to learn her name.

She leaned over and kissed his cheek. He didn't resist, but there was no response. It was like kissing a warm, beautiful statue.

She stared at him and saw now, for the first time, that a subtle change had come over his features. They were softer, more boyish, as though his body had somehow regressed along with his mind.

He had turned to stare out into the garden again, and when she spoke his name this time,

314

she got no response. She rose, and saw Ledee and Leesa in the doorway. He was never left alone, although no one believed he would harm himself. He tended to his own needs, though he sometimes needed to be reminded to eat.

Strangely, the one thing he did without fail was to rise each morning and go through his exercise routine. Ketta had told Emily that the habit was probably so deeply ingrained that it required no thought. Those moments when she watched him were the most painful of all, because he seemed to be his old self.

She walked into the house to join the two women. They inquired about her father and she told them he'd fully recovered, then passed on to them the Mevoshees' concern about Alec.

"I told Mesav that I would come next week to visit them. He thinks it would be a good idea—to show that there is no anger on our part about Alec."

The two women exchanged what were clearly relieved looks, and Emily frowned at them questioningly.

"Emily, we believe it would be best for you to leave the valley for a time."

"Why? And for how long?" Emily panicked, fearing they would say "forever."

It was Ledee who answered. "While you were gone, something happened that may have been caused by your absence. Alyeka became . . . what is the word, Leesa?"

"Agitated, I believe."

"Yes, that is it. He roamed through the garden, especially the part you created, and he kept repeating your name over and over. In fact, we knew you must be back in the valley because he suddenly became quiet again just before you appeared.

"I looked into his mind, Emily, and I felt something. Very vague, but more than I've felt before. I've spoken with the others and we believe that this agitation was a good sign—the sign of one who is beginning to struggle within himself."

"And you think that if I'm not here, he might continue that struggle?" Emily asked in confusion—a confusion that held a measure of hope.

"It may be that he is aware of your presence even when he doesn't seem to be, and perhaps he is too much comforted by it to fight his way back." Ledee shrugged. "It is only a theory, of course, but I believe it is worth pursuing."

"But what if my absence simply makes him more agitated?" Emily asked fearfully. She'd been told that he wasn't suffering, but surely such a thing must indicate pain.

"We can soothe him. He won't suffer. That is part of bringing someone back. Just so much struggle within the mind is permitted, and then we intervene."

Emily had her back to the doorway, but she turned when she saw both women look in that direction. Alec was standing uncertainly in the doorway.

"Emily."

She hurried to him. For a moment she thought his hand moved, as though to reach out to her. But perhaps it was only her imagination. She reached for his hand and led him back out to the garden.

"Alec, I am going away. I love you and I want to stay with you, but I am leaving. You must want me back, Alec—and then I will come."

She stared into his eyes as she said this. She wanted desperately to reach into his mind, but she'd been forbidden to do that. In his precarious mental state, only the nastranos could risk it.

He said her name again, then fell silent. She searched his face for some hint that he'd understood her, but found none. She decided she would have Leesa help her get the words right in their language and she would say them to him again. Then she would leave.

Leaving Alec was the most difficult thing Emily had ever done, the assurances of the others notwithstanding. No sooner had she 'ported herself out of the valley than she had an overwhelming urge to return. She carried with her all the way back to Connecticut a heart-rending image of him wandering about in his garden, saying her name over and over in that strange, flat voice.

Then, despite her trust and affection for Ledee, Leesa, Ketta, and the others, Emily began to suspect that they would never allow her to return, that they had been harboring a secret hatred for her because they blamed her for what had happened to Alec.

Worst of all, she blamed herself. It was because of her that he had taken such a risk in the first place. He would never have ventured so close to the Mevoshee land if she hadn't been there. She should have insisted that he return to his home, instead of asking him to remain close by. Why had she done such a thing—she who had always fended for herself?

She should have understood his confusion over feelings he'd never had before; instead, she'd been absurdly flattered. She'd convinced herself that he was invincible, nearly godlike. It was as though she'd never quite rid herself of that initial impression of him. Why hadn't she seen him for what he was? A man with truly extraordinary gifts, but still only a man.

Emily went home—or rather, returned to a place that had once been home. Now it felt only like a familiar place, better than a hotel only because it provided more comforts and she knew where everything was.

Her neighbor Peggy was delighted to see her and immediately asked about Alec, commenting that surely Emily wasn't going to let him get away. Chaucer couldn't quite decide whether to be happy about her return or angry over his lengthy abandonment. He vacillated between rubbing against her and moving out of her reach when she tried to pet him. She solved that problem by going out and buying him fresh scallops, his favorite food.

She made calls, picking up the scattered pieces of her earlier life. The friends she could reach were delighted to hear from her, but when she made promises to get together, she knew they were false. She had moved beyond them, into a world they could never understand.

She called Hank and apologized for her premature departure. Remembering her excuse that there'd been a "family emergency" only at the last possible moment, she was forced to manufacture a story about her mother's sudden illness.

Hank reported that Toby showed great promise as a researcher, often picking up on things the others had overlooked. Emily actually smiled at that—and didn't doubt it for one minute.

Then she made the most difficult call of all—to her parents. They asked her to join them for a weekend at their summer home on Fire Island, and included Alec in the invitation. Emily told them she would come, but that Alec had gone off to Europe. It promised to be a very difficult weekend, since they obviously considered Alec to be prime son-in-law material.

She also had a decision to make, one she hadn't even considered until she drove past the college on her way to her house. School was due to start in a month and she was scheduled to teach four courses. Furthermore, the upcoming academic year was very important to her; tenure was in the offing. The department chair was solidly in her camp, but she knew that several others on the committee felt that her prime field of interest was little more than fluff to please students.

Finally she went to see the department chair and requested a year off, using her mother's "illness" as her excuse. Her request was granted, of course, but by the time Emily left the woman's house, she knew she might well have ended any hopes of a tenured position.

She envisioned herself as a pathetic figure, going around cutting every tie she'd previously cherished—and for what? To spend the rest of her life with a man who didn't even know she was there most of the time, in a place where she could never truly fit in?

Sometimes an ugly resentment would come

over her. Why had he taken such a risk? How could he do this to her, after dragging her into a life from which she could now never truly escape?

But in her dreams, the Alec she had known was always there, his dark eyes alight with love, his thoughts perfectly attuned to hers, his love-making so perfect, so beautiful.

She went with her parents to Fire Island, where she was vague about her relationship with Alec and where she found herself watching her mother nervously, lest her lie actually become the truth. And she felt herself slipping further and further from these two wonderful people who had raised her and loved her.

She returned to Connecticut with relief, then left soon after for Scotland. There, in the Mevoshee valley, she was able for a time to set aside her pain and fears as she saw for herself that her father had indeed recovered.

Because of their unique bond, Turan understood and accepted her reluctance to talk about Alec, so two days passed before she finally raised the issue by initiating a discussion of that terrible day on the hilltop.

"Did you follow us because you knew what Noel was going to do?" she asked.

"I knew only that there was evil in his thoughts. I caught a suggestion of it just before you 'ported out of the valley. But at the time, I thought it might be directed against you.

"When I arrived and saw his true intention, my first thought was to protect you from being caught in the battle between them. I was angry with Noelo, but I do not think I could have attacked him—even to save Alyeka.

"But something happened, Emily—something I will never understand. I felt a totally alien force grip me. I don't think I ever made a conscious decision to strike out at Noelo. I think, rather, that that decision was made for me."

"Could that force you felt have been me?" she asked. "I wanted to kill Noel. I remember that same terrible rage coming over me that caused me to hurt Ledee."

"It could have been," he said uncertainly. "But I doubt it. Still, there were so many forces loose on that hill. And Alyeka . . ." He paused, shaking his head.

"Emily, the power I felt flowing from Alyeka that day was far greater than I had ever felt in any battle. It should not have been—but it was. Whatever stories are told of that day, none will ever be truer than that Alyeka wielded more power than any of us—Mevoshee or Azonyee—has ever held."

"And for that he has lost himself," she said in a shaky voice.

Turan nodded sadly. "Yes, I think it was that, and not Noelo, that struck him down."

Emily remained with her father and his people for nearly a month. Their kindness and love soothed her, and there were long periods when she was able to set aside her pain. She had begun to train as a dancer with the Azonyee, and now continued training with the Mevoshee, who also pronounced her very gifted.

Because of their closeness, she could sense her father's hope that she might decide to remain there, although he never spoke of it. The thought was tempting, but Emily could make no commitments. Her life had been put on hold.

They talked about Alec. She confessed her resentment at his talk of Janna.

"Their relationship was more perfect than ours could ever have been, and if he has gone back to that time, why should he want to return? He is living in a world that's happy for him, instead of one that confused him and caused him to do something irrational."

Turan shook his head slowly. "No, Emily, you are wrong. If Alyeka had found true perfection with Janna, he would never have taken you for his mate. That's why I—and others as well—have remained alone after losing a mate. We know that anything else would be less. Shekaz in particular tend to be that way, because the quest for perfection is at the heart of our training.

"No doubt Alyeka believed that his marriage with Janna was perfect. He probably even resented your appearance in his life for a time, because you unknowingly challenged that assumption.

"You said you were angry with yourself for having idealized him, but you fail to realize that we Shekaz do the same thing to ourselves. In that sense, the sin of pride that was Noelo's ruin was different only by degree from the feelings of other Shekaz.

"Because he was clearly the most powerful of Shekaz, Alyeka too might have been guilty of that sin. He might well have believed that he could approach our lands and escape unscathed. And the truth is that he was probably right. His powers were clearly not diminished. They actually increased."

Then he stared at her intently. "My concern now is for *you*, child. If Alyeka remains beyond reach, what is to happen to you?"

When Emily merely shrugged, he went on. "Emily, I do not want you to live the life I have lived, although I cannot ask you to do other than you want. For me, there was the demanding life of a Shekaz and then the almost equally demanding task of a mentor.

"When the very best part of our lives has been taken from us, it is important to find, not a substitution—for that can never be—but something that gives life meaning, something to which we can give ourselves."

"I have my teaching and writing," she said. "Before I met him, it would have been enough. Perhaps it still could be, if I thought I could live in the outer world. But I have difficulty doing that now. I feel too different."

"Then you must craft for yourself an existence within our worlds—perhaps both our worlds."

"But how can I do that? You said yourself that the time would probably come when I could no longer come here?"

"Yes, but that was when Alyeka was himself. I think you could continue to move between our worlds as you have done. And you could give lectures or do research in the outer world when it pleases you."

He paused, and his blue eyes twinkled. "You could in fact write an authoritative history of our people, using resources out there augmented by information to which only you would have access.

And money would be no problem, of course. You will have unlimited funds at your disposal anytime you wish."

Emily smiled and admitted that she had once thought of doing just that.

It wasn't until later that Emily realized how her father had, in his gentle way, pointed out a future for her. At first she resented it, but in the end she accepted that he was challenging her to face the truth: that the life with Alec she had envisioned would not be and she must rebuild her dreams.

A few days later Emily attended a wedding celebration for one of her cousins. Her gift was to be part of the dance troupe and she'd been practicing hard.

Her practice paid off, since she felt herself in perfect harmony with her companions as they performed their intricate creation. But she was tired when the dance was over, and after accepting the thanks of the honored couple, she sought a quiet spot to relax.

She'd apparently fallen asleep at some point, because when something brushed lightly against her mind, she opened her eyes to discover that the sun was setting. Her father stood before her. She had, of course, been dreaming about Alec.

Turan sank down across from her. "Dreams are a great gift. They give back to us for a little while what we have lost."

She nodded, blinking away a sudden onrush of tears. "But I still can't accept that that's all I'll ever have of him."

"Perhaps it isn't," he said gently. "You will leave soon."

She nodded. For the past few days she had

known it was time to go. She wanted to return to the other valley, but she wasn't ready to face the pain that awaited her there.

Emily was so lost in her thoughts that she was slow to pick up on Turan's mental agitation. When she did, she assumed that he was upset because she was leaving.

He shook his head. "It isn't that. I understand that you must go. I have just been speaking to Pharra and he has some strange things to say."

"What sort of things?" Emily knew that Pharra was Ledee's opposite number: the Mevoshees' chief nastrano.

"Pharra says they have been sensing strange movements within the forces, shifts whose patterns none of them can decipher. But they're not imbalances. No Shekaz have been called to battle since the day Alyeka and Noelo fought."

"Is that unusual?" Emily wasn't sure how often these battles occurred, although Alec had once told her that he generally fought four or five times a year.

"Yes and no," he replied. "It's unusual to go so long, but not unprecedented. That isn't what's troubling. It's these strange shifts that don't fit any pattern known to the nastranos. And Pharra has a strong sense of a gathering in, of the forces being channeled to some particular place. But they don't know where that place is."

"Could it have something to do with the battle between Alec and Noel?"

"That would certainly be the logical conclusion," Turan agreed. "But there's never been any discernible logic to the forces. They simply *are*."

Emily felt an inner shudder. "Could the forces

be angry with all of you—for having broken the rules?"

He smiled. "You give them a human aspect that we do not. If that were the case, they would certainly have been angry when your mother and I broke the rules. But nothing happened then—except for you, of course—and I don't believe you were the result of their anger."

He smiled again, but Emily felt his thoughts and gasped. "You're afraid they might destroy you, destroy this place."

He nodded. "It is one interpretation that is being discussed. That's why it would be best if you go. You're not fully one of us, Emily, however much we love you. None of us could live—or would want to live—out there, but you can. And those who suggest this theory believe it might only be us who would be punished, for we are the ones who broke the rules."

"But Alec broke a rule as well," she protested as an icy terror crept over her.

"What Alyeka did was mere foolishness, not really a breaking of the rules. He could not have harmed anyone other than himself by coming so close to our land. It was Noelo who broke the rule by trying to kill him—and I who broke it by fighting one of my own."

When he saw her stricken look and felt her fear, Turan put out a hand to touch hers. "Emily, this is only conjecture. But you had already decided it was time to leave, and I think that is wise."

And so Emily was once again forced into a painful leavetaking. She felt somewhat better when she learned from others that many different theories about the strangeness in the forces were being discussed. Some claimed that it was nothing more than a sort of aftershock from the mammoth battle. Others even suggested that the nastranos were misreading the forces after being subjected to an overload on the day of the battle. Most were concerned, but certainly not panicked.

Emily took heart from this as she said her good-byes and left the valley, but as she flew home she realized that she had misunderstood that lack of panic. She'd been seeing them as ordinary people—and they weren't. "What will be will be" was one of the tenets of their belief in the forces. And as her father had said, they would not want to live in the outer world. Left unsaid was that they would prefer death.

She returned to Connecticut, intending to go on quickly to the Azonyee valley. But instead, she lingered at home. As long as she didn't go to the valley, she could cling to the hope that she would find Alec waiting for her, his dark eyes ablaze at the sight of her and his arms welcoming.

A curious languor came over her. For three days she awoke each morning determined to journey back to the Adirondacks, and yet the day would pass without her departure. Finally, on the fourth day, she awoke knowing that it was time to go.

"Hope for the best; expect the worst." She repeated that tired cliché over and over as she made her way back.

She even played stupid games with herself. If she were coming here now for the first time, knowing what she now knew, would she turn around and forget about Neville and his book?

But that wouldn't have worked. Alec would have found her in any event. So she tried another gambit: What if she could go back to that day when she'd decided to go to the bookstore instead of to Elizabeth Arden's with Susan?

Dumb as they are, such "what ifs" have value. Emily discovered that no matter what the future cost, she would not have missed the happiness she'd known with Alec. It was the only comforting thought she had on the entire journey.

Then at last she was on the road to Traverton's Mill and the luminous road opened for her. She drove onto it, then abandoned her car and began to climb the hill toward the valley.

By now she was clinging tightly to her hopes, as though they had the power of truth within them. He would be there waiting for her—not as a broken shadow of a man, but as the charismatic sorcerer who'd changed her life.

The valley lay there shimmering faintly in the heat-haze, far less dark and forbidding than when she'd first seen it. There were even the first small touches of approaching autumn to be seen in the scarlet of some sumac bushes.

"He will be waiting," she said to herself, and gathered her energy to 'port across the barrier.

Nothing happened! She opened her eyes and saw only the silent valley that hid that other valley. Then she closed them again, deciding that she obviously hadn't concentrated enough. 'Porting across the barrier was considerably more difficult than ordinary 'porting.

Still nothing happened. She fought off her rising panic and tried a third time. Then she sank onto the rocky ledge and practiced deep-breathing exercises to calm herself. She forced herself to wait fifteen minutes after she'd slowed her pulse rate and eased her breathing. Then she tried again. Nothing!

Still unwilling to accept the truth that was peering out from the dark corners of her mind, Emily became convinced that she had lost her powers completely. But with no effort at all, she 'ported herself to the far side of the valley, and even down into its center.

Then she faced the nearly equal, terrible alternatives. Either the valley no longer existed, or it had been closed off from the outside world.

Turan had been wrong when he'd said that only the Mevoshee would be punished. The forces had turned against both. And did it really matter which alternative were true? Could this be a punishment directed at her, for having barged into their lives with utter disregard for their ancient traditions and rules? What would it be like for them if they still existed but remained forever locked in their valleys, no longer the guarantors of stability in the forces?

And if their beliefs were correct, she didn't even want to consider what that could mean for the outer world.

As daylight began to fade, she made one more futile attempt, then returned to her car. As she drove back on the shining road, her hopes suddenly soared. The valley *must* still exist. The road was still here.

But the hope died quickly. She was making assumptions again—being logical about an illogical subject. If she came back tomorrow, the road might well be gone, too.

She managed to get a room at Mrs. Davison's. Conversation with her welcoming hostess was nearly impossible, and she didn't correct the woman's statement that she seemed tired. She was, in truth, not tired; instead, she felt increasing agitation as conflicting thoughts collided in her mind. The Azonyees were gone; they were only gone for a while. They weren't gone at all, just sequestered for a time. Alec had recovered and he would find a way to reach her; he hadn't recovered and it was better that way, since he wouldn't know what had happened.

On and on it went, the clashes in her mind. She stayed in the area for three days, returning to the valley each day and prowling through stores in the area where she knew they shopped from time to time. She slept poorly and ate only because her solicitous hostess would have been offended if she didn't.

Then she returned once more to Connecticut, to a place she no longer considered home but that at least afforded her privacy. Sometimes she thought that maybe the time away had never been. But she knew it had; she still had her powers. She became obsessed with them, 'porting herself from room to room and even outside late at night. She levitated, sometimes sitting for hours in mid-air and causing Chaucer to emit worried sounds.

She'd been home for two days when she remembered the telepaths and the answering service. She called the service, then spent an entire day sending frantic messages, taxing her powers to the point of exhaustion. There was no response.

Calls came and she let her machine deal with them. Her parents had gone to Europe. Her neighbor Peggy had gone to Cape Cod.

Unremembered days and nights passed. She slept only when exhaustion overtook her, dropping off into troubled sleep wherever she happened to be at the moment. She would not have fed herself if not for Chaucer's noisy reminders that it was mealtime.

Then she ran out of cat food and had to go out. She grabbed her car keys and was on her way to the garage when it occurred to her to check her appearance.

The face that stared back at her from the mirror shocked her back to reality for a time. She looked like a madwoman: her hair was lank and greasy-looking; her eyes seemed to have taken over her entire face and were ringed in dark circles. There were spots on her shirt because when she forced herself to eat, her hands trembled. She wasn't even sure when she had last showered.

The simple acts of making herself presentable had a soothing effect on her. She went grocery shopping, then stopped by her hairdresser for a trim. Being forced to deal with people helped, although it strained her meager resources.

Unfortunately, she ran into several faculty colleagues, and by that evening she was being besieged by phone calls from well-intentioned friends, all of whom inquired after her mother's health. She lied and lied some more.

Ben did not call; instead, he showed up at her

door. Even though it had now been three days since she'd tried to contact the telepaths, when the bell sounded, she was sure they'd come to her at last. She couldn't hide her disappointment when she saw Ben.

His visit was mercifully brief. He had heard about her mother and was worried about Emily herself. He wanted more, but he also wanted to be her friend. Emily wished he could be, but what good is a friend in whom you can't confide?

She spent countless hours reliving her brief time with Alec, as though she could hold on to him by carefully parceling out each moment.

She thought about the first time she'd seen him, in the bookstore, and about her absolute certainty even then that this was an extraordinary man. But that memory was shattered when it became mixed up with a more recent memory of a quiet, broken man sitting in his magical garden, perhaps not even remembering that he'd created it.

She dwelled on that moment at the edge of the valley when she'd turned to find him standing there, leaning against a tree with that lazy smile on his face. Much later, she'd brought up that day and told him that he'd been insufferably arrogant. He'd laughed and admitted that he had indeed. It had been a unique opportunity to show off for a Tiyazh, and he'd been unable to resist carrying it to extremes.

And of course there was the love-making, that unique and wondrous fusion of bodies and minds—the pure joy of creating a whole from two separate parts.

Finally Emily did what she knew she had to do:

she returned to Scotland. This time she had no hopes to be dashed, so when she parked her rented car in front of the old barn and walked around to the back, she was prepared for what she found. She didn't even try a second time, and she didn't linger.

Chapter Thirteen

Days and then weeks passed. The heat of late summer gave way to cooler days and chilled nights. The breathtaking beauty of New England enveloped her. Her parents returned, and she spent a weekend with them in Manhattan, letting her mother drag her on shopping trips and to visit museums and galleries.

On Monday morning, after leaving her parents' townhouse, Emily found that without any conscious intent she was headed downtown, toward the Village.

She parked her car and walked slowly but determinedly to the bookstore. The owner was just unlocking the door when she got there. She wandered through the rows of shelves, then finally bought several books she didn't want because she felt ridiculous about spending so much time there and then walking away empty-handed.

When she carried the books to the checkout counter, she saw that the owner was hand-printing a sign.

"You're closing?"

He nodded. "I finally sold a book and decided to call myself a writer. I'm moving up to Maine."

Another ending.

A few days later Emily became aware of a strangeness in herself. It came first in the form of turbulent dreams she could never quite recall—dreams vastly different from her pleasurable dreams of Alec. Then it began to assault her in her waking hours too. Strange, deep vibrations would well up in her, trembling through body and mind. At such moments she would lose her awareness of herself and feel as though she were being pulled along by invisible currents.

She stayed close to home, fearing what she might look like at such times. Twice, she even 'ported herself to the supermarket in the middle of the night, ignoring the fact that she had become a thief.

Was she going mad? In the hours when the forces receded into a low hum, she considered that possibility. After all, if the earth forces had taken their revenge upon the Azonyee and the Mevoshee, did it make sense that they would leave her alone—she, who had started it all?

October gave way to November and it got neither better nor worse. Were they toying with her, trying to decide if she should be destroyed completely or just made mad?

Then a morning came when she awoke to a

sensation she couldn't at first identify. Only when she had gotten out of bed did she recognize it: peace. No frightening dreams. No low vibrations humming menacingly within her.

Several days passed and she felt better and better. When she studied herself in the mirror, she thought she looked quite normal. Her energy level soared, the result of regular meals and untroubled sleep. She even went to her health club and worked out, and she returned to work on her long-neglected book.

There were times when she questioned this sudden transformation, but not for long and not too deeply. She'd been introspective for too long.

Her department chair called, asking if she would consider filling in on this week's Sunday Afternoon Series lecture. The scheduled lecturer had been in an auto accident. Emily hesitated, then agreed. It felt right—another step back to reality.

The lecture went well. A gratifyingly large crowd was gathered, including several of her faculty colleagues. The question period lasted nearly as long as the lecture. Afterwards her colleagues invited her to join them for dinner at a new Japanese restaurant. She accepted without hesitation.

But it had been a long time since Emily had exposed herself to socializing, and by the time she said good night to her friends, she was exhausted from the effort required just to be herself.

Chaucer greeted her with more than his usual volubility, but Emily assumed it was because he wanted his food dish filled. Even when he ignored his food and continued to harangue her all the way up the stairs, she didn't heed it.

She walked into her bedroom and reached automatically for the wall light switch—then froze! In the dim light from the hallway she could see the rumpled bed and the dark head on the pillow.

She caught the cry in her throat and backed quickly out of the room. So this was to be the new torture: hallucinations. She staggered down the hallway to her office and sank into her desk chair.

He's not there, she told herself. They're playing a cruel game with you—trying to drive you insane.

She got up and went to the bathroom, then walked determinedly to the guest room, carrying blankets she'd taken from the linen closet. Too tired to be frightened about what they might do to her, she lay down on the futon sofa and pulled the blankets over her. But before she could fall asleep, Chaucer leapt onto the sofa, startling a sharp cry from her.

She reached out to pet him and belatedly recalled his agitated state when she'd come home. He only behaved that way when someone had been in the house.

And then she felt it. "No!" she cried, pressing her hands to the sides of her head. She had been prepared for anything but this. They were mimicking that soft brushing of his mind against hers.

Then, abruptly, Chaucer turned his head toward the doorway and jumped down from the sofa. Emily turned very slowly, letting the denial build within her.

He stood in the doorway, silhouetted by the light from the hall. He was naked and his face was in shadows, but Emily knew she was seeing him as he'd been before the battle. Something in his stance. Something about the way he held his head. She covered her eyes and began to sob.

The sofa dipped beneath his weight. His arms came around her, drawing her stiff, resisting body against his warm, solid flesh. And she felt again that soft touch against her mind even as he spoke in a voice roughened by passion.

"Emily, rezha, I'm not a ghost. I'm *real*."

"Rezha." An untranslatable word. More than wife—far more than lover. Soul-mate. She heard it echo endlessly through her mind even as she continued to sob uncontrollably.

He sat there holding her, edging more and more deeply into her mind until his thoughts mingled freely with hers—and at last she knew he was real.

"How?" she asked hoarsely.

He smoothed her tangled hair and brushed away the last of the tears. "I'm very tired, rezha. It was perhaps too soon to make such a journey. Come back to your bed with me. I will explain in the morning. For tonight, it is enough that we are together again."

"You'll . . . you'll be gone in the morning, won't you?"

"No," he whispered against her ear. "I'll never be gone again."

They stumbled down the hallway, unable to let go of each other. She had so many questions, but she was asleep within seconds, curled in his arms. The last thing she remembered was

Chaucer's loud purring as he settled himself at the foot of the bed.

Emily felt herself being nudged out of the depths of sleep by something she couldn't quite identify, something that spoke of the past. She muttered a protest and tried to shift about in her bed. But something pressed against her: large and hard and warm. With the hazy certainty of dreaming, she sought oblivion again.

But that subtle prodding at her mind continued, and lips began to trace a line across her ear, down over her neck and into the hollow between her breasts. A hand caught her about the waist and turned her, then began making its slow, caressing way along the curve of her hip and across to the juncture of her thighs.

She awoke with a startled cry to find his face looming above hers in the semidarkness. She blinked uncertainly, struggling to grasp a memory, unwilling to accept reality just yet.

He smiled at her but said nothing. She stared at him, seeing a face that had regained its true age and seeing even in the shadowy light the unmistakable gleam in his dark eyes.

Then his need filled her mind with liquid fire, flowing through her, setting off still more fire.

They were both still very tired, but that tiredness did nothing more than take the rough, ragged edges off their passion, giving it instead a slow, voluptuous heat.

No words passed between them as flesh caressed flesh, as warm, secret places burst into flame at a touch. A thought began with one and ended with the other, blending perfectly. It felt like a first time—and it seemed as though it had always been this way.

He lifted her to meet his thrusts, his hands digging deeply into her softness while hers clutched the hard points of his shoulders and curved about smooth muscles. She arched to welcome him with small cries that were answered by his deep, hoarse groans. And two became completely, incomparably one.

Within moments, they were both asleep again, bodies still entwined, minds still touching as they fell away into oblivion.

Warm water cascaded over them in the steamy shower stall. She murmured something about its running out if they stayed there much longer, and he replied with a low chuckle that what good was magic if it couldn't produce an endless supply of hot water?

They stroked each other with soap-lathered hands as wet mouths hungrily sought each other. He lifted her, supporting her as she wrapped her legs around him and struggled to stay put in the slipperiness of two wet bodies. He reminded her teasingly of her special talent, and she managed to focus her thoughts well enough to stay there without his support. But it was difficult to defy gravity when she was being consumed by erotic flames. Somehow, though, they managed—and the water remained warm.

She sat at her small kitchen table, following his every move as he fixed breakfast. She loved to watch him cook. He effortlessly mixed magic with normal skills, flipping the bacon with a glance as he scrambled eggs. What cook hasn't dreamed of having an extra pair of hands?

They ate their breakfast with bare feet caressing each other beneath the table. The mind touch wasn't enough now; they both craved the physical.

Emily glanced up at the kitchen clock, shocked to see that it was one-fifteen. There was a delicious decadence implied to eating breakfast at such an hour, when the rest of the world was bustling about. They'd probably still be in bed if it hadn't been for Chaucer's increasingly aggressive assaults and loud demands to be fed. Alec might have used his magic to accomplish that, but they discovered that they were hungry, too.

Her need grew stronger to know how Alec had gotten well and returned to her. He led her into her living room, where he lit a fire and drew her down beside him.

Something unique in Azonyee history had occurred, he told her. In the course of one day, every Azonyee who had been in the outer world returned to the valley, saying they'd felt a sudden urgency to come home. Students left classes, vacationers chartered flights—even the telepaths abandoned their posts.

And then when all had returned, the barrier had become impassable, locking them into their enchanted land.

Soon after, the vibrations began, touching them all—the same deep chords that would later make themselves felt to Emily. The nastranos were forced to withdraw from their constant monitoring of the forces beneath them. People slept poorly. It was a bad time for them all. Such turbulence was unknown to them. Theories as to the cause flew about, but no one really knew.

"But what about you?" she asked. "Did you feel all this? When did you . . . come back?"

"I didn't feel what they were feeling," he admitted. "But it was during this time that I began to come back." He paused, then slipped into her mind to let her see what it had been like for him.

She saw darkness, shadows moving languidly. And she heard unfamiliar voices—then her own. But they sounded muffled, confused, speaking gibberish with an occasional recognizable word.

But there were brief bursts of lucidity. Through him, she saw herself as she'd been then: pale, frightened, and yet trying to pretend she was happy. She saw frozen moments she hadn't known he'd been aware of, times when she'd cried silently at the hopelessness of it all.

"Leesa and Ledee told me that within a few days after you had gone, I began to walk around aimlessly, repeating your name. I remember only being confused and frightened. Ledee was sure that I was coming back and she stayed with me day and night, drawing me back and easing the pain and confusion.

"It felt to me as though you were the sun," he said, reaching out to touch her pale golden hair. "I could see you up there, surrounded by light, while I was down in the dark and cold.

"After a while, there were periods when I was myself, and during those periods I too felt the vibrations, although they didn't seem to affect me as they did the others. I think I felt energized by them. Then I'd just slip away again into the darkness.

"By the time I came back to stay, the vibrations had ceased and the barrier had been opened. The nastranos began monitoring the forces again, but there were no imbalances anywhere. There hadn't been any since my battle with Noelo.

"I was and am weak," he went on. "I can 'port myself short distances, but I needed help to get through the barrier when it reopened. No one knows if I will ever regain the powers required to be a Shekaz."

Emily felt the pain in him and covered his hand with hers. "But there are no imbalances, so perhaps it doesn't matter."

"I'm sure it's only a temporary lull. I can't believe there will never be a need again."

Emily felt his lingering confusion, his disbelief that he would never pursue his profession again.

"Do you think all this happened because of your battle with Noel?"

He shrugged. "It's impossible to know—but yes, I think so. That battle was felt by every Azonyee all over the world, and I assume the Mevoshee felt it as well."

She confirmed that they had, then told him about her journey back to Scotland when she'd left him and her more recent trip after she'd discovered his valley was closed. She told him as well about her father's theory that only the Mevoshee would be punished.

"I agree that they were more to blame, but I cannot believe that they would be destroyed and we would be left intact. What would be the point? We are opposing forces."

"But if there are no more battles to be fought?" she asked gently.

He merely nodded.

"Why did you put yourself at risk?" she asked, not accusingly, but out of a need to understand.

"I don't know. I might have been foolish enough to believe that the rules didn't apply to me, the most powerful of Shekaz. If so, I was scarcely any better than Noelo, whose pride led him to try to kill me.

"Or it might have been because I was half-mad with wanting you. I needed you so badly, even though I understood that you needed your father, too.

"My memories of those days are clouded, so I'll never really know. But it seems to me that there was a compulsion in me to go there, to be there at that time. Or maybe that's just my pride again—wanting to blame anything but myself."

"How much do you remember about the battle itself?" she asked curiously.

"Only a little. I don't really know how Noelo was killed, but perhaps I did it. I do remember that the power that flowed through me was enormous, as your father said. And I remember his being there, too. I knew he was trying to kill Noelo as well."

"So was I," she said, as shame crept into her voice. "I felt that same rage I felt when Ledee probed my mind, and I know I flung it at him just before I passed out."

"Don't blame yourself, Emily. You could not have killed him. What felt like great power to you was nothing. There were three Shekaz present. It would have been like throwing a pebble against a nuclear missile."

* * *

They spent the remainder of the day quietly, dozing before the fireplace, making slow and tender love and just lying there holding each other and drifting with their commingled thoughts.

It was during these periods of thought-sharing that Emily came to the realization that whatever had taken place had not yet ended. She'd allowed herself to believe that it was over; after all, she had Alec back. But he was certain there was more to come, and his certainty convinced her.

It was during this time too that she came to know the vulnerability in him. No matter how he might appear to others, Alec had lost a substantial amount of his powers—and might never regain them. If she had not been able to share his thoughts, she knew she would never have suspected that change.

He'd always accepted that his powers would wane one day; all Shekaz knew that. But he'd believed that he had some years left before the slow decline set in. And beneath all that was the continuing uncertainty about whether or not those powers would even be needed again.

Two calls interrupted them. The first was from her mother, whose tone indicated increasing concern for her daughter. Emily told her that Alec had returned and they were leaving soon to take a quiet vacation in the Adirondacks. Then she said that they were going to be married as soon as their schedules permitted. Her mother was delighted by the announcement.

Shortly after, there was another call. When Emily heard the caller's voice, joy burst forth, drawing Alec quickly to her side.

"Mesav! I'm so glad you called. Is everyone all right? What about Father?"

Mesav assured her that all was well, then told her the same story she'd heard from Alec. Like the Azonyee, the Mevoshee were certain that more was to come.

"Alec is here," she told him. "He's come back, Mesav. But he needs to get back to the valley, so we'll be leaving tomorrow. Please tell Father that I'll visit him as soon as I can."

"Your news will please him—and all of us. And of course it will add to the endless speculation."

Then he put his sister, Kalera, on the phone. They chatted comfortably for quite a while, but Emily could sense some of the same confusion in Kalera as she'd felt in Alec. She too was a Shekaz, and perhaps in a way it was worse for her, since she was younger and had believed she had many years left in her profession.

After they hung up, she told Alec who Mesav and Kalera were and explained how Mesav had helped her get him away from the Mevoshee lands. She said that Kalera was a Shekaz, but was not quite able to conceal her cousin's revelation about her meeting with an Azonyee Shekaz.

Alec's brows furrowed in thought. "I wonder if there have been other meetings as well. Perhaps the changes began long ago—even before your father and mother met."

"Does that trouble you?"

He shook his head. "If it happened, it was meant to happen."

"Alec, I want to understand this," Emily said urgently as they walked up the path to the Council building. "I don't feel anything."

They'd been back in the valley for a month. Winter had come to the enchanted land and snow covered the gardens. Chaucer had adapted well to his new home, although Alec was certainly going to have to make some repairs to his garden in the spring.

As the weather grew colder, the Azonyee tended to 'port themselves from place to place, but Emily and Alec had walked partway here in order to talk. A few hours ago, a gradual certainty had come over Alec that they would have to leave the valley, that there was a place they had to go. Emily was frightened because she felt no such compulsion and feared he might go without her. But he insisted that wherever he went, she would go too.

Then, just a short time ago, they'd been summoned before the Council.

When they entered and Emily's eyes became accustomed to the dazzle of all the gold, she saw that a small group had gathered before the long table where the Council members sat. As they went to join them, Emily looked curiously at the group.

There was Ketta, his presence always a pleasure for her. She thought that all the nastranos were there, though she didn't know for sure. Lilleet was there, the young woman who had helped Emily get Alec home after the battle, and three others she belatedly recognized as having been at the battle. There were several more she didn't know, all of them about her age or younger.

Menda called the meeting to order, her voice

rising above the babble. When her gaze swept over Emily, it seemed, if not exactly friendly, then at least neutral. At the far end of the table, her grandmother's smile couldn't quite hide her concern.

Emily soon discovered that all of the assembled guests—except herself—had felt what Alec had felt: there was something they had to do, a place they had to go to. And it seemed that the nastranos knew where that place was.

"We cannot determine the exact location," Ledee told them, "but we know that it is somewhere in the South Pacific. We will know more as we approach it."

Menda and the Council, who had not felt what the others felt, demanded more information. Ledee and the nastranos could not provide it. Great rivers of power were flowing to that place, stronger currents than they'd ever felt before. It was different from the recent turbulence, which had been unfocused. And there was no sense of a buildup of opposing forces that signals a need to send out a Shekaz.

The discussion went on for an hour. At first Emily thought that the Council would prohibit this journey, but she soon realized that when it came to anything involving the forces, the decision of the nastranos took precedence. A few on the Council, naturally including Menda, obviously resented this usurpation of their authority.

Emily remained silent and looked around her again. Why this group? Why had these people been chosen? And why had she herself felt nothing?

She was slow to react to Menda's question, and looked her way only when she heard her name being spoken with the Leader's customary imperiousness.

"Have you felt this, Emily?"

Emily hesitated, then shook her head. "I've felt nothing."

"Then why are you here?" the woman demanded. "This obviously does not concern you."

"She stays with me," Alec stated firmly.

A brief silence followed during which Menda and Alec faced each other. Then Ledee intervened in a strong voice.

"Emily might not have felt anything, but she is to be part of the group. We are all agreed on that." She glanced at her fellow nastranos and they all nodded.

Finally it was over. Someone was dispatched to the outer world to make the arrangements for the journey. They would leave the next day.

Snow was falling when the group left the Council building; then promptly vanished as they 'ported themselves to their homes. Alec and Emily wrapped their arms about each other and did likewise.

"Why this particular group of people?" Emily asked when they had settled into bed a short time later. "I've been trying to come up with something that links us all. Everyone who had anything to do with the battle and its aftermath was there—but that doesn't explain the rest, except for the nastranos, who are obviously needed to guide us."

He shifted onto his side and began to run his

fingers along the silky curve of her hip. "Stop worrying about it, rezha. We'll know soon enough."

"Aren't you at all concerned?" It struck her then that none of them had seemed fearful; in fact, they'd seemed quite excited.

"No, it feels good—though not as good as I intend to feel in a few minutes." He bent to kiss her and at the same time slid his hand across her belly and down into the tangle of curls at its base.

Emily laughed throatily. Alec might have described himself as being still weak when they'd come back to the valley, but the "weakness" had nothing to do with his need for her. It seemed to her that they'd done little but make love for the past month. She'd told him at one point that no man his age should be capable of making love two or three times a day for days on end.

"Magic," he'd replied, reaching for her again.

And it was—always.

Emily stared down at the winter-barren fields of the Midwest and smiled at the thought of a planeload of sorcerers winging their way to the South Pacific aboard a chartered luxury jet.

An eruption of laughter, followed by outbursts in their own language, drew her back again. She saw them hastily switch to English when the two flight attendants looked puzzled, and wondered what they thought of this group. Curious, she listened in to their thoughts for a moment.

The attendants were clearly bewildered by this richly dressed group who had chartered a jet large enough to carry them to the South Pacific, seemingly on a whim. They weren't Arabs, who'd been known to do such things. But they weren't American, either—or at least some of them weren't because their accents were strange.

The one who fascinated them most was the tall, dark-haired man who was now in the cockpit talking to the flight crew. Emily caught a bit of her own initial thoughts about Alec in the mental musings of the two attendants.

The female attendant turned as Alec reappeared, and the drinks tray she was carrying began to slip from her hand. Emily didn't know who stopped it, but it was Ketta who belatedly slid his hand beneath it as it hung suspended in mid-air. The attendant looked momentarily confused, but then her expression became calm as someone apparently smoothed over the incident.

They made a brief stopover in Hawaii, where they changed crews and the passengers broke up into groups to get some exercise. Alec and Emily walked on the beach, then hired a car to take them sightseeing before returning to the plane just ahead of the others, most of whom appeared to have spent their time shopping.

The plane was quiet as it continued across the Pacific to its next destination: Tahiti. A traditional luau had been brought aboard, and after devouring so many exotic foods, they all settled into their roomy, reclining seats and slept.

Emily remained awake longer than the others, still confused at this crazy voyage and bemused by the childlike eagerness of her companions. Only Alec retained some degree of solemnity, and she suspected that was because of her.

As she too succumbed to sleep, Emily wondered if madness awaited them at the end of this journey. Certainly they seemed to be approaching that.

No one saw much of Tahiti, since their eagerness had reached near fever pitch. The nastranos by now knew exactly where they were going, and several of the group were dispatched to find a sailboat.

"Does anyone here know how to sail?" Emily asked curiously.

It turned out that Alec was the "seasoned" sailor among them, having sailed once, years ago, in these very waters with Janna.

"But how can we take a crew with us?" she inquired, looking from one unconcerned face to the next.

"I will buy a book," Ketta pronounced, and left the group to find one.

And so they set sail on a beautiful seventy-five-foot boat about which no one knew anything. The charter company seemed completely unconcerned about turning over the boat, which led Emily to the suspicion that more magic had been employed.

"This is crazy," Emily muttered as she stood with Alec, who had taken the helm. "What if we run into bad weather?"

"We won't." He wrapped an arm around her. "Emily, I know you think we're insane, but we are only doing what we are meant to do. And we know that whatever lies ahead is good."

"Then why don't *I* feel that as well?"

"What *do* you feel?" he asked, slipping easily into her mind.

She wasn't really afraid, only confused at the behavior of the others, and perhaps a little annoyed that she couldn't share their pleasure. The truth was that she felt more than ever an outsider.

No, he said in her mind—not an outsider. You are here because it is important that you be here. You will see.

But what she saw at the moment looked like a bunch of overgrown kids on a school outing. Several of them were taking turns 'porting themselves up to the top of the main mast. Ledee was standing in the bow, her nastrano dignity reduced somewhat by her attire: a wildly printed minuscule bikini. Ketta sat on a deck chair wearing the loudest Hawaiian print shirt Emily had ever seen. Even with sunglasses, Emily's eyes hurt when she looked at it. He had a small cassette recorder beside him that was instructing him how to play the ukulele he'd purchased.

Then someone else wanted to take a turn at the helm, and Alec suggested they go swimming. Emily stared from him to the open sea in disbelief. "Here? You can't be serious."

But he was. A few minutes later they dove into the water. By the time they had exhausted themselves, the boat was only a speck on the horizon. Arms around each other, they 'ported themselves back to the deck and landed in a tangled heap in front of Ketta, who had dozed off with his ukulele on his lap.

"A bit clumsy," he remarked as he woke up and saw them.

The antics stopped late the next afternoon. Even Emily thought she felt something now, although she couldn't be sure it wasn't just a reflection of Alec's suddenly serious mood.

"Just ahead," Ledee announced from the bow.

She had changed back into the formal robes of a nastrano.

"I don't see anything." Emily frowned, peering out at endless blue waters.

A few moments later, the scene before them began to shimmer slightly. The silvery blur grew until it seemed to surround them. Emily moved closer to Alec as a brightness washed over them.

And then an island lay before them: dark green and ringed with a wide beach. It was still some distance away, but she could make out a dock—and another boat. Alec picked up a pair of binoculars as Ketta came to join them. After a moment, he handed them to her with a smile.

"My father!" she gasped. "And that's Mesav and Kalera with him." Before she could focus on the others, Ketta asked to borrow the glasses.

"Turan looks fit," he remarked as he handed them back again.

A sudden fear shot through Emily as she remembered that these two men had fought to a draw—twice. But Ketta shook his white head.

"No, Emily, those days are past. I think there will be no more battles."

Ledee joined them, while the others clustered in the bow. They were already close enough to see the group at the dock without glasses.

Ledee, who had overheard Ketta's remark, nodded. "There is a confluence of forces here unlike anything we have felt before. I think you are right, Ketta."

"A reunion," Emily said softly. "That's what it is, isn't it?"

"So we believe," Ledee smiled.

The boat glided up to the dock. Lines were

tossed by Azonyee and secured by the Mevoshee. After that, no one moved for a long moment until Emily ran across the deck and leapt onto the dock into Turan's waiting arms.

The others followed her off the boat, but in a considerably more restrained fashion. Alec was the last. Then the two groups simply stood there watching each other, keeping their distance.

Emily stared at Alec, silently imploring him to come to her as she stood with an arm around her father's waist. After what seemed an eternity, he did. Turan stepped forward, his hand out.

"We meet under better circumstances this time, Alyeka. And I extend the deep regrets of my people over the wrong that was done to you."

"That wrong was to some extent of my own doing, Turan—but I thank you nonetheless."

Emily stood there between the two men she loved and thought that they sounded like diplomats from warring nations. But at least they were talking.

More introductions were made just as formally, with both sides speaking careful English even though they shared a language. Hands were extended tentatively, then withdrawn just as quickly. The nastranos from each side merely nodded to each other.

"Well," said Emily brightly when both sides had lapsed into an uneasy silence again, "perhaps someone would like to offer their thoughts on why we've all come halfway around the world. Surely it's for more than *this*." She gave them all a look of faint disgust.

"It may be that *you* are the one responsible for all this, Emily," Mesav said.

"Me? I had nothing to do with this. I didn't even have an urge to come here, although I'm certainly happy about it." *Happier than any of you are*, she said to herself.

But two men were present who could pick up on that thought easily—and both burst into laughter at the same time. That eased the tension somewhat, but still no one moved or spoke.

"Does anyone know how this place was created?" she asked, determined to get them talking. "Are there any houses?"

Again it was Mesav who seemed most willing to talk. "Madam, when we do something, we do it right. The island arrived ready for occupancy. The houses are just over the crest of the hill, surrounding a lagoon."

"Wonderful," she responded. "But did *you* do this—or was it done for you?"

"It is one and the same, Emily," said Ledee. "When it was decided that we should come here, a place was created for us."

They all walked up the path to the crest of the hill, where they saw before them a beautiful, nearly circular lagoon surrounded by small houses exactly like the ones in both valleys. Slightly apart at the far end of the lagoon was a larger building much like both Council buildings. Emily assumed that it too would be smothered in gold.

It was—and it also held a feast of fruits and cheeses and bread so fresh she could smell it even before she saw it. Hammered gold wine carafes and goblets were set about on the big round table. When Mesav had said the place was ready for occupancy, he'd meant it.

They all sat down to eat, and Emily sighed inwardly at the way they continued to keep themselves separate. She was seated between her father and Alec, and as she complained to herself, she felt both men touch her mind, creating a babble that finally resolved itself into a suggestion that she might be expecting too much too soon.

Still, she was determined to force them to face up to this change in their lives. "You could not have always lived separately," she announced. "How could you possibly believe that, when you share the same language, the same customs—even the same architecture? That doesn't make sense."

This time it was one of the Mevoshee nastranos who responded. "You raise a question that each of us has certainly considered, Emily—although we've rarely spoken of it." He looked around the table and the others nodded slowly.

Then Ketta chuckled quietly. "We are not so unlike the Tiyazh in some ways, Emily. We too avoid asking each other the difficult questions."

There were smiles all around, and Emily felt the tension drain away still more. She hurried on.

"What I still don't understand is why all of *us* are here? Why were we chosen to come here—rather than the Councils, for example?"

"We don't know, Emily. But speaking for our Council, if they'd come, we wouldn't even be sitting here together. They'd be off plotting how to take advantage of the situation."

General laughter greeted Turan's comment—laughter from both sides.

Mesav had obviously been pondering that question as well. "At least some of us may be here because we had some part in the battle between Noelo and Alyeka."

Emily, who had already noted that, now realized that several of the others who looked familiar were among those who'd come to the hilltop after the battle to take the unconscious Turan and the body of Noel home.

"And the nastranos are here because they had to guide us to this place," Mesav added. "But that still leaves some unexplained."

"Me, for one," Ketta stated. "I was Alyeka's mentor, but I played no role in the battle."

"There is another link, Ketta," Turan said.

The two men stared at each other, and Ketta nodded. "Yes, you are right, Turan. A powerful bond was forged in those two battles. I feel it even after all these years."

"As do I," Turan acknowledged.

Emily was busy sorting out the two groups, to see whose presence was still unexplained. Her gaze rested briefly on her cousin Kalera, who looked quickly away. And it was then she knew.

"I think we may be wrong to believe it was the battle that provided the link," Emily announced, drawing everyone's attention.

"I think you were all chosen—except for the nastranos—because each of you has had some contact with a member of the opposite group."

She felt Alec's understanding, but Turan frowned. Emily shot a beseeching glance at her cousin, and with a quick glance at a man who sat a few seats away, Kalera cleared her throat softly.

"I think Emily is right. At least she's right about *me*."

There was general consternation around the

table, followed by confessions from the rest of the group: eight people, four Azonyees and four Mevoshees—all of them Shekaz, none of whom had ever fought each other.

But they *had* met, just as Kalera had met Daneek, a handsome young man who quickly owned up to his transgression. In Paris, in Rio, on the Harvard campus, at Cambridge. Chance meetings had been allowed to move beyond the rules. One of the couples had met three times, another twice.

"It seems," said Turan, "that the rules have been breaking down for some time."

"Perhaps even before you and Susurra met," Ketta responded. "Although yours was certainly the most spectacular, since it gave us Emily."

With the veil of secrecy lifted, the couples in question left the group, still rather shy but talking in low voices. The nastranos of both sides moved off as well, seating themselves on a terrace that overlooked the lagoon. Mesav and Pheera, the young Azonyee who had shown up to help Emily after the battle, renewed their brief acquaintance as they too strolled out to the terrace.

Ketta and Turan both stood up at the same time. Turan gestured to his old foe.

"Ketta, old men like us need to stretch our legs a bit after meals to help the digestion."

Ketta smiled. "And old men like to talk of old battles. Let's walk on the beach."

Emily watched the two of them walk off, already deep in animated conversation. She knew she was seeing the beginning of a friendship. The two men were much alike.

Alec drew her to her feet. "Let's explore the

island a bit."

They circled the placid lagoon and found another path leading off into the thick jungle. Emily turned briefly to look back at the terrace, where several groups were deep in conversation. Now, finally, she too felt that joy.

"Do you think this is a place where we can all live?" she asked as they plunged into the jungle.

"No, if it were intended to be that, it would have to be much larger."

"Well, can't you just *make* it larger?"

He laughed. "No, rezha, it doesn't work that way. I think this is intended to be a place where we can meet."

"Well, it certainly isn't very convenient," she pointed out.

"Perhaps it was intended to be inconvenient. We have lived apart for a long time, and there must be a will to get together again."

"'Nothing worth having is ever easy,'" She quoted. "Is that what you mean?"

"Exactly."

"But what will you do? So much of your culture is built around the need to oppose each other."

"I think the future is ours to decide," he said slowly.

"Well, you might try working your combined magic on some of the world's problems," she suggested.

"The Tiyazh world is beyond even our magic. But perhaps you are right. There may be a few things we could do."

The path led them to a small cove with a crescent of pure white sand. They walked down to the water's edge, then kicked off their shoes and began to wade in the surf. The setting sun was fiery red, trailing glittery fingers across the darkening waters.

"I think I could stay here for a while," Emily said with a happy sigh.

A wave rolled in and soaked them both. They ran laughing from the water and fell onto the sand together.

"Making love on a beach could be interesting," he commented as he began to fumble with her shirt buttons.

"It's already been done. There was a famous old movie with . . . "

"We'll improve upon it," he promised as he slid the wet shirt from her shoulders. "What else is magic for?"

"CONNIE MASON WRITES THE STUFF THAT FANTASIES ARE MADE OF!" — *Romantic Times*

CONNIE MASON

"Ye cannot kill the devil," whispered the awestruck throng at the hanging of the notorious Diablo. And, indeed, moments later the pirate had not only escaped the noose, but had abducted Lady Devon, whisking her aboard his ship, the DEVIL DANCER. Devon swore she would have nothing to do with rakishly handsome captor. But long days at sea, and even longer nights beneath the tropical stars, brought Devon ever closer to surrender. Diablo was a master of seduction, an experienced lover who knew every imaginable way to please a woman — and some that she had never imagined. Devon knew she would find ecstasy in his arms, but dare she tempt the devil?

__2958-8 $4.50

LEISURE BOOKS

ATTN: Customer Service Dept.

276 5th Avenue, New York, NY 10001

Please add $1.25 for shipping and handling of the first book and $.30 for each book thereafter. All orders shipped within 6 weeks via postal service book rate.

Canadian orders must reflect Canadian price, when indicated, and must be paid in U.S. dollars through a U.S. banking facility.

Name _____

Address _____

City _____ State _____ Zip _____

I have enclosed $ _____ in payment for the books checked above.

Payment <u>must</u> accompany all orders.   ❑Please send a free catalogue.